PENGUIN

THE FIANCÉE AND

ANTON PAVLOVICH CHEKHOV, the son of a former serf, was born in 1860 in Taganrog, a port on the Sea of Azov. He received a classical education at the Taganrog Secondary School, then in 1879 he went to Moscow, where he entered the medical faculty of the university, graduating in 1884. During his university years he supported his family by contributing humorous stories and sketches to magazines. He published his first volume of stories, *Motley Stories*, in 1886 and a year later his second volume, *In the Twilight*, for which he was awarded the Pushkin Prize by the Russian Academy. His most famous stories were written after his return from the convict island of Sakhalin, which he visited in 1890. For five years he lived on his small country estate near Moscow, but when his health began to fail he moved to the Crimea. After 1900, the rest of his life was spent at Yalta, where he met Tolstoy and Gorky. He wrote very few stories during the last years of his life, devoting most of his time to a thorough revision of his stories for a collected edition of his works, published in 1901, and to the writing of his great plays. In 1901 Chekhov married Olga Knipper, an actress of the Moscow Art Theatre. He died of consumption in 1904.

RONALD WILKS studied Russian language and literature at Trinity College, Cambridge, and later Russian literature at London University, where he received his Ph.D. in 1972. He has also translated 'The Little Demon' by Sologub, and, for the Penguin Classics, *My Childhood*, *My Apprenticeship* and *My Universities* by Gorky, *Diary of a Madman* by Gogol and three other volumes of stories by Chekhov, *The Kiss and Other Stories*, *The Duel and Other Stories* and *The Party and Other Stories*.

Chekhov

ॐ

THE FIANCÉE

AND OTHER STORIES

ॐ

TRANSLATED WITH AN INTRODUCTION BY
RONALD WILKS

ॐ

PENGUIN BOOKS

PENGUIN BOOKS

Published by the Penguin Group
27 Wrights Lane, London w8 5tz, England
Viking Penguin Inc., 40 West 23rd Street, New York, New York 10010, USA
Penguin Books Australia Ltd, Ringwood, Victoria, Australia
Penguin Books Canada Ltd, 2801 John Street, Markham, Ontario, Canada l3r 1b4
Penguin Books (NZ) Ltd, 182–190 Wairau Road, Auckland 10, New Zealand

Penguin Books Ltd, Registered Offices: Harmondsworth, Middlesex, England

This translation first published 1986
3 5 7 9 10 8 6 4

Made and printed in Great Britain by
Richard Clay Ltd, Bungay, Suffolk
Typeset in Monophoto Photina

In memory of Erna

Contents

Introduction

In January 1903 Chekhov wrote to Olga Knipper, 'I'm writing a story for the *Journal for All*, in the antiquated style of the seventies. I don't know how it will turn out.' A few days later he wrote to his wife again, 'I'm writing a story, but very slowly, a table-spoonful an hour – possibly because there's a lot of characters or because I've lost the knack. I must recover it.'

The Fiancée was the last story that Chekhov wrote. He revised the text many times, and no fewer than five versions exist. Many critics saw this story as a turning-point in Chekhov's work, showing a trend towards a more optimistic, healthy perception of reality. Indeed, the 'upward' movement of the story, with its conclusion that leaves us full of hope, is unusual for Chekhov and strikes a new note in his stories. The social significance of the heroine's abandonment of the philistine, materialistic background where she has grown up for the pure bright path of self-denial and hard work was not missed by contemporary critics. Maximilian Voloshin, a minor poet of the time, suggested that whereas the lives of Turgenev's heroines are almost invariably grounded on love, Chekhov's heroines seek the meaning of life, as Nadya does in this story: she is a 'positive woman of action' and it is no wonder that she was taken as an exemplar of re-volutionary zeal by the later Soviet critics.

The Fiancée was written at the same time as *The Cherry Orchard* and there are many similarities between Trofimov's and Sasha's tirades against the philistinism, squalor, ignorance and back-wardness that surround them. Sasha's impossible visions of the future, with its remarkable people and beautiful towns where truth reigns supreme, are closely paralleled in Trofimov's Utopian dreams. In Sasha, who persuades Nadya to abandon her dull, pompous, self-satisfied fiancé and escape to the city, it is possible that Chekhov has to some extent portrayed himself: both Chekhov and his fictional hero were dying of consumption.

On Official Business, first published in *The Week*, in 1899, tells of a young coroner and a doctor who are dispatched from the city to a remote village to carry out an inquest on a suicide. The story is constructed from many contrasting themes—such as the gap separating the professional, educated classes from the benighted peasantry, and the young coroner's hopes for a fascinating life in Moscow set against the dreariness of the functions he has to carry out, in a desolate backwater. Typically Chekhovian is the contrast between the introspective, sensitive coroner and the hearty, extrovert doctor. And there are further contrasts between the misery of the 'council offices' where doctor and coroner are doomed to spend the night and the warmth and luxury of the friend's house they go to visit. The character of the village constable – 'that administrative *perpetuum mobile*' as a friend of Tolstoy called him – is particularly vividly drawn, as Chekhov's brother Mikhail records, from an actual constable who delivered government papers to Chekhov when he was active in the local council at Melikhovo.

Rothschild's Fiddle (1894), one of a group of stories set in the world of small tradesmen, tells of a coffin-maker who, on his deathbed, leaves his most treasured possession (his fiddle) to a Jewish musician for whom he had felt only contempt. This story sounds a sentimental note unusual in Chekhov, although there are some very amusing passages, especially the confrontation between the coffin-maker and the obtuse hospital orderly.

First published in Suvorin's *New Times* in 1891, *Peasant Women* was regarded by Tolstoy as one of Chekhov's best stories. Completed soon after his return from Sakhalin, the story concerns a peasant woman who murders her husband, is sentenced to hard labour in Siberia, but dies on the way. The story is related by a small trader, Matvey, who had seduced the murdered man's wife and who now takes the orphan son with him on his travels. Staying overnight at the house of a farmer, Dyudya, who lets the upper rooms to travellers, Matvey gives a most vivid account of the events leading up to the murder. Among his audience are Dyudya's daughters-in-law – one of them ugly, with a husband who is almost permanently away, the other pretty, with an idiot for a husband. After hearing Matvey's story, one of them is inspired with thoughts of doing away with her own husband and her father-in-law, and Chekhov succeeds in creating a sinister atmosphere as the two women sleep outside on the warm night, while mysterious figures lurk in the shadows by the church, with a 'fathomless sky and scudding clouds and moon' above.

Three Years, the most 'novelistic' in scope and length of Chekhov's stories, was first published in the journal *Russian Thought* in 1895, and underwent heavy revision for the collected edition, especially the characterization of Laptev and his friends, and his relationship with Julia. In 1894 Chekhov wrote to his sister that he was writing a 'novel of Moscow life' and he described his work on it as 'laborious'.

The story, embodying much material from Chekhov's own childhood, presented a new theme in Russian literature: the portrayal of greed and exploitation against a merchant background. It was published at approximately the same time as the powerful *A Woman's Kingdom*, which has a commercial setting. Both stories were highly acclaimed by contemporary critics, who hailed Chekhov as the 'representative of the new literature' and called him the heir of Russia's great writers.

The central character, Laptev – called a 'suburban Muscovite Hamlet' by one critic – and heir to the haberdashery business, had grown up in that same atmosphere of stifling religious ritual that Chekhov knew as a boy, and there is much in him that is auto-biographical – especially the references to boyhood thrashings as a chorister. The impressive description of the warehouse owned by the Laptevs most probably owes much to Chekhov's memories of the Gavrilov warehouse, where his father once worked. One of Chekhov's longest stories, *Three Years* shows every sign of originally having been intended as a novel. However, Chekhov wrote that his story had turned out 'satin, not silk' and it seems he was temperamentally and artistically unsuited to creating a work with the epic plenitude of a family saga, on the Tolstoyan scale. Interestingly, Laptev's reconciliation with his wife Julia is strongly reminiscent of the similar conclusion to Tolstoy's *Family Happiness*.

The cheating and exploitation in the haberdashery warehouse and the domineering, hypocritical Old Laptev are superbly portrayed, and the rather stifling atmosphere of the story is relieved by glimpses of a more poetical Moscow, with beautiful evocations of fragrant, moonlit nights, gardens with bird-cherry in bloom and suburban retreats. Chekhov's deep love for Moscow is voiced in passages such as:

They [Yartsev and Kostya] were convinced that Moscow was a remarkable city, and Russia a remarkable country. Away in the Crimea or the Caucasus, or abroad, they felt bored, uncomfortable, out of place, and their beloved Moscow's dreary grey weather was the most pleasant and healthy of all, they thought. Days when the cold rain beats on windows and dusk comes on early, when walls of houses and churches take on a sombre, brownish colour, when you don't know what to wear when you go out into the street – days like these pleasantly stimulated them.

With Friends, first published in the journal *Cosmopolis*, in 1898, was written at the request of its editor, the literary historian F. D. Batyushkov. Chekhov, in Nice at the time, replied revealingly to Batyushkov's request for an 'international story, drawn from the local Riviera life': 'I can only write such a story in Russia, from memory. I can only write from memory and I never wrote directly from nature. My memory has to sieve the subject, so that only what is important or typical remains on it, like a filter.' This was the only one of Chekhov's late stories to be excluded from the Collected Edition – for some reason he took a dislike to it. *With Friends*, however, cannot in any way be considered inferior to other stories of this period and is an excellent portrayal of a declining landowning family, and of a love affair that goes wrong. As in *Ionych*, written later that same year, a prosaic, unromantic hero cannot respond to the beautiful girl who is in love with him, even in the poetic setting of a country estate with its fragrant moonlit garden. Indeed, the idyllic atmosphere is destroyed by prosaic intrusions – for example, the discussions of legal and financial matters. The owner of the bankrupt estate, Losev, is a particularly pathetic figure, with his maudlin self-pity and over-indulgence. The description of the moonlit garden at the end of the story distinctly recalls the scene at Otradnoye in *War and Peace* and is invested with a dreamlike quality.

The Bet first appeared in Suvorin's *New Times* in 1889, and was later published in the Collected Edition, with many stylistic changes and the omission of a third chapter which, according to critics such as Grigorovich, obscured the story's intended meaning, creating an impression of the glorification of wealth. The conclusion shows how, at this time, Chekhov was influenced by Tolstoy, and in its didacticism and its treatment of the vanity of earthly riches and human knowledge the story is close to *A Nervous Breakdown* and *The Shoemaker and the Devil*.

The following story, *New Villa*, published in *Russian Annals* in 1899, provides graphic illustration of the great rift between landowner and peasant. An engineer who decides to build a villa in the country, and who earnestly wishes to live in harmony with the local peasants, encounters nothing but hostility and incomprehension, and ends up by despising them and leaving. In this there are marked similarities to scenes in *My Life*, where a well-meaning couple from the upper classes settle in the country and are robbed and cheated. The engineer (who becomes what we may call the village squire after building his villa) had originally come to the district to build a bridge, but the peasants claim they need neither a bridge nor a squire who has their interests at heart. The breakdown in communication exists on a purely linguistic plane too, with the thick-witted peasant Rodion misunderstanding what the squire tells him (which provides a daunting task for the translator). No possibility of any *rapprochement* between peasant and landowner exists and the engineer sells his villa, only to be replaced by a self-important minor civil servant who completely ignores the peasants – probably the best line of defence in the circumstances.

In *At a Country House* Chekhov portrays a reactionary old bore who likes nothing better than the sound of his own voice. Extolling the virtues of 'blue blood' he delivers an interminable harangue to his visitor, who turns out to be of rather plebeian origins and is deeply insulted: as a study of logorrhoea combined with complete tactlessness the story has few equals.

The plotless story (sketch, rather) *Beauties* appeared in *New Times*, in 1888, and its first section most probably incorporates biographical material relating to Chekhov's childhood in the south of Russia. The story contrasts two differing types of ideal feminine beauty. Firstly, there is Masha, the Armenian girl whom the narrator meets in a dusty village, during an exhausting journey over the steppe: her beauty is of the classical variety, with perfectly moulded features, dark eyes with long lashes, delicate white complexion and curly black hair. In contrast the Russian girl whom the narrator meets at a remote railway station has a flat featureless profile, a snub nose and a small mouth. The magical thing about her is her delicate, 'infinitely graceful' movements, her glancing smile, her youthfulness and vivacity.

Both types of beauty have a saddening effect on the narrator and the other onlookers, arousing a train of melancholy, wistful thoughts, a profound regret for lost youth and wasted opportunities. The two girls in *Beauties* are like exotic flowers providing life and colour against the harsh background of existence in the wilderness. The sudden, totally unexpected glimpses of beauty only serve to reinforce in the onlookers' minds a sense of the transience of existence, of the drabness and futility of their own lives. The thoughts of the wretched guard as he contemplates the beautiful young girl embody the whole sadness of human existence:

A guard was standing on the little open platform at the end of our carriage, his elbows propped on the railings. He was looking towards the girl and his flabby, unpleasantly puffy face, exhausted by sleepless nights and the jolting of the train, expressed intense joy and the deepest sorrow, as if he were seeing his own youth, his happiness, sobriety, purity, his wife and children in that girl. He was regretting his sins, it seemed, and he apparently felt with his whole being that the girl was not his and that for him, with his premature ageing, his clumsiness and flabby face, the happiness enjoyed by ordinary people, by train passengers, was as far away as the heavens.

The subject for the following story, *His Wife* (1895), was provided by Chekhov's brother Mikhail and concerns the wretched existence of a henpecked husband. The unfortunate real-life husband was a government official in Yaroslavl by the name of Sablin, who was tormented by a most dreadful wife. Chekhov's brother considered this story as a biography, almost, of Sablin, and Tolstoy thought it one of Chekhov's best. It is a compelling study in marital discord and in the dissolute, flighty, rapacious wife we can see an obvious precursor of Irina in *The Seagull* and of Natasha in *The Three Sisters*.

The Student, originally entitled *Evening*, was first published in *Russian Annals* in 1894. Chekhov had a great love for this story and Bunin records Chekhov saying it was his favourite. A theology student makes his way home across some water meadows, in a desolate tract of country. Despite the fact that it is Easter, a cold wind blows and winter seems to have returned. The very bleakness of nature leads the student to meditate on Russia's remote, barbaric past and he concludes that little has really changed over hundreds of years: all around was that same 'ignorance and suffering, the same wilderness . . . the same gloom and feeling of oppression'. After meeting two widows (mother and daughter) by a bonfire he retells the story of Christ's Betrayal, in highly poetic language. The women are deeply moved, especially the mother. The student sees that there is a strong link between the remote past and the present, for events of almost two thousand years ago have a vital significance for the women listening to him – and for everyone in the world. Indeed, it was not his actual narrative that moved the old woman to tears, but the fact that Peter (Christ's disciple) was 'close to her and because she was concerned, from the bottom of her heart, with his most intimate feelings'. The link between past and present is thus unbroken – the truth and beauty that had prevailed in Christ's time were still valid for humanity and were the most important elements of man's life. This most lyrical of Chekhov's works, a prose poem perhaps, closes with words of optimism: 'A feeling of youthfulness, health, strength – he was only twenty-two – and an inexpressibly sweet anticipation of happiness, of a mysterious, unfamiliar happiness, gradually took possession of him. And life seemed entrancing, wonderful and endowed with sublime meaning.'

The Fiancée

It was ten o'clock in the evening and a full moon was shining over the garden. At the Shumins' the service held at Grandmother's request had just finished. Nadya had gone out into the garden for a moment and now she could see them laying the table for supper, with Grandmother fussing about in her splendid silk dress. Father Andrey, a cathedral dean, was chatting to Nina, Nadya's mother. In the window, in the evening light, her mother looked somehow very young. Father Andrey's son (also called Andrey) was standing nearby listening attentively.

The garden was quiet and cool, and deep, restful shadows lay on the earth. Somewhere, far, far away, probably on the other side of town, she could hear frogs croaking. May, beautiful May was all around! She could breathe deeply and she liked to imagine that somewhere else, beneath the sky, above the trees, far beyond the town, in the fields and forests, spring was unfolding its own secret life, so lovely, rich and sacred, beyond the understanding of weak, sinful man. And she felt rather like crying.

Nadya was twenty-three now. Since the age of sixteen she had longed passionately for marriage and now, at last, she was engaged to that Andrey (Father Andrey's son), whom she could see through the window. She liked him, the wedding was fixed for 7 July, and yet she felt no joy, slept badly and was miserable. Through an open window she could hear people rushing about, knives clattering, a door banging on its block and pulley in the basement where the kitchen was. There was a smell of roast turkey and pickled cherries. She felt that life would go on for ever like this, never changing.

Just then someone came out of the house and stopped on the steps. It was Alexander Timofeyevich, or Sasha for short; he was one of the guests who had arrived from Moscow about ten days before. Once, a long time ago, a distant relative of Grandmother's by the name of Marya Petrovna – an impoverished, widowed gentlewoman, small, thin and in poor health – used to call on her and be given money. Sasha was her son. People said for some mysterious reason that he was a fine artist, and when his mother died Grandmother sent him off to the Komissarov School in Moscow, for the good of her soul. About two years later he transferred to the Fine Arts Institute, where he stayed almost fifteen years, just managing in the end to qualify in architecture. But he did not practise architecture and worked for a firm of lithographers in Moscow instead. Seriously ill most of the time, he would come and stay at Grandmother's nearly every summer to rest and recuperate.

He was wearing a buttoned-up frock-coat and shabby canvas trousers that were ragged at the bottoms. His shirt had not been ironed and on the whole he looked somewhat grubby. Although very thin, with large eyes, long gaunt fingers, a beard and swarthy complexion, he was still a handsome man. He was like one of the family with the Shumins and felt quite at home with them. The room in which he stayed had been known as Sasha's for years.

As he stood in the porch he caught sight of Nadya and went up to her.

'Nice here, isn't it?' he remarked.

'Why, of course. You ought to stay until the autumn.'

'Yes, I might have to. Yes, I may well stay until September.'

For no reason he laughed and sat down next to her.

'Here I am sitting watching Mother,' Nadya said. 'She looks so young from here!' After a brief silence she added, 'Mother does have her weak points. Despite that, she's a remarkable woman.'

'Yes, she's a good woman,' Sasha agreed. 'In her own way your mother's very kind and charming of course, but . . . how can I put it? . . . early this morning I popped into the kitchen and four of the servants were asleep on the bare floor. They don't have beds; instead of bedding all they have is rags, stench, bugs, cockroaches. It's all exactly the same as twenty years ago – nothing's changed. Well, don't blame your grandmother, it's not

18

her fault. But your mother speaks French, doesn't she? She takes part in amateur dramatics. You would have thought that *she* would understand.'

When Sasha spoke he would point two long, emaciated fingers towards the person he was talking to.

'When you're not used to it here it all seems a bit primitive,' he went on. 'No one does a damned thing! Your mother spends the whole day running around enjoying herself like some duchess. Your grandmother doesn't do anything either, nor do you. The same goes for your fiancé Andrey.'

Nadya had heard all this last year and the year before that, she thought. She knew that Sasha just could not think in any other way. This was amusing once; now it rather irritated her.

'That's all old hat, so boring,' she said, getting up. 'You might try and think of something new.'

He laughed as he too got up and both of them walked towards the house. Tall, pretty, with a good figure, she looked so healthy, so attractive next to him. She sensed this and felt sorry for him and somewhat embarrassed. 'You're always going too far!' she said. 'Just now you said something about my Andrey, for example. But you don't know him, do you?'

' "*My*" Andrey! Blow *your* Andrey! It's your *youth* I feel sorry for.'

As they entered the large dining-room, everyone was already sitting down to supper. Grandmother, known as 'Grannie' by everyone in that house, was a very stout, ugly woman with bushy eyebrows and whiskers. She spoke loudly and it was plain from her voice and manner who was head of the house. She owned rows of stalls in the market, and this old house with its columns and garden, but every morning she asked God to spare her from bankruptcy, crying as she prayed. And then there was her daughter-in-law Nina (Nadya's mother), a fair-haired, tightly corseted woman with pince-nez, and diamonds on every finger. There was Father Andrey, a skinny toothless old man, who always seemed about to tell some very funny story. And there was his son Andrey, Nadya's fiancé: he was stout, handsome, with curly hair, and he looked like an actor or an artist. All three of them were discussing hypnotism.

'One week here with me and you'll be better,' Grannie told Sasha. 'But you must eat more – what do you look like!' she sighed. 'Really awful, a true Prodigal Son.'

'He wasted his substance with riotous living,' Father Andrey observed slowly, with laughter in his eyes. 'He filled his belly with the husks that the swine did eat.'

'I do love that dear old father of mine,' Andrey said, touching his father's shoulder. 'He's wonderful – so kind.'

No one said a word. Sasha suddenly burst out laughing and pressed a serviette to his mouth.

'So you believe in hypnotism?' Father Andrey asked Nina.

'I wouldn't venture to assert, of course, that I believe in it,' Nina replied, assuming a deadly serious, almost grim expression. 'But I must admit that nature is full of mysterious, incomprehensible things.'

'I agree entirely, only I would add that religion significantly reduces the domain of the Mysterious.'

A large, extremely plump turkey was served. Father Andrey and Nina carried on talking. The diamonds sparkled on Nina's fingers, then tears sparkled in her eyes. She was excited.

'I daren't even argue with you,' she said. 'Still, you must agree that life has so many insoluble puzzles.'

'Not one, may I assure you.'

After supper young Andrey played the violin and Nina accompanied him on the piano. Ten years ago he had taken a degree in modern languages, but he had never worked anywhere and had no fixed occupation apart from occasionally participating in charity concerts. In town he was called 'The Musician'.

They all listened in silence as Andrey played. The samovar quietly bubbled on the table – only Sasha drank tea. Then, when twelve o'clock struck, a violin string suddenly snapped. Everyone burst out laughing, rushed around and began to say farewell.

After she had seen her fiancé out, Nadya went upstairs, where she and her mother lived (Grandmother occupied the lower floor). Downstairs, in the dining-room, they had started putting the lights out, but Sasha still sat there drinking his tea. He always took a long time over it, Moscow style, and would drink seven glasses at one sitting. For a long while after she had undressed and gone to bed, Nadya could hear the servants clearing away downstairs and Grannie getting cross. Finally, everything was quiet, except for the occasional sound of Sasha's deep cough from his room downstairs.

II

It must have been about two in the morning when Nadya woke up. Dawn was breaking. Somewhere in the distance a night watchman was banging away. She did not feel sleepy. The bed was uncomfortable – much too soft. As she used to do on May nights in the past she sat up in bed to take stock. Her thoughts were just the same as last night's – monotonous, barren, obsessive thoughts about Andrey courting her and proposing, about her accepting him and then gradually coming to appreciate the true worth of that kind, clever man. But now, with the wedding less than a month away, she began to feel scared for some reason, uneasy, as if something vaguely unpleasant lay in store for her.

Once again she heard the watchman lazily beating his stick.

Through the large old window, she could see the garden and then, a little further away, the richly blossoming lilac bushes, sleepy and lifeless in the cold. A dense white mist was drifting towards the lilac, wanting to envelop it. Drowsy crows cawed in far-off trees.

'God, why am I so miserable?'

Perhaps every bride felt like this before her wedding – who knows? Or was it Sasha's influence? But hadn't he been saying the same old thing for years now, as if reciting from a book? He sounded so naïve, so peculiar. Then why couldn't she get Sasha out of her head? Why?

The watchman had long stopped banging. Birds began to chirp beneath the window, and in the garden the mist disappeared and everything around was illumined in the smiling spring sunlight. Soon the whole garden, warmed and caressed by the sun, came to life, and dewdrops glittered on leaves like diamonds. That morning the old, long-neglected garden seemed so young, so decked out.

Grannie was already awake. Sasha was producing his deep

rough cough. She could hear them downstairs putting on the samovar and moving the chairs.

The hours passed slowly. Nadya had been up and taken her garden stroll long ago, but still the morning dragged on.

Then Nina came out with a glass of mineral water, her eyes full of tears. She practised spiritualism and homoeopathy, read a great deal and liked talking about the doubts that were plaguing her – all this (so she thought) had some profound, mysterious meaning. Nadya kissed her mother and walked along with her.

'What were you crying about, Mother?' she asked.

'Last night I started reading a story about an old man and his daughter. The old man was working somewhere and his boss fell in love with his daughter. I didn't finish it, but there was one part you couldn't help crying over.' Nina took a sip from her glass. 'I remembered it this morning and started crying again.'

'I've been feeling so miserable recently,' Nadya said. 'Why can't I sleep at night?'

'I don't know, my dearest. Whenever I can't sleep I close my eyes ever so tight – like this – and imagine Anna Karenina walking and talking. Or I think of something from history, from the ancient world.' Nadya felt that her mother did not and could not understand her – this she felt for the first time in her life, and it really frightened her. She wanted to hide, so she went up to her room.

They had lunch at two. As it was a Wednesday – a Fast Day – Grandmother was served borshch and then bream with buckwheat.

To tease Grandmother, Sasha ate both the borshch and some meat broth of his own concoction. All through lunch he joked, but his clumsy, moralizing witticisms misfired. When he lifted those long, emaciated, corpse-like fingers before launching some joke and you could see how very ill he was – not long for this world perhaps – the effect was far from funny, and you felt so sorry you could have cried.

After lunch Grandmother went to her room to lie down. Nina played the piano for a short while and then she too left.

'Oh, my dear Nadya,' Sasha said, embarking on his customary after-lunch speech. 'If you would only, if you would only ... listen to me ...'

She was deep in an antique armchair, eyes closed, while he slowly paced the room.

'If you would only go away and study!' he said. 'The only interesting people are the educated and idealistic, they're the ones we need. The more there are of these people, the quicker God's kingdom will come on earth – agreed? Very gradually, not one stone of your town will be left on another, everything will be turned upside down, everything will change as if by magic. And then there will be magnificent, huge houses, wonderful gardens, splendid fountains, remarkable people. But that's not the most important part of it. The main thing is, the mob, as we know it, as it exists now – that evil will be no more, since every man will have something to believe in, everyone will know what the purpose of his life is and no one will seek support from the masses. My dear, darling girl, get away from here! Show everyone that you're sick of this vegetating, dull, shameful existence! At least show *yourself*!'

'I can't, Sasha. I'm getting married.'

'That's a fat lot of good! You can't mean it!'

They went out into the garden and walked a little.

'You can say what you like, my dear,' Sasha continued, 'but you must try and realize how squalid and immoral this idle existence of yours is. You must see that! If you, your mother and that Grannie of yours, for example, never do a stroke of work, it means others are doing the work for you, you're ruining the lives of people you've never even met. Isn't that squalid, dishonourable?'

Nadya felt like saying, 'Yes, that's the truth.' She wanted to tell him that she understood, but her eyes filled with tears, and she suddenly grew quiet, hunched her shoulders and went to her room.

Andrey arrived in the late afternoon and gave his usual lengthy performance on the violin. On the whole he was rather taciturn and perhaps he liked playing the violin because then he didn't have to talk. After ten o'clock, when he was preparing to leave and had already put on his coat, he embraced Nadya, hungrily kissing her face, shoulders and hands. 'My dear beautiful darling!' he muttered. 'Oh, how happy I am! I'm going mad with ecstasy!'

Nadya thought that she had heard all this long, long ago – or that she had read it somewhere, in an old, dog-eared, long-abandoned novel.

Sasha was sitting at the dining-room table drinking tea with the saucer balanced on his five long fingers. Grannie was playing patience, Nina was reading. The icon-lamp sputtered and everything seemed serene and happy. Nadya said goodnight and went up to her room, got into bed and fell asleep immediately. However, as on the previous night, she awoke at the first glimmer of dawn. She wasn't sleepy and felt uneasy and depressed. Her head on her knees, she sat thinking about her fiancé, about the wedding. For some reason she recalled that her mother hadn't loved her husband (he had died), that now she had nothing, being completely dependent on Grannie, Nina's mother-in-law. However hard she thought about it Nadya just could not understand why, up to now, she had looked on her mother as someone special, unusual. Why hadn't she realized that she was just a very simple, ordinary, unhappy sort of woman?

Downstairs, Sasha couldn't sleep either. She could hear him coughing. He was a strange, naïve person, thought Nadya, and there was something absurd in those dreams of his, in all those marvellous gardens and extraordinary fountains. But somehow, in that very naïvety – even in his absurdity – there was so much that was fine that the mere thought of going away to study was enough to send a cold shiver through her heart and breast and flood her whole being with joy and rapture.

'But it's best not to think about it,' she whispered. 'I mustn't think about it.'

Far off she could hear the nightwatchman's knocking.

III

In the middle of June, Sasha suddenly felt bored and prepared to leave for Moscow.

'I just can't live in this town,' he said gloomily. 'There's no running water, no drains. And I'm a bit squeamish about eating meals here – that kitchen's positively filthy!'

'Now, wait a minute, Prodigal Son,' Grandmother urged, whispering for some reason. 'The wedding's on the seventh!'

'I don't want to stay any longer.'

'But I thought you'd be here until September!'

'Well, I don't want to stay now. I have work to do.'

Summer had turned out cold and damp, the trees were soaking wet and the whole garden looked miserable and uninviting: it really did make you feel like working. In the upstairs and downstairs rooms unfamiliar women's voices rang out. The sewing-machine in Grandmother's room rattled away – they were hurrying to get the trousseau finished. There were no fewer than six fur coats and the cheapest was costing three hundred roubles, according to Grandmother. All this fuss irritated Sasha, who stayed in his room getting very cross. All the same they persuaded him to stay on and he gave his word not to leave before 1 July.

Time flew. On St Peter's Day, after lunch, Andrey went to Moscow Street with Nadya to have another look at the house that had been rented and prepared for the young couple a long time before. There were two floors, but so far only the upper one had been decorated. There was a glittering floor painted to look like parquet in the lounge, bentwood chairs, a grand piano and a violin-stand. The room smelled of paint. A large oil painting of a naked lady with a broken-handled, violet-coloured vase by her side hung in its gilt frame on the wall.

'Marvellous!' Andrey said with a respectful sigh. 'It's a Shishmachevsky.'

After that came a sitting-room, with a round table, sofa and armchairs upholstered in a bright blue material. A large photograph of Father Andrey, in priest's hat and wearing decorations, hung over the sofa. Then they entered the dining-room, with its sideboard, and then the bedroom. Here in the half-light, two beds stood side by side, giving the impression that the room had been furnished with the intention that everything there would always be perfect and could never be otherwise. Andrey led Nadya through the whole house, keeping his arm around her waist all the time. But she felt weak and guilty, hating all those rooms, beds and armchairs, and nauseated by that naked lady. Now she clearly understood that she no longer loved Andrey and that perhaps she never had. But how could she put it into words, whom could she tell and what good would it do? This was something she did not and could not understand, although she had thought about it for days and nights on end. He was holding her round the waist, talking to her so affectionately, so modestly – he was happy walking around his new house. But all she saw was vulgarity, stupid, fatuous, intolerable vulgarity, and that arm round her waist seemed as hard and cold as an iron hoop. Every minute she was on the verge of running away, sobbing, throwing herself out of the window. Andrey led her to the bathroom, where he placed his hand on a tap set in the wall – and suddenly water flowed.

'What do you think of that?' he said, laughing. 'I had a two-hundred-gallon tank put in the loft. Now you and I shall have water.'

They strolled around the yard and then went out into the street, where they took a cab. Thick clouds of dust blew about, and it looked like rain.

'Don't you feel cold?' Andrey asked, screwing up his eyes from the dust.

She did not reply.

'Do you remember how Sasha told me off yesterday for doing nothing?' he asked after a short silence. 'Well, he's absolutely right! I never do a thing, I just can't. Why is it, my dear? Why does the mere thought of pinning a cockade on my hat and entering government service repel me so much? Why do I feel so edgy when I see a lawyer, a Latin teacher or a local councillor? Oh, Russia, Russia! What a lot of useless idlers you carry on your shoulders! My dear, long-suffering native land, there's so many like me you have to tolerate!'

He was trying to turn the fact that he did nothing into a general truth, seeing it as a sign of the times.

'When we're married,' he continued, 'we'll both go into the country and we'll work! We'll buy a small plot of land with a garden, near a river, we'll slave away and observe the life all around us. Oh, that will be so wonderful!'

He took off his hat and his hair streamed in the wind. As she listened she thought, 'Good God, I want to go back home!'

They were almost back at the house when they overtook Father Andrey.

'There's Father!' Andrey said, joyfully waving his hat. 'I'm so fond of my old man, I really am,' he said as he paid the cab-driver. 'He's such a kind old boy.'

Nadya entered the house feeling angry and unwell. She thought about the guests she would have to entertain all evening – she would have to smile, listen to that violin and all sorts of rubbish, and talk of nothing except that wedding.

Impressive and splendid in her silk dress, Grandmother was sitting by the samovar. She looked haughty, as she invariably did to her guests. Father Andrey came in, smiling his crafty smile.

'I have the pleasure and inestimable satisfaction of seeing you in good health,' he told Grandmother, and it was hard to tell if this was meant seriously or as a joke.

IV

The wind beat against the windows and roof. There was a whistling noise and the hobgoblin in the stove sang its song, plaintively, mournfully. It was past midnight. Everyone in the house had gone to bed, but no one slept and Nadya fancied she could hear someone playing the violin downstairs. Then there was a sharp bang – a shutter must have been torn off its hinges. A minute later Nina entered in her nightdress, with a candle.

'Nadya, what was that bang?' she asked.

With her hair done up in a single plait and smiling timidly, her mother looked older, uglier and shorter on that stormy night. Nadya recalled how, not long ago, she had looked on her mother as an extraordinary woman and had listened proudly to her every word. But now she could not remember those words: everything that came to mind was so feeble and useless.

Suddenly, several deep voices began droning in the stove and she could even make out the words, 'O-oh! Good Go-od!' Nadya sat up in bed, suddenly clutched her head and burst out sobbing.

'Dearest Mother,' she sobbed, 'if only you knew what's happening to me! I beg you, implore you, let me go away from here. Please!'

'But where?' Nina asked, not understanding. 'Where to?'

Nadya wept for a long time, and could not say one word. 'Please let me leave this town!' she said at last. 'There can't be any wedding, there shan't be any wedding, so there! I don't love that man and I can't bear talking about him.'

'No, my darling, no,' Nina said quickly, absolutely horrified. 'Please calm down. You're not yourself at the moment, it will pass. These things happen. You've probably had a little argument with Andrey, but love's not complete without a quarrel.'

'Please leave me alone, Mother. Please!' sobbed Nadya.

'Yes,' Nina said after a brief silence. 'Not long ago you were a child, just a little girl, and now you're going to be married. This transmutation of matter is constantly taking place in nature. Without even noticing it, you'll be a mother yourself, then an old lady – and then you'll have a stubborn little daughter like I have.'

'My sweet darling, you *are* clever, but you're unhappy,' Nadya said. 'You're very unhappy, but why say such nasty things? In heaven's name why?'

Nina wanted to speak, but she was unable to utter one word. Sobbing, she went to her room. Those deep voices began droning in the stove again and Nadya suddenly felt terrified. She leapt out of bed and dashed to her mother's room. Nina was lying under a light blue quilt, book in hand; her eyes were filled with tears.

'Mother, please hear what I have to say!' Nadya said. 'Now think and try to see my point of view. Just look how petty and degrading our lives are. My eyes have been opened, I can see everything clearly now. What's so special about Andrey? He's not very clever, is he, Mother? Heavens, can't you see that he's stupid!'

Nina sat up abruptly.

'You and your grandmother are torturing me,' she sobbed. 'I want some life . . . some life!' she repeated, striking herself twice on the chest with her fist. 'Give me my freedom. I'm still young, I want some life, but you two have made an old woman out of me.'

She wept bitterly, lay down and curled up under the quilt – she seemed so small, pathetic, stupid. Nadya went to her room, dressed, and sat by the window to wait for morning. All night long she sat there brooding, while someone seemed to be banging the shutter from outside and whistling.

In the morning Grandmother complained that the wind had blown all the apples off the trees during the night and broken an old plum tree. Everything was so grey, dull and cheerless, it seemed dark enough for lighting the lamps. Everyone complained of the cold, and the rain lashed the windows. After her morning tea, Nadya went to Sasha's room. Without a word she knelt in the corner by his armchair and covered her face in her hands.

'What's the matter?' Sasha asked.

'I can't stand it any more,' she said. 'I just don't understand how I could ever have lived in this place. It's beyond me. I despise my fiancé, I despise myself and I despise this idle existence.'

'It's all right now,' Sasha said, not yet realizing what was wrong. 'It's all right. Everything's fine.'

For a minute, Sasha looked at her in amazement. Finally he understood and was as happy as a little boy. He waved his arms and delightedly performed a tap-dance in his slippers.

'Wonderful!' he said, rubbing his hands. 'God, that's wonderful!'

Like one enchanted, her large eyes full of love, she looked at him unblinking, expecting him to tell her something vitally, immensely important there and then. He had not told her anything yet, but she felt that a new, boundless world that she had never known was opening up before her. She watched him, full of expectation and ready for anything – even death.

'I'm leaving tomorrow,' he said after a moment's thought, 'and you can come to the station, so that it looks as if you're seeing me off. I'll put your luggage in my trunk and get your ticket. When the departure bell rings, on you get and off we go. Come with me as far as Moscow, then travel on to St Petersburg on your own. Do you have a passport?'

'Yes.'

'You won't be sorry, I swear it. You won't have any regrets,' Sasha said enthusiastically. 'You'll start your studies and then it's all in the hands of fate. Drastically alter your way of life and then everything else will change too. The most important thing is to make a completely fresh start, the rest doesn't matter. So, we'll leave tomorrow then?'

'Oh yes, for God's sake yes!'

Nadya felt very agitated, more depressed than ever before – and now there was the prospect of going through sheer mental hell until the time came to leave. But the moment she went upstairs and lay on her bed she fell asleep. And she slept soundly, right until the evening, and there was a smile on her tear-stained face.

V

A cab had been ordered. With her hat and coat on, Nadya went upstairs for one more look at her mother, at all that had been hers. In her own room she stood by the bed – still warm – looked around and then went to her mother's room without making a sound. Nina was asleep and it was quiet there. Nadya kissed her mother, smoothed her hair and stood still for a couple of minutes. Then she slowly went downstairs.

It was pelting with rain. The cab's top was up and the driver was standing near the porch, soaking wet.

'There won't be enough room for you, Nadya,' Grandmother said when the servants started putting the luggage in. 'Fancy seeing someone off in this weather! You should stay at home! Heavens, just look at that rain!'

Nadya wanted to say something, but she couldn't. Sasha helped her to sit down, covered her legs with a rug and sat beside her.

'Good luck! God bless!' Grandmother shouted from the porch. 'Mind you write to us from Moscow, Sasha.'

'Of course. Cheerio, Grannie.'

'May God protect you!'

'What lousy weather,' Sasha said.

Only now did Nadya begin to cry. Only now did she realize that she was actually leaving – even when she had said goodbye to Grandmother and looked at her mother she still hadn't believed it. Farewell, dear old town! Suddenly she remembered everything: Andrey, his father, the new house, the naked lady with the vase.

None of these things frightened or oppressed her any more – it all seemed so mindless and trivial, and was receding ever further into the past. When they climbed into the carriage and the train moved off, all that past existence which had seemed so large, so serious, now dwindled into insignificance, and a vast, broad future opened out before her, a future she had hardly dreamt of. The rain beat against the carriage windows and all she could see was green fields, with glimpses of telegraph poles and birds on the wires. Suddenly she gasped for joy: she remembered that she was travelling to freedom, that she was going to study – it was exactly the same as running away to join the Cossacks, as it was called long, long ago. She laughed, she wept, she prayed.

'Don't worry!' Sasha said, grinning. 'Everything's going to be all right!'

VI

Autumn passed, winter followed. Nadya felt very homesick. Every day she thought about Mother and Grandmother, and about Sasha. The letters from home were calm and affectionate and it seemed that all had been forgiven and forgotten. After the May examinations she went home feeling healthy and cheerful, stopping at Moscow on the way to see Sasha. He looked just the same as last summer: bearded, hair dishevelled, with the same frock-coat and canvas trousers, the same big, handsome eyes. But he looked ill and worn-out, and he had aged, grown thinner and was always coughing. Somehow he struck Nadya as dull, provincial.

'Good God, Nadya's here!' he said, laughing cheerfully. 'My dear little darling!'

They sat in the smoky printing-room with its suffocating, overwhelming smell of Indian ink and paint. Then they went to his room, also full of the smell of stale tobacco, and with saliva stains. On the table, next to a cold samovar, lay a broken plate and a piece of dark paper. Both table and floor were covered with dead flies. Everything showed what a slipshod existence Sasha led – he was living any old how, with a profound contempt for creature comforts. If someone had spoken to him about his personal happiness, his private life, about someone being in love with him, he wouldn't have understood – he would have just laughed.

'It's all right, everything's turned out nicely,' Nadya said hurriedly. 'Last autumn Mother came to St Petersburg to see me. She told me that Grandmother isn't angry, but she keeps going to my room and making the sign of the cross over the walls.'

Sasha looked at her cheerfully, but he kept coughing and spoke in a cracked voice. Nadya watched him closely, unable to tell whether he really was seriously ill or if she was imagining it.

'Dear Sasha, you really *are* ill, aren't you?' she asked.

'No, it's nothing. I'm ill, but not terribly . . .'

'Good God,' Nadya said, deeply disturbed. 'Why don't you go and see a doctor, why don't you look after your health? My dear, sweet Sasha!' The tears spurted from her eyes. For some strange reason, Andrey, that naked lady with the vase, her entire past which now seemed as remote as her childhood – all this loomed in her imagination now. She wept because Sasha did not seem as abreast of things, as intellectual, as interesting as last year.

'Dear Sasha, you are very, very ill. I would do anything in the world to stop you being so pale and thin. I owe you so much. You can't imagine how much you've done for me, my good Sasha! Really, you're my very nearest and dearest now.'

They sat talking for a while. But now, after that winter she had spent in St Petersburg, everything about Sasha – his words, his smile, his whole presence – seemed outmoded, old-fashioned, obsolete and lifeless.

'I'm going down to the Volga the day after tomorrow,' Sasha said, 'and then I'll be taking the fermented mare's milk cure – drinking *koumiss*. A friend of mine and his wife are coming with me. The wife's quite amazing. I've been trying to win her over and persuade her to go and study. I want her life to be transformed.'

After their talk they went to the station. Sasha treated her to tea and some apples. As he stood there smiling and waving his handkerchief while the train pulled out, one could tell just by looking at his legs that he was desperately ill and did not have long to live.

Nadya arrived at her home town at noon. As she drove from the station, the streets seemed very wide, but the houses small and squat. No one was about, except for a German piano-tuner in his brown coat. All the houses seemed covered in dust. Grandmother, who was really quite ancient now and as plump and ugly as ever, flung her arms round Nadya and wept for a long time, pressing her face to her shoulder and unable to tear herself away. Nina also looked a great deal older and had deteriorated considerably. She had a hunched-up look, but was still as tightly corseted as before and diamonds still sparkled on her fingers.

'My darling!' she exclaimed, trembling all over. 'My darling!'

They sat down, silently weeping. Grandmother and Mother plainly sensed that the past had gone for ever, that nothing could bring it back. No longer did they have any position in society, reputation, the right to entertain guests. It was rather like when, in the midst of a life without cares, the police raid the house suddenly one night and the master turns out to be an embezzler and forger – then it's goodbye for ever to any carefree, untroubled exitence!

Nadya went upstairs and saw that same bed, those same windows with their simple white curtains, that same cheerful, noisy garden bathed in sunlight. She touched her table, sat down and pondered. Then she ate a fine lunch and drank tea with delicious rich cream. But something was missing, however – the rooms seemed empty and the ceilings low. That night, when she went to bed and pulled up the blankets, it was somehow rather funny lying in that warm, very soft bed again.

Nina came in for a moment and sat down guiltily, timidly glancing around her.

'Well, how are you, Nadya?' she asked after a brief silence. 'Are you happy? Very happy?'

'Yes I am, Mother.'

Nina stood up and made the sign of the cross over Nadya and the windows.

'As you see, I've become religious. You know, I'm studying philosophy now and I think a great deal. Many things have become as clear as daylight now. Filter your whole life through a prism – that's the most important thing.'

'Tell me, Mother, how's Grandmother's health these days?'

'Not too bad, it seems. After you left with Sasha and your telegram arrived, Grandmother collapsed when she read it. She lay for three days without moving. Then she kept praying and crying. But she's all right now.'

She stood up and paced the room.

That knocking could be heard again – it was the night-watchman.

'Your whole life must be filtered through a prism, that's what's most important,' Nina said. 'In other words, one's perception of life must be broken down into its simplest elements, like the seven primary colours, and each element must be studied separately.'

Whatever else Nina said, Nadya didn't hear. And she didn't hear her leave either, as she was soon fast asleep.

May passed, June began. Nadya had grown used to that house again. Grandmother fussed over the samovar, heaving deep sighs, and Nina talked about her philosophy in the evenings. She was still in the ignominious position of hanger-on in that household and had to turn to Grandmother for every twenty-copeck piece. The house was full of flies and the ceilings seemed to get lower and lower. Grannie and Nina never went out into the street for fear of meeting Father Andrey, or Andrey his son. Nadya would walk around the garden, down the street, look at the houses, the grey fences. Everything in that town struck her as ancient, obsolete – either it was awaiting its own demise or perhaps some fresh beginning. Oh, if only that bright new life would come quickly, then one could face one's destiny boldly, cheerful and free in the knowledge that one was right! That life would come, sooner or later. Surely the time would come when not a trace would remain of Grandmother's house, where four servants were forced to live in one filthy basement room – it would be forgotten, erased from the memory. The only distraction for Nadya was the small boys from next door. Whenever she strolled in the garden they would bang on the fence, laugh and taunt her with the words, 'And she thought she was going to get married, she did!'

A letter came from Sasha – from Saratov. In that sprightly, dancing hand of his he wrote that his trip on the Volga had been a huge success, but that he hadn't been well in Saratov, had lost his voice and had been in hospital for two weeks. Nadya understood what this meant and felt a deep foreboding that was very similar to absolute certainty. But her forebodings and thoughts about Sasha did not trouble her as much as before, and this she found disagreeable. She passionately wanted a full life and to go to St Petersburg again, and her friendship with Sasha seemed a thing of the far distant past, even though she still cherished it. She lay awake the whole night and next morning sat by the window listening. And she did hear voices down below – Grandmother, highly agitated, was asking one question after another.

Then someone began to cry. When Nadya went downstairs she saw Grandmother standing in a corner praying, her face tear-stained. On the table lay a telegram.

Nadya paced the room for a long time listening to Grandmother crying, then she picked up the telegram and read it. The news was that yesterday morning Alexander Timofeyevich (or Sasha for short) had died of tuberculosis in Saratov.

Grandmother and Nina went to church to arrange a prayer service, while Nadya kept pacing the house, thinking things over. She saw quite clearly that her life had been turned upside down, as Sasha had wanted, that she was a stranger in this place, unwanted, and that there was nothing in fact that *she* needed from it. She saw how her whole past had been torn away, had vanished as if burnt and the ashes scattered in the wind.

She went to Sasha's room and stood there for a while.

'Goodbye, dear Sasha!' she thought, and before her there opened up a new, full and rich life. As yet vague and mysterious, this life beckoned and lured her.

She went upstairs to pack and next morning said goodbye to her family. In a lively, cheerful mood she left that town – for ever, so she thought.

On Official Business

 භළ

An acting coroner and a country doctor were travelling to the village of Syrnya to carry out an inquest. On the way they were caught in a snowstorm and for a long time they drove around in circles. Instead of reaching their destination at noon, as had been intended, they arrived in the evening, when it was dark. Their lodging for the night was a hut – the rural council 'offices'. It so happened that in these 'offices' lay the corpse – that of Lesnitsky, the council's insurance agent who had come to Syrnya three days before, settled in the hut, asked for a samovar and then, to everyone's amazement, shot himself. The strange circumstances of his death – over a samovar, after spreading out his food on the table – led many to believe that he had been murdered. An inquest was necessary.

The doctor and coroner stamped their feet in the passage to shake off the snow, while next to them stood old Ilya Loshadin (the village constable) holding a tin lamp as a light for them. There was a strong smell of paraffin.

'And who may you be?' the doctor asked.

'The consterball,' replied the constable.

And that was how he signed himself at the post-office: *consterball*.

'And where are the witnesses?'

'Probably gone to tea, sir.'

To the right was the front room or 'reception', for the gentry, while on the left was the common people's room, with its large stove and sleeping-benches. The doctor and coroner, followed by the constable with his lamp above his head, entered the 'reception'. Here on the floor, by the table legs, was a long, motionless body, covered in a white sheet. Besides the white covering some new rubber galoshes were clearly visible in the dim lamplight and the whole scene was chilling and macabre, what with those dark walls, the silence, the galoshes and the immobility of the body. On the table there was the samovar, long cold, with packets of what was presumably food lying around it.

'Shooting oneself in a *council* hut – how tactless,' the doctor said. 'If he had the urge to put a bullet in his brains, he could have done it at home, in a shed somewhere.' Just as he was, in his fur cap, coat and felt boots, he sank on to a bench. His companion the coroner sat opposite.

'These hysterical, neurotic types are such terrible egotists,' the doctor continued bitterly. 'When a neurotic sleeps in the same room as you, he'll start rustling a newspaper. When he dines with you, he'll make a scene with his wife – oblivious of your presence. And when he has the urge to shoot himself, he does it in a village, in a council hut, to create as much inconvenience as possible. Whatever the circumstances, these gentlemen think only of themselves. Themselves! That's why old people hate this so-called "neurotic age" so much.'

'But there's just no end to what old folk dislike,' the coroner said, yawning. 'Go and point out to these old people the difference between suicides as they used to be and those we get nowadays. Formerly, your so-called respectable gent would shoot himself because he'd embezzled government funds, but contemporary suicides do it because they're sick of life, depressed. Tell me, who's superior?'

'The man who's sick of life and depressed. But you must agree, this one might at least have shot himself somewhere else – not in a council hut.'

'It's all so terrible,' the constable said, 'like punishment from above. The people are very upset – it be three nights since they slept. The children don't stop crying. There's cows to be milked, but the women be too scared to go into the shed, in case they sees that gentleman's ghost in the dark. Yes, they're stupid women all right, but some of the men be scared too. Come evening they won't go past this hut on their own, they'll sort of herd themselves into a bunch. It be the same with the witnesses . . .'

Dr Starchenko, middle-aged, with a dark beard and spectacles, and the young fair-haired coroner Lyzhin, who had graduated only two years before and looked more like a student than an official, sat silently, deep in thought. They were annoyed at having been delayed. Now they would have to wait until morning and spend the night here. But it was still only between five and six o'clock and they were faced with a long evening, then a long, dark night, boredom, an uncomfortable place to sleep, cockroaches and the early morning cold. As they listened to the blizzard howling in the chimney and loft, both thought how remote it all was from the kind of life they had really wanted for themselves and of which they had once dreamed. And how different they were from their contemporaries, who were at that very moment strolling down brightly lit streets not caring about bad weather, or getting ready for the theatre, or sitting over a book in their study. How much would they have given to be walking down Nevsky Avenue in St Petersburg or Petrovka Street in Moscow, to hear some decent singing or to sit for an hour or two in a restaurant!

The blizzard wailed in the loft and something outside banged angrily – most likely the council hut's signboard.

'Please yourself what you do, but I don't feel like spending the night here,' Starchenko said, getting up. 'It's not six yet – it's too early for bed. I'm going out. Von Taunitz doesn't live far from here, only about two miles from Syrnya. I'll drive over and spend the evening with him. Constable, go and tell the driver not to unharness the horses. Well, what will you do?' he asked Lyzhin.

'I don't know. Go to sleep, I think.'

The doctor wrapped himself in his fur coat and left. He could be heard talking to the driver, and sleigh-bells jingled on horses numb with cold. He drove off.

'Sir, it won't do for you to be spending the night in this room,' the constable said. 'Go into the other one. It's not clean, but that won't matter for one night. I'll get a samovar from one of the men here and put it on. Then I'll make up a nice little pile of hay for you, sir, so's you can have a good sleep.'

Shortly afterwards the coroner was sitting at a table in the 'common' room, drinking tea, while constable Loshadin stood by the door and talked. He was an old man – past sixty – not tall, very thin, hunchbacked, pale, with an innocent smile and eyes that watered. He was always smacking his lips as if sucking a boiled sweet. He wore a short sheepskin coat and felt boots, and he was always holding a stick. Evidently he was touched at seeing such a young coroner and this was probably why he spoke to him so familiarly.

'Fyodor, what's in charge in the village, told me to report to him as soon as the police officer or coroner arrived,' he said. 'So, I'd better be going. He lives about three miles from here, and there's a blizzard blowing and drifting. Very nasty – I don't think I'll make it before midnight. D'ye hear that howling?'

'I don't need your boss,' Lyzhin said. 'There's nothing he can do here.'

He gave the old man a quizzical look and asked, 'Tell me, old chap, how long have you been village constable in these parts?'

'How long? Well, must be nigh on thirty year. It was about five year after the serfs was freed that I began, so you can work it out for yourself. Since then I've been doing it every day. Folk may be holidaying, but I have to keep going. Folks might be celebrating Easter, church bells ringing and Christ being resurrected, but I keeps going around with me little bag. To the treasurer's department, the post-office, the police inspector's house, the magistrate, council offices, tax inspector, gentlefolk, village folk and all God-fearing Christians. I carry parcels, summonses, tax papers, letters, all kinds of forms and lists. Nowadays, my good sir, there's no end to these forms – yellow, white, red – all for writing figures on. Every squire, parson and rich farmer has to write down, ten times a year, how much he's sown or reaped, how many bushels or hundredweight of rye he's got, how much oats and hay, what the weather's like, and about different sorts of insects. They please themselves what they write of course, it's only just forms, but I has to run round handing them sheets of paper out – and then it's me what has to collect 'em all in. Now, that dead gent over there. There's no need to slit him open, you yourself knows it's a waste of time and you'd only get your hands dirty. But you've had to go to the bother, sir, you've driven out here, all because of them *forms*. It's all right in summer, then it's warm and dry, but in winter or autumn it's nasty. Time was when I fair near drowned and froze – all sorts of things happened. Once some rotten devils stole me bag in the forest and beat me up. And I've been in court too.'

'In *court*? What for?'

'Fraud.'

'What do you mean, "fraud"?'

'Well now, our clerk Khrisanf Grigoryev happens to sell a contractor some planks what didn't belong to him – cheats him, I mean. I was there at the time, they sends me over to the pub for vodka. Well, the clerk wouldn't deal me in, didn't even treat me to a drink. He could see I was poor, not reliable-looking, a bit of no good. So the two of us ends up in court. He goes to prison but they let me off on all charges, thank God. They read one of them forms out in court and they were all wearing uniforms. In court, I mean. Now, I'm telling you sir, for anyone not used to it, the job I do is real hell, though it don't worry us what does it, God help me. Your feet starts aching when you're *not* on your rounds! And it's worse indoors. At the council offices you have to make up the clerk's stove, fetch the clerk's water, clean the clerk's boots.'

'And how much do you earn?' Lyzhin asked.

'Eighty-four roubles a year.'

'Surely there's a few perks, though?'

'*What* perks? Nowadays gentlefolk seldom gives you a tip. These days gentlefolk are hard, very touchy they are. Keep going off the deep end if you takes them some forms and they get mad if you doffs your hat to them. They'll say you came in by the wrong door, call you a drunkard, say you stink of onion, call you blockhead and son of a bitch. Of course, there's some decent ones, but you won't get much out of them. They'll laugh and call you names. Squire Altukhin, for example. He's a kind man and seems sober enough, and there's no flies on him. But the moment he sees you coming he starts shouting things he don't even understand himself. He gave me a nickname. "You," says he, "are a —"'

The constable pronounced a word, but so softly it was impossible to make it out.

'What?' Lyzhin asked. 'Say that again.'

'*Administrator!*' the constable repeated out loud. 'He's been

calling me that for ages, for six years. "Hullo, administrator!"
he'll say. But I don't mind, to hell with him. Now and again a
lady'll send out a glass of vodka or a piece of pie and you drink
her health. But peasants give you most. Peasants are more kindly,
they fear God. One'll give you some bread, another a drop of
cabbage soup or a little drink. The village elders'll treat you to tea
in the pub, like those witnesses here who've gone off for tea.
"Loshadin," they say, "you wait here and keep a look out" –
then they give me a copeck each. They're frightened because
they're not used to this kind of thing. Yesterday they gave me
fifteen copecks and a glass of tea.'

'But don't *you* feel scared?'

'Oh yes, sir, but that's all part of the job, there's no escaping it.
Last year I was taking a prisoner to town and he starts knocking
the living daylights out of me. All around there was just fields
and forest, nowhere to run to. Now, about these here goings-on.
I remember this gentleman Lesnitsky when he was only this high
and I remember his dad and mum. I'm from Nedoshchotovo and
the Lesnitskys live half a mile away, less I think – our land
borders on theirs. This Mr Lesnitsky had an unmarried sister, a
God-fearing merciful woman. Remember, O Lord, Thy servant
Julia, may her memory never die! She didn't marry and when
she was dying she divided up all her property. She left two
hundred and fifty acres to the monastery and to us peasants in
Nedoshchotovo she left five hundred, to remember her by. But
some say her brother, the squire, hid the piece of paper and burnt
it in the stove, collaring all the land for himself. Thought it was
for his own good, but he was wrong. You can't prosper by wrong-
doing in this world, friend. For twenty years the squire didn't go
to confession, he stayed away from the church and died without
repenting. He just burst right open he did – he was as fat as could
be. He burst right the way down. Then they took everything
away from the young gentleman over there – Seryozha's the
name – to pay the debts. Now, he didn't have much education,
wasn't much good at anything really. So his uncle, head of the
local council, says: "I'll take Seryozha on as an insurance agent,
let him try it, it's not difficult." But the young gent was proud,
wanted something with a bit more scope, more free and easy.

Well, it's sinking a bit low to go dragging yourself all over the place in some lousy old cart and talking to ordinary peasants. When he went round he would always keep looking at the ground, not saying nothing. If you shouted right in his ear, "Mr Seryozha!" he'd look round and all you'd get was "Eh?" And now he's done away with himself. It's very awkward, sir, it's not right. Can't make this sort of thing out, for the life of me I can't. Just supposing your father was rich and you was poor. Well, all very tough, of course, but you have to grin and bear it. Time was when I lived well, sir. Had two horses, three cows, twenty head of sheep. But later on all I had left was me little bag – and that wasn't really mine, it was the government's. And now, come to mention it, I've the lousiest house in the whole of Nedoshchotovo village. King one day, servant the next, I've come right down in the world I have.'

'How did you become so poor?' the coroner asked.

'My sons are all on the vodka, drink like fish they do. You'd never believe how much they knock back.'

As he listened, Lyzhin realized that *he* would be returning to Moscow sooner or later, but that this old man would never move from here, forever doing his rounds. And how many more of these scruffy, unkempt, 'no good' old men he would meet in life, men in whose minds thoughts of fifteen-copeck coins, glasses of tea, the belief that dishonesty gets you nowhere had somehow inseparably merged into a single idea. Bored with listening to the old man, he ordered him to bring some hay for the bedding. In the 'reception' stood an iron bedstead with a pillow and blanket that could have been moved in for him, but the corpse of the man who had possibly sat on it before he died had been lying next to it for three days. Sleeping in it now wouldn't have been very pleasant . . .

'It's still only half past seven,' Lyzhin thought, glancing at his watch. 'That's awful!'

He did not feel sleepy, but, since he had nothing else to do, and in order to kill time, he lay down and covered himself with a rug. Loshadin came in and out several times to clear away the tea things, smacking his lips, sighing and fussing around the table. Finally he took his lamp and left. As he looked at his long grey hair and hunched-up body from behind Lyzhin thought, 'He's just like a wizard in an opera.'

It was dark now. The moon must have been behind the clouds, since the windows and snow on the frames were clearly visible.

Still the blizzard howled. 'Heavens above!' a woman moaned up in the loft – this was what he thought he could hear.

Then there came a great crash as something hit the wall outside. The coroner listened hard. No woman was up there – it was the wind howling. He felt chilly, so he put his fur coat over the rug. As he warmed himself, he thought how all this – the blizzard, the hut, the old man, the corpse in the next room – was so remote from the life he had wanted to lead. How alien, petty and dreary it was! If that man had killed himself in Moscow or thereabouts and if he had been put in charge of the inquest, it would have been so interesting, so important – he might even have been scared of sleeping in the room next to a corpse. But in this place, over six hundred miles from Moscow, everything appeared in a different light: this wasn't real life, these weren't real people, they were just items entered 'on forms' as Loshadin would have said. None of this would leave the slightest trace in his memory – all would be forgotten the moment Lyzhin drove out of Syrnya. His native land, the *real* Russia – that was Moscow, St Petersburg; but here he was in some provincial outpost. When you dream of being important, popular – a top investigator, for example, a chief prosecutor at the assizes, a darling of society – then Moscow was the only conceivable place to be. Everything was happening in Moscow, but here you wanted nothing – you became very easily reconciled to obscurity and all you asked of life was for it to pass, the sooner the better. Lyzhin's imagination carried him down Moscow's streets and he called at houses he knew so well, met relatives and colleagues, and experienced a delicious thrill at the thought that he was only twenty-six and that if he could get away from here and end up in Moscow within five or ten years, then it still wouldn't be too late, his whole life would be ahead of him. Slipping deeper into unconsciousness, his thoughts growing more and more confused, he imagined the long corridors in the Moscow courts, delivering a speech, his sisters, an orchestra which kept humming away for some reason ... It was the howling of the blizzard. Then he heard that crashing and banging from outside again.

Suddenly he remembered how he was once talking to a bookkeeper at the council offices when a pale, thin gentleman, dark-eyed and black-haired, had come up to the counter. His eyes had that unpleasant look you find in people who have had a long sleep after lunch, and it spoiled his fine, clever profile. The jackboots he wore did not suit him, they were roughly made. 'This is our insurance agent,' the bookkeeper had said by way of introduction.

'So *that* was Lesnitsky . . . the very same . . .' Lyzhin reasoned.

He recalled Lesnitsky's quiet voice, pictured the way he walked and had the feeling that someone was walking quite near him now – the way Lesnitsky used to walk. He was terrified. His head went cold. 'Who's there?' he asked in alarm.

'The consterball.'

'What do you want?'

'Just something I wanted to ask, sir. You said you don't need the man what's in charge round here, but I'm scared he might get angry. He told me to go and fetch him. I'd better go, eh?'

'Blow you! I'm fed up with you!' Lyzhin said irritably, covering himself again.

'He might get angry . . . I'll be on my way now, sir, you make yourself comfortable.'

And Loshadin went. The sound of coughing and whispering came from the passage. The witnesses had returned, no doubt. 'Tomorrow we'll let those poor devils go early,' the coroner thought. 'We'll start the inquest as soon as it's light.'

He was sinking into unconsciousness when suddenly there were steps again – not timid ones, but swift and noisy. A door slammed, he could hear voices, someone striking a match.

'So, asleep then? Are you asleep?' Dr Starchenko was asking hurriedly and angrily, and cold air seemed to emanate from him. 'Asleep then? Get up. We're driving over to Von Taunitz's. He's sent his own horses for you. Let's go – at least you'll get supper there and a proper bed to sleep in. As you see, I've come to collect you myself. They're fine horses, we'll do it in twenty minutes.'

'What time is it?'

'A quarter past ten.'

Sleepy and sulky, Lyzhin put on his felt boots, fur coat, hat and hood and went outside with the doctor. It wasn't freezing cold, but a strong, biting wind was blowing, driving clouds of snow along the street – they seemed to be running away in terror. Deep drifts had already piled up by fences and front doors. The doctor and coroner sat in the sledge and the white driver bent over to button up the travelling rug. Both felt hot.

'Off we go!'

Through the village street they went. Watching the trace-horse's legs working away, the coroner thought of the lines from Pushkin's *Eugene Onegin*: 'He clove the snow in powdered furrows'. Lights were burning in every hut, as though on the eve of some important festival: the villagers hadn't gone to bed, they were all too scared of the corpse. The coachman maintained a gloomy silence – no doubt he had grown bored waiting outside the council hut and was also thinking about the corpse.

'As soon as they heard at Taunitz's that you were staying the night in that hut, they all came down on me like a ton of bricks for not bringing you with me.'

Rounding a bend as they drove out of the village, the driver suddenly shouted at the top of his voice, 'Get out of the way!'

They glimpsed some man up to his knees in snow – he'd stepped off the road and was watching the sledge with its three-horse team. The coroner saw a crooked stick, a beard and a bag at the man's side – it was Loshadin, it seemed, and he even appeared to be smiling. It was only a fleeting glimpse, then he disappeared.

The road ran along the edge of a wood at first, then down a cutting. They glimpsed old pines, young birches, lofty young gnarled oaks standing alone in clearings where trees had recently been felled, but soon everything was blurred in swirling snow. The driver said that he could see the forest, but all the coroner could see was the trace-horse. The wind blew in their backs.

Suddenly the horses stopped.

'Well, what is it now?' Starchenko asked angrily.

The driver silently climbed from the box and ran round the sledge, treading with his heels. He described ever-widening

45

circles, moving further and further from the sledge, and he seemed to be dancing. Finally he came back and turned right.

'Lost the way?' Starchenko asked.

'It's all right.'

Now they came to some wretched little village without a single light. Then more woods and fields. Again they lost the way and the driver climbed from his box and did some more dancing. The three-horse team tore down a dark avenue and continued at great speed, while the heated trace-horse kept kicking against the front of the sledge. Here the trees made a terrifying hollow roar and it was pitch black – just as if they were all plunging into an abyss. But then, suddenly, the bright light of a drive and windows struck their eyes, a friendly bark rang out, there were voices. They had arrived.

While they were taking off their fur coats and felt boots in the hall, someone played *Un petit verre de Cliquot* on a piano upstairs, and they could hear children stamping about. Immediately, the guests encountered the warmth and smell of old manor-house rooms where, whatever the weather outside, life is always so cosy, clean and comfortable.

'Splendid!' exclaimed Von Taunitz – a fat man with an unbelievably broad neck and side whiskers – as he shook the coroner's hand. 'Splendid! Welcome! I'm delighted to meet you. You and I could really be called colleagues, couldn't we? Once I was a deputy prosecutor, but not for long, two years in all. I came here to run this estate and I've grown old here. An old fogy, in short.' Obviously trying to speak softly he continued, 'Welcome to my house!' and he went upstairs with his guests. 'I haven't any wife, she died, but may I introduce you to my daughters.' Turning round he shouted downstairs in a thunderous voice, 'Tell Ignaty to bring the sledge round at eight o'clock tomorrow morning.'

In the drawing-room were his four daughters, all young and pretty, all in grey dresses and with identical hair styles. With them was a young cousin and her children – she was young and attractive too. Starchenko, who knew them already, immediately asked them to sing something and two of the young ladies gave him lengthy assurances that they couldn't sing and that they had no music. Then the cousin sat at the piano and they sang a duet from *The Queen of Spades*, voices trembling. Then *Un petit verre de Cliquot* was played again and the children skipped, beating time with their feet. Starchenko started skipping too. Everyone laughed.

Then the children said goodnight and went off to bed. The coroner laughed, danced a quadrille, flirted with the ladies and wondered if it was all a dream. The ordinary peasants' room in that council hut, the heap of hay in the corner, the rustling cockroaches, the revolting, wretched surroundings, the witnesses' voices, the wind, the snowstorm, the danger of losing the way – and then, suddenly, these magnificent bright rooms, piano music, pretty girls, curly-haired children and cheerful, happy laughter: it was a fairy-tale transformation and it just didn't seem possible that this could happen within two miles or so, within one hour. And depressing thoughts dampened his gaiety and he reflected that these were mere scraps of existence all around, fragments and not life at all. Everything here was fortuitous, it seemed – you could draw no firm conclusions from it. He even felt sorry for these young girls, who were living and who would end their lives here in this provincial backwater, remote from civilized surroundings where nothing happened by chance, where everything had been thought out and obeyed the laws of logic, where any suicide, for example, could be explained, its meaning in the general flow of life demonstrated. He supposed that if he couldn't understand the life in this backwater, if he couldn't see it, then this meant it just didn't exist.

Over supper they discussed Lesnitsky.

'He left a wife and child,' Starchenko said. '*I* wouldn't allow neurotics and mentally disturbed people to marry. I would deprive them of the right and opportunity to reproduce their own kind. It's criminal bringing mentally disturbed children into this world.'

'That poor young man,' Von Taunitz said, softly sighing and shaking his head. 'How much heart-searching and suffering must one experience before finally deciding to take one's life. Such tragedies can happen in any family and it's absolutely shocking. These things are hard to take, they're unbearable.'

Glancing at their father, all the girls listened in silence, with serious faces. Lyzhin felt that he should have offered his point of view, but all he could say was, 'Yes, suicide is an undesirable phenomenon.'

He slept in a soft bed, in a warm room, with a quilt over him and fine fresh linen underneath. For some reason, though, these comforts were lost on him. Perhaps it was because the doctor and Von Taunitz were having a long conversation in the next room, or because the blizzard was howling above the ceiling and in the stove, just as it had done in the hut – and as mournfully as ever.

Von Taunitz's wife had died two years before and he hadn't yet resigned himself to the fact. Whatever he happened to be talking about he invariably mentioned her. There wasn't a trace of the prosecuting lawyer in him any more.

'Could I ever come to that?' Lyzhin thought as he fell asleep, hearing Von Taunitz's subdued, almost orphan-like voice through the wall.

The coroner had a bad night. It was hot and uncomfortable, and he dreamed that he wasn't in a soft, clean bed at Von Taunitz's, but back in the hut, lying on hay, listening to the witnesses whispering. Lesnitsky seemed quite close – about fifteen paces away. In his dreams he once again remembered the black-haired, pale-faced insurance agent going up to the counter in his dusty jackboots. ('This is our insurance agent.') Then he pictured Lesnitsky and Loshadin walking side by side across a snowy field, supporting each other. The blizzard whirled above, the wind blew in their backs, but they kept going, singing as they went, 'We're marching, marching, marching along.'

The old man resembled a wizard from some opera and both of them in fact sang as if performing in a theatre. 'We're marching, marching, marching along. You are warm, you have bright lights, you are comfortable, but we are striding into the icy cold and the blizzard, through the deep snow. We know no peace or joy, we bear all life's burdens, both ours and yours. Oh, we're marching, marching, marching along . . .'

Lyzhin woke and sat up in bed. What a confused, nasty dream! Why had he dreamt of the insurance agent and village constable *together?* What nonsense! But now, with his heart pounding as he sat up in bed clutching his head, Lyzhin felt that the insurance agent and constable did indeed have something in common. Hadn't *they* been walking through life, side by side, holding on to one another? Some invisible, but significant and essential bond existed between the two of them, between them and Von Taunitz even, and between everyone. Nothing in this life is accidental, even in the remotest backwater, everything is permeated by one common idea, one spirit, one purpose. Thinking and reasoning alone cannot help one understand this – one should most probably have the gift of penetrating to life's very essence, a gift which is not bestowed on all. That wretched, broken-down suicide – that 'neurotic', as the doctor had called him – that old peasant who had spent every day of his life going from one person to another: these were random events, fragments of life only for someone looking upon his own life as purely fortuitous. For someone who sees and understands his own life as part of the common whole, these things are part of some single, marvellous, rational organism. These were Lyzhin's thoughts – thoughts that he had secretly been nurturing for some time: only now had they unfurled themselves so fully and lucidly in his mind.

He lay down and began to doze off. Suddenly those two were striding along together again and singing, 'We're marching, marching, marching along . . . We bear the burden of all that is most oppressive and bitter in life, leaving you with the easy, joyful things. You can sit over your supper, coldly and logically debating why *we* are the ones who suffer and perish, why we're not as healthy and contented as you.' The gist of their song had occurred to him before, but the thought had always somehow been eclipsed by others, timidly flickering like a distant light in foggy weather. Now he felt that this suicide, the peasants' misery, lay on his conscience. How dreadful to accept the fact that these people, resigned to their fate, were shouldering all that was most oppressive and black in life. To accept all this, while at the same time desiring a bright, active life for oneself among happy, contented people and perpetually dreaming of such a life – that was tantamount to wanting fresh suicides among people crushed by toil and care, among weak, abandoned people whom one might sometimes mention in annoyance or with derision over supper and who got no help from anyone. Once again he heard that singing, 'We're marching, marching, marching along.' It was as if someone was beating his temples with a hammer.

Next morning he woke up early with a headache – some noise had aroused him. In the next room Von Taunitz was shouting at the doctor, 'You can't leave now. Just take a look outside! Don't argue, go and ask the driver if you like. He won't take you in this weather, not for a million roubles.'

'But it's only two miles, after all,' the doctor pleaded.

'I don't care if it's two hundred yards. What can't be done, can't be done. Just go through the gates and you'll see that it's absolute hell out there. You'll be off the road in a minute. I won't let you go for anything, whatever you say.'

'It'll calm down come evening,' said the peasant who was seeing to the stove.

In the next room the doctor started discussing the influence of the severe climate on the Russian character, the long winters that cramped one's movements and therefore retarded people's intellectual development. But Lyzhin was annoyed listening to these discourses and he looked through the windows at the snowdrifts piled high against the fence, at that white dust filling all visible space, at the trees bending in despair, first right, then left. He listened to the howling and banging, and gloomily wondered, 'What sort of moral can you draw from all this? That there's a blizzard, nothing else.'

They had lunch at noon, then they wandered aimlessly around the house and kept going up to the windows.

'Lesnitsky's lying there . . .' Lyzhin thought, as he watched the clouds of snow whirling furiously over the drifts. 'Lesnitsky's lying there, the witnesses are waiting . . .'

They discussed the weather, commenting that blizzards usually last forty-eight hours, rarely longer. They dined at six, then they played cards, sang, danced and finally had supper. The day was over and they went to bed.

By daybreak everything was calm. When they got up and looked out of the windows, bare willows with weakly drooping branches were standing quite motionless. It was overcast and quiet, just as if nature was ashamed now of its wild outburst, of those nights of madness, of giving full rein to her passions. The horses, harnessed in single file, had been waiting at the front door since five o'clock. When it was completely light, the doctor and coroner put on their fur coats and felt boots, said goodbye to their host and left the house. At the front door, next to the driver, that familiar figure of 'consterball' Loshadin was standing, covered with snow. An old leather bag was slung over his shoulder. His face was red and wet with sweat. The footman who had come out to help the guests into the sledge and wrap their feet up gave him a forbidding look and said, 'Why are you standing around here, you old devil? Clear off!'

'Please sir, the people in the village are very worried,' Loshadin said with an innocent smile all over his face. He was clearly delighted to see those for whom he had been waiting for so long. 'Very restless those villagers, and the children are crying. They thought you'd gone off back to town, sir. Please help them, good kind gentlemen!'

The doctor and coroner said nothing, got into their sledge and drove off to Syrnya.

Rothschild's Fiddle

ཚ

It was a small town, more miserable than a village, inhabited almost exclusively by old men who died so seldom it was very annoying. Moreover, very few coffins were needed at the hospital and gaol. In short, business was bad. If Yakov Ivanov had been a coffin-maker in some large, provincial town he would most likely have owned a house and been called 'Mr Ivanov'. But in this wretched dump he was simply Yakov, his street nickname was Bronze for some reason and he lived wretchedly, like any common peasant, in a tiny old one-roomed cottage, which housed himself, Marfa, a stove, a double bed, coffins, work-bench and all his household goods.

Yakov produced fine, solid coffins. For the male peasants and ordinary tradesmen, he made them the same length as himself, never making a mistake, as he was taller and stronger than anyone else – even those in the gaol – despite his seventy years. For ladies and gentlemen, on the other hand, he made his coffins to measure, using an iron rule. He was most reluctant to take orders for children's coffins and would contemptuously turn them out, without even taking measurements. Every time he was paid for these he would remark, 'I really don't like wasting my time on such nonsense.'

Besides his business, his fiddle brought him in a small income. Usually a Jewish band played at weddings in the town, led by one Moses Shakhkes the tinker, who kept half the takings for himself. Since Yakov played the fiddle excellently, Shakhkes sometimes invited him to play with the band for fifty copecks a day, plus tips from guests. Immediately he took his place with the band his face would become covered in sweat and turn crimson. It was hot, there was a stifling smell of garlic, the fiddle screeched, the double-bass wheezed by his right ear – by his left a flute sobbed, played by a red-haired skinny Jew with a network of red and blue veins all over his face. He was called Rothschild, after the famous millionaire. This lousy little Jew managed to make the most cheerful tune sound mournful. For no apparent reason, Yakov gradually began to feel nothing but hatred and contempt for Jews – especially this Rothschild. He started finding fault with him, swearing at him, and once was even on the point of hitting him, at which Rothschild took offence. Eyeing him furiously he said, 'If I was not respecting your talents I vould be throwing you long ago out of vindow.'

At which he burst into tears. Consequently, Bronze wasn't often invited to join the band – only in an extreme emergency, when one of the Jews was unable to come.

Yakov was never in a good mood, since he was always having to put up with losing an awful lot of money. For example, it was a sin to work on Sundays or church festivals, Mondays were unlucky, and in one year this amounted to two hundred days when he was forced to sit twiddling his thumbs. All of it was profit down the drain. If someone in town held a wedding without music, or if Shakhkes didn't ask for Yakov's services, that was money lost too. The local police inspector had been ill for two years now and was wasting away. Yakov had impatiently waited for him to die, but the inspector moved to the main town in the district for treatment, and he darned well gave up the ghost there. This meant a loss of at least ten roubles, since the coffin would have been an expensive one lined with brocade. It was at night that Yakov was particularly plagued by thoughts of these losses. He would put his fiddle by his side on the bed and whenever he was haunted by any unpalatable thoughts, he would touch the strings, the fiddle would twang in the dark and he would feel better.

On 6 May the previous year, Marfa had suddenly become ill. The old woman breathed heavily, drank a lot of water and was unsteady on her feet. Despite this, she saw to the stove herself in the mornings and even fetched water. But by the time evening came she would be in bed. All day long Yakov played his fiddle. But when it was quite dark he picked up the book in which he entered his losses every day and from sheer boredom totted up the annual amount. This came to more than one thousand roubles. He was so shaken by this that he threw the abacus on the floor and stamped his feet. Then he picked up his abacus and clicked away for a long time, heaving really deep sighs. His face was purple and bathed in sweat. If he had put those lost thousand roubles in the bank, he thought, the interest for one year would have been at least forty roubles. So that was forty more roubles gone begging. In brief, whichever way he turned, he was the loser.

'Yakov!' Marfa suddenly called. 'I'm dying!'

He looked round at his wife. Her face was pink from the heat, and unusually bright and joyful. Bronze, who had always been used to seeing a pale, timid, unhappy face, was taken aback. She really did seem to be dying, glad that she was finally leaving that cottage, the coffins and Yakov for ever. As she glanced up at the ceiling, moving her lips, her face was happy, as if she could actually see Death her deliverer and was whispering to him.

It was dawn and through the window the first rays of light were visible. As he looked at the old woman, it crossed Yakov's mind that he had never shown her any affection in his whole life. Not once had he spared her a kind thought, not once had it occurred to him to buy her a scarf or bring her back something nice and sweet from a wedding. He had only shouted at her, blamed her for lost profits, shaken his fists at her. True, he had never struck her, but he had scared her all the same and on each occasion she had gone numb with terror. Yes, he didn't allow her any tea, since they had expenses enough and all she drank was hot water. Now he understood why her face was so peculiarly joyous and this made him go cold all over.

When it was quite light he borrowed a horse from a neighbour and drove Marfa to hospital. There were very few patients, so he didn't have to wait long – only about three hours. To his inestimable joy, this time the doctor wasn't there to see patients – he was ill himself – but his orderly Maxim was, an old man reputed by everyone in town to know more medicine than the doctor, although he was always drinking and fighting.

'Good day, sir,' Yakov said as he led his old woman into the consulting-room. 'Please forgive us, sir, for troubling you with our silly little worries. As you can see, sir, my old missus is sick. Pardon the expression, but, as they say, she's my helpmate.'

Knitting his white eyebrows and stroking his side-whiskers, the orderly started examining the old woman as she sat there hunched up on a stool, haggard, sharp-nosed, open-mouthed, with the profile of a hungry bird.

'Mmmmmmm ... well now,' the orderly slowly pronounced, sighing. 'It's influenza, possibly fever. And there's typhus going round the town now. Well now, the old woman's lived her life, thanks be to God. How old is she?'

'One year short of seventy, sir.'

'So, she's lived her life, time she was going.'

'Of course, what you say is right, sir,' Yakov said, 'and we thank you from the bottom of our hearts for being so nice. But, begging your pardon, every insect wants to live.'

'You don't say!' the orderly exclaimed in a tone that suggested it was up to him whether the old woman lived or died. 'Now, my dear man, you go and put a cold compress on her head and give her some of this powder twice a day. So, ta-ta for now. Bong jour to you.'

Yakov could tell from his face that it was a lost cause, that no powder on earth would help. He realized that Marfa would die any day now. Nudging the orderly's elbow, he winked and said in a low voice, 'Perhaps we ought to bleed her, Mr Maxim.'

'I just haven't the time, my dear man. Take your old woman and be on your way. So long!'

'Please do me a favour,' Yakov pleaded. 'As you know, sir, if something was wrong with her belly or innards then powders and drops would do the trick. But she's got a chill. The first thing you do with chills is bleed them, sir.'

But the orderly had already called in the next patient and a peasant woman with her little boy entered the consulting-room.

'Clear off, get out of here!' he told Yakov, frowning. 'Don't you try and confuse the issue!'

'Then at least apply some leeches! I'll always be grateful, that I will!'

Suddenly the orderly flared up. 'Just one more squeak out of you!' he shouted. 'You fathead!'

Yakov flared up too and his whole face turned crimson. But he did not say one word. Grabbing Marfa's arm, he led her out of the room. Only when they were climbing into their cart did he give that hospital a stern, mocking look and say, 'They're a stuck-up lot in that place! He'd have bled a rich man, I dare say, but he begrudges someone what's poor even one leech. Swine!'

When they were home, Marfa went inside and stood holding on to the stove for about ten minutes. She thought that if she lay down Yakov would start talking about all the money he had lost and tell her off for lazing around and not wanting to work. Yakov looked at her dejectedly and remembered that tomorrow was St John's Day, that it was St Nicholas's Day after that, and then it was Sunday and Monday – both unlucky days. For four days he wouldn't be able to work. But Marfa was bound to die on one of those days, which meant the coffin had to be made today. He took his steel rule, went over to the old woman and measured her. After she had lain down he crossed himself and started making the coffin.

When it was finished Bronze put on his spectacles and wrote in his book: 'For Marfa Ivanovna. One coffin, 2 roubles 40 copecks.' And he sighed. All this time the old woman lay there silently, her eyes closed. But when evening came and it grew dark, she suddenly called the old man.

'Yakov, do you remember?' she asked, looking at him joyfully. 'Do you remember, fifty years ago God gave us a little baby, fair-haired it was? In those days we were always sitting by the river, just the two of us, under the willows, singing songs.' Laughing bitterly she went on, 'The little girl died.'

Yakov racked his brains but just could not remember any baby or willow trees. 'You're imagining things,' he said.

The priest came and administered the last rites. After that Marfa started mumbling some nonsense and she passed away towards morning.

Some old women neighbours washed and dressed her, and laid her in the coffin. To avoid having to pay a lay reader Yakov read the prayers himself and he wasn't charged for the grave, since the cemetery caretaker was an old pal of his. Four peasants bore the coffin to the cemetery, out of respect and not for money. Old women, beggars and two village idiots followed it, and people in the street crossed themselves. Yakov was terribly pleased that it had all been conducted so decently, with such decorum, and that it had cost very little and had offended no one. As he said farewell to Marfa for the last time he touched the coffin and thought, 'Nice job, that!'

But on the way home from the cemetery he became dreadfully sad. He felt rather ill – his breath was hot and heavy, his legs were weak and he was thirsty. All kinds of thoughts came flooding into his mind. He remembered once again that he had never in all his life shown Marfa sympathy or affection. The fifty-two years they had lived together in the same cottage seemed an eternity, but somehow, during all that time, he had never spared her a thought and had taken no more notice of her than a cat or dog. But hadn't she tended the stove every day, cooked and baked, fetched water, chopped wood, slept in the same bed with him? And whenever he had returned drunk from a wedding she would reverently hang his fiddle on the wall and put him to bed, all of which she did in silence, with a timid, anxious look on her face.

Rothschild went over to Yakov, smiling and bowing.

'I've been looking for you, sir!' he said. 'Mr Moisey sends his regards, he vants to see you right avay.'

Yakov didn't feel up to it. He felt like crying. 'Leave me alone,' he replied and went on his way.

'But vot you think you're doing!' Rothschild said in alarm, running on ahead. 'Mr Moisey will be offended. He said you're to come at vunce!'

Yakov was disgusted by that Jew, his puffing and panting, his blinking, his profusion of red freckles. His green frock-coat with dark patches and his whole fragile, feeble-looking figure were a repulsive sight.

'What do you keep pestering me for, Garlic Mouth?' Yakov shouted. 'Leave me alone.'

The Jew became angry and shouted too. 'Now, you shut your mouth, pliz, or I make you fly over fence!'

'Out of my sight!' Yakov roared, going for him with his fists. 'Life's hell with you rotten bastards around!'

Petrified with fear, Rothschild crouched, then waved his arms over his head as if warding off blows. Then he leapt up and tore off as fast as he could, hopping and throwing his arms up as he ran. His long skinny back was visibly shaking. The street urchins were overjoyed at the opportunity and dashed after him shouting, 'Dirty Jew!' Barking dogs also took up the chase. Someone guffawed, then whistled and the dogs barked louder and more in concert. One of the dogs must have bitten Rothschild, as a desperate cry of pain rang out.

Yakov wandered on to the common, then walked along the edge of the town, not knowing exactly where he was going. The street boys shouted, 'Bronze's coming! Bronze's coming!' He reached the river. Here sandpipers circled and twittered, ducks quacked. The sun was scorching and the water so dazzling it hurt one's eyes. Yakov went down the tow-path and saw a plump, red-cheeked woman emerge from a bathing-hut. 'Ugh, you ugly old otter!' he thought.

Not far from the bathing-hut some boys were fishing for crayfish, using meat for bait. The moment they saw him they started shouting viciously, 'Look, it's that old Yakov!' Then he passed the broad old willow with its huge hollow and crows' nests. And his memory conjured up a vivid picture of that fair-haired child and the old willow that Marfa had talked about. Yes, it was the same willow, so green, peaceful, sad . . . How the poor thing had aged!

He sat beneath it and tried to remember. On the far bank, now a water meadow, there used to be a large birch forest, and further off, on that bare hill outlined on the horizon, was the dark blue mass of an immensely old pine forest. Barges used to travel up and down the river. But now everything was smooth and bare, with a solitary little birch tree on the near side, shapely and slender as a young girl. Now there were only ducks and geese on the river and it didn't seem possible that barges had once passed by. And there seemed to be fewer geese. Yakov closed his eyes and imagined huge flocks of white geese rushing towards each other.

He just couldn't make out why he had never gone down to the river during the past forty or fifty years. If he had in fact gone, then it hadn't affected him at all. After all, it was a real river, not just a little stream. You could go fishing there, sell the fish to merchants, clerks and the buffet manager at the station, and then bank the proceeds. You could sail along it from one estate to another playing the fiddle, and all sorts of people would pay you. You could set up in the barge business again – that was better than coffin-making. Finally, you could raise geese, slaughter them and send them to Moscow in the winter. Probably the down alone would bring in ten roubles a year. But he had let the grass grow under his feet and done none of this. The money he had lost! If you added it all up – fishing, playing the fiddle, keeping barges, slaughtering geese – what a packet he'd have made! But none of this had happened, even in his dreams. Life had passed without profit, without pleasure; it had gone by aimlessly, to no purpose. There was nothing to look forward to, and if you looked back, there was a terrible waste of money, enough to make your flesh creep. Why couldn't a man live without all that loss and waste? Why had they cut down the birch and pine forests? Why wasn't the common pasture used at all? Why were people always doing the wrong thing? Why had Yakov done nothing in his life but swear, snarl, shake his fists at people, insult his wife? Why – yes, *why* – did he have to frighten and insult that Jew not so long ago? Why couldn't people ever let one another alone? It only led to so much money being wasted, didn't it? A terrible waste! If hatred and spite didn't exist, people would profit enormously from each other.

That evening and night he was haunted by visions of the child, willow, fish, slaughtered geese, of Marfa with the profile of a thirsty bird, and Rothschild's pale, pathetic face. And grotesque faces bore down on him from all sides, muttering about wasted money. He tossed and turned and got out of bed about five times to play his fiddle.

In the morning he forced himself to get up and go to the hospital. That same Maxim instructed him to put a cold compress on his head and gave him powders. But Yakov could tell from his expression and tone that his was a lost cause and that no powder could help him now. Afterwards, on his way home, he concluded that he stood only to profit by dying: he wouldn't have to eat, drink, pay taxes, insult people. Since a man lies in the grave not only for one year, but for hundreds and thousands, the profit would be enormous. Man's life is loss, his death is profit. This conclusion was correct, of course, but dreadfully unpalatable none the less. Why were things so strangely organized in this world, when you lived only once and had nothing to show for it?

He didn't regret dying, but as soon as he was home and spotted his fiddle, his heart sank and he did feel sorry. He couldn't take that fiddle with him to the grave and it would become an orphan and suffer the same fate as the birch and pine forests. Everything in this world has always come to naught and that's how it would always be. Yakov left the cottage and sat in the doorway, pressing the fiddle to his chest. As he contemplated his wasted, unprofitable life, he started playing – he couldn't say what it was, but it sounded plaintive and moving – and the tears flowed down his cheeks. The harder he thought, the sadder the fiddle's song became.

The latch squeaked twice and Rothschild appeared at the garden gate. Boldly, he crossed half of the yard, but as soon as he saw Yakov he stopped, hunched himself up and (probably from fear) started making signs with his hands, as if trying to indicate the time with his fingers.

'Come over here, it's all right,' Yakov said welcomingly as he beckoned him. 'Come on.'

With a frightened, suspicious look, Rothschild began approaching him, but stopped about six feet away. 'Please, sir, don't beat me, I beg you!' he said, crouching. 'Mr Moisey sent me again. "Don't be scared," he told me, "go and see Yakov again and tell him we can't do without him." There's a vedding on Vednesday . . . Ye-es! Mr Shapovalov's marrying his daughter to a nice young man. Oiy, vot a rich vedding that will be!' the Jew added, screwing up one eye.

'I can't go,' Yakov said, breathing heavily. 'I'm not well, my dear friend.'

He struck up again – and the tears spurted on to his fiddle. Rothschild listened attentively, standing sideways on, his arms crossed over his chest. His frightened, bewildered expression gradually turned into a sorrowful, martyred look and he rolled his eyes

60

in agonized delight. 'Oh, oh!' he exclaimed. And tears slowly trickled down his cheeks, spotting his green frock-coat.

Afterwards, Yakov lay down all day in a miserable frame of mind. When the priest confessing him that evening asked whether he remembered committing any particular sin, he strained his failing memory and once more recollected Marfa's unhappy face and the desperate shout of the Jew bitten by a dog. Barely audibly he said, 'Give my fiddle to Rothschild.'

'All right then,' the priest replied.

And now everyone in the town keeps asking: where did Rothschild get such a fine fiddle? Did he buy or steal it? Perhaps someone had given it as a pledge? He gave up the flute long ago and only plays the fiddle now. The same mournful melodies that once came from his flute pour from his bow. But whenever he tries to repeat the tune Yakov used to play sitting in his doorway, it sounds so melancholy and doleful his audience weep, and he finishes by rolling his eyes and uttering, 'Oh, oh!'

Everyone in town likes this new tune so much, there's intense rivalry among merchants and civil servants, and they're always inviting him to their houses, where they force him to play it a dozen times.

Peasant Women

ನಾಲ

In the village of Raybuzh, just opposite the church, stands a two-storeyed house with stone foundations and an iron roof. Filip Ivanov Kashin, the owner, nicknamed Dyudya, lives with his family on the ground floor, while passing officials, merchants and landowners stay on the upper floor, where it's very hot in summer and freezing in winter. Dyudya rents plots of land, keeps a pub on the main road, trades in tar, honey, cattle and peasant women's hats, and has saved up about eight thousand roubles, which are kept in the town bank.

His elder son Fyodor is a senior mechanic in a factory. As the peasants say, he has gone up in the world and left everyone far behind. Fyodor's wife Sofya, a homely, sickly woman, lives in her father-in-law's house, is always crying and drives over to the hospital every Sunday for treatment. Dyudya's second son, hunchbacked Alyoshka, lives at home with his father. Recently he married Barbara, a girl from a poor family – she's pretty, enjoys good health and is fond of smart clothes. When officials and merchants stop at the house, they invariably ask for Barbara to serve the samovar and make their beds.

One evening in June, when the sun was setting and the air was full of the smell of hay, warm manure and fresh milk, a simple cart with three people in it drove into Dyudya's yard. There was a man of about thirty in a canvas suit, a seven- or eight-year-old boy in a long black coat with large bone buttons beside him, and a lad in a red shirt – the driver.

The lad unharnessed the horses and walked them up and down the street, while the man washed, turned towards the church to offer a prayer, then spread out a rug by the cart and sat down to supper with the young boy.

He ate solemnly, unhurriedly, and Dyudya, who had seen

62

many travellers in his day, could tell from his manners that he was a serious, businesslike man who knew his own worth.

Dyudya sat in his porch in his waistcoat, without a cap, waiting for the traveller to say something. He was used to travellers telling all sorts of stories in the evenings before going to bed; it was something he loved. His elderly wife Afanasyevna and Sofya his daughter-in-law were milking the cows in the shed. Barbara, the other daughter-in-law, was sitting upstairs by an open window eating sunflower seeds.

'Would that little boy be your son, eh?" Dyudya asked the traveller.

'No, he's adopted, an orphan. I took him in for the good of my soul.'

They got into conversation. The traveller turned out to be a talkative man who had a way with words. Dyudya learned that he was a small trader and house-owner, that his name was Matvey Savvich, that he was on his way to inspect some orchards he had rented from German settlers, and that the boy was called Kuzka. It was a hot, close evening and no one felt like sleeping. When it grew dark and pale stars twinkled here and there in the sky, Matvey Savvich began to relate how Kuzka had come to be with him. Afanasyevna and Sofya stood a little way off listening, while Kuzka went to the gate.

'It's an exceedingly complicated story, old man,' Matvey Savvich began, 'and if I were to tell you everything that happened, the night wouldn't be long enough. Ten years ago in our street, in the cottage next to mine – where there's a candle-works and dairy now – there lived an old widow called Martha Kapluntseva and she had two sons. One was a railway guard, the other, Vasya, was the same age as me and lived at home with his mother. Old man Kapluntsev used to keep about five pairs of horses and had a carting business in the town. The widow kept it going and was just as good at controlling her carriers as the old man, so that some days they made five roubles clear profit. And the lad made himself a few roubles too – bred pedigree pigeons and sold them to fanciers. He was always standing on the roof, flinging a broom up and whistling, and his tumblers would soar right up in the sky. But it wouldn't be high enough for him and he wanted them to fly even higher. He caught finches and starlings and made cages for them. You might have thought there was nothing in it, but this messing about with birds was bringing in ten roubles a month before long. Well now, with the passing of time the old lady loses the use of her legs and has to take to her bed, by reason of which fact that house had no woman running it – and that's about the same as a man without eyes! So the old lady gets busy and decides to marry off her Vasya. A matchmaker's called in right away, then it's one thing after the other, the women confer together and off goes Vasya to inspect the local prospects. He chooses Mashenka, Widow Samokhvalina's daughter. They don't hang about, the couple receive everyone's blessing and the whole thing was fixed up within one week. She's a young girl, about seventeen, small and dumpy, but with a fair complexion and nice-looking – a real lady-to-be. And the dowry's not bad – five hundred roubles, a cow, a bed. But the old lady senses what's going to happen and two days after the wedding she departs for that heavenly Jerusalem where there's neither illness nor lamentation. The young couple see to her funeral and say a prayer for her soul and settle down together. For about six months everything's marvellous, and then suddenly disaster strikes again – it never rains but it pours. Vasya has to go to the recruiting-office, his lot is drawn and the poor lad is taken into the army and they don't even allow him exemption. They shave his head and send him to Poland. It was God's will, nothing could be done about it. As he says goodbye to his wife in the yard he feels all right, but as soon as he takes a last look at his pigeon-loft the tears just come in floods. It was a sorry sight. At first Mashenka takes her mother to live with her for company and her mother stays on till the lying-in, when this Kuzka you see here was born. Then she drives off to her other married daughter in Oboyan and Mashenka's left alone with her baby. Now, there's the five carriers, a drunken, rowdy lot, there's the horses and drays to see to, her fence is falling down or the chimney's catching fire – do you get me? It's no woman's work, that. So, seeing as we're neighbours, she starts asking me to help with every little thing. Well, I go and give her a hand and a spot of advice. Well, you know how it goes, you go into a place, have a cup of tea and a chat. I'm a young man, I'm no fool and I like chatting about this and that. She too is educated, and well-mannered. She dresses smartly and carries a sunshade in summer. I'd start talking about religion or politics, which flatters her, and she gives me tea and jam. So, old man, to cut a long story short, before the year's out, the devil, mankind's adversary, has me mixed up good and proper. I begin to notice that when I don't go to see her, I feel out of sorts, bored. And I keep trying to think of some excuse to see her. I'd tell her, "It's time the winter window-frames were fixed," and all day I'd lounge around her place putting the frames in, making sure I had two left to do the next day. "I think I should count Vasya's pigeons," I'd say, "in case any get lost" – and so on. I'd be forever talking to her across the fence and in the end I made a little gate in it to save going right round. A great deal of the evil and rottenness in this world comes from the female sex – not only we ordinary sinners, but even saints have been led astray. Mashenka doesn't let me far from her side and instead of thinking of her husband and saving herself for him she falls in love with me. I begin to notice that she's bored without me too, and she keeps hanging around the fence and looking into my yard through the holes. She really had me in a spin. Early one Thursday during Easter week, at the crack of dawn, I'm passing her gate on my way to market when, lo and behold, there's the Devil. I look through the sort of trellis at the top of her gate and there she is, already up and about, feeding her ducks in the middle of the yard. I can't stop myself calling out to her. She comes over and looks at me through the trellis. Her little face is pale, her eyes tender and sleepy. She attracts me very much and I start paying her compliments as if we weren't standing by a gate but at some festive gathering. She blushes, laughs and looks me right in the eye without blinking. I lose all reason and start declaring my amorous feelings. She opens the gate and lets me in, and from that morning we live as man and wife.'

Just then hunchbacked Alyoshka came into the yard from the street and ran breathlessly into the house without looking at anyone. A minute later he came running out with his accordion and then vanished through the gate, jingling copper coins in his pockets and cracking sunflower seeds.

'Who's that?' Matvey Savvich asked.

'My son Alyoshka,' Dyudya replied. 'He's gone off to enjoy himself, the little devil. God afflicted him with a hunched back, so we're not too hard on him.'

'He's always with the lads, always having a good time,' Afanasyevna sighed. 'Before Shrovetide we married him off, thinking he'd mend his ways, but he's even worse, that's plain to see.'

'Yes, it was no use. All we did was make a strange girl rich, and to no purpose,' Dyudya said.

Somewhere beyond the church they started singing a wonderful, sad song. It was impossible to make the words out, only the voices could be heard – two tenors and a bass. With everyone listening hard, the yard became absolutely quiet. Two of the singers suddenly broke off with peals of laughter while the third, a tenor, continued and took such a high note that everyone just had to look up, as if the voice had soared to heaven itself. Barbara came out of the house and shaded her eyes with her hand as she looked at the church, as though blinded by the sun. 'It's the priest's sons and their teacher,' she said.

Once again the three voices sang in unison. Matvey Savvich sighed.

'So that's how it was, old man,' he went on. 'Two years later we get a letter from Vasya in Warsaw. He writes that he's being invalided out of the army, he's not well. By that time I've put all the nonsense out of my head and they're preparing to marry me to a nice young girl. But I don't know how to break that lousy little affair off. Every day I decide to go and talk to Mashenka, but I don't know how to do it without having a woman's screams in my ears. That letter unties my hands. Mashenka and I read it, she turns white as a ghost and I say to her, "Thank God for that, now you can be a respectable married woman again." But she says, "I don't want to live with him."

'"But he's your husband, isn't he?" I say.

'"It's not as simple as that. I never loved him, I married him against my will. Mother made me do it ..." And I say, "Now don't try and get out of it, you little fool. Tell me, were you married in church or weren't you?" "I was," she replies, "but it's you I love and I'll live with you till my dying day. Let them laugh, I couldn't care less." And I say, "But you fear God, don't you, you know what the Bible says, don't you?"'

'A married woman must stay with her husband,' Dyudya said.

'Husband and wife are one flesh. "We have sinned," I say, "and now it's enough. We must repent and fear God. Let's confess everything to Vasya. He's a quiet, peaceful sort of man, he won't kill us. And it's better" – I tell her – "to suffer pain from a lawful husband in this world than gnash your teeth on the Day of Judgement." But the woman won't listen, she insists on having it her own way, whatever I say. "I love you," she says – and that was that. Vasya arrived early on the Saturday before Trinity Sunday. I can see everything through the fence. He runs into the house and a minute later comes out with Kuzka in his arms, laughing and crying, kissing Kuzka and looking at his pigeon-loft. He just doesn't want to put Kuzka down but at the same time he wants to see his pigeons. He's a soft-hearted, sentimental sort of man. The day passes without any trouble, quietly and peacefully. The bells are rung for evening service and I start thinking to myself, "Tomorrow's Trinity Sunday, why haven't they decorated their gate and fence with greenery? Something's wrong." So I go over to see them. There he is sitting in the middle of the floor, rolling his eyes as if he's drunk, tears streaming down his cheeks and hands trembling. He takes some rolls, necklaces, gingerbread and all sorts of sweets out of his bundle and throws them all over the floor. Kuzka – he was about three then – crawls about chewing gingerbread, while Mashenka stands by the stove, pale and shaking all over.

'"I'm no wife of yours," she mutters, "I don't want to live with you" – and all sorts of silly things. I bow low to Vasya and say, "We're to blame, Vasya. Forgive us, for Christ's sake!" Then I get up and say the following to Mashenka: "You, Mashenka, must wash Vasya's feet now and drink the water. You must be his obedient wife and pray to God for me that He may be merciful and forgive me my sins." It was as if I was inspired by an angel from heaven. I lecture her, speaking with such feeling that I'm overcome and burst into tears. Well then, two days later Vasya comes over. "I forgive you, Matvey, and my wife as well, God help you. She's a soldier's wife. Young women behave like that – they find it hard to keep to themselves. She's not the first and she won't be the last. All I ask," he says, "is for you to pretend there's never been anything between you and keep quiet about it. As for me, I'll do all I can to please her and make her love me again." He shakes hands, drinks some tea and leaves quite happy. Well, I think, thank God for that! I'm so pleased it's all turned out so well. But the moment Vasya is out of my yard, in comes Mashenka. It was something shocking! She hangs on my neck, starts crying and begs me, "For God's sake, don't leave me, I can't live without you!"'

'The slut!' Dyudya said, sighing.

'I shout at her, stamp my feet, drag her out into the hall and put the door on the latch. "Go to your husband!" I shout. "Don't shame me in public, fear God!" And every day it's the same story. One morning I'm standing in my yard near the stable mending a bridle. Suddenly I see her running through the gate, barefoot, in her petticoat, heading straight for me. She grabs the bridle and gets covered in tar, trembles and cries, "I can't live with that hateful man, I just can't! If you don't love me you'd better kill me!" I get mad and hit her twice with the bridle. Just then Vasya comes running through the gate, shouting desperately, "Don't hit her, don't hit her!" But he runs to her himself and starts swinging his fists like a madman, hitting her as hard as he can. Then he throws her down and starts stamping on her. I try and defend her, but he grabs some reins and lets her have it with them. All the time he's beating her he lets out wild squeals and whinnies like a foal.'

'I'd give you a taste of some reins if I could!' Barbara growled as she moved away. 'You torture the life out of us women, you rotten bastards!'

'Shut up, you cow!' Dyudya shouted.

'So, there he was squealing away,' Matvey Savvich continued. 'A carter comes running out of his yard, I call my own workman and all three of us take Mashenka away from him and lead her

68

home by her arms. What a disgrace! That same evening I go to see her. She's lying in bed all wrapped up and covered with fomentations. All I can see are her eyes and nose, and she's gazing up at the ceiling. "Hallo, Mashenka," I say. She doesn't answer. Vasya's sitting in the next room clutching his head and weeping: "I'm a wicked person! I've ruined my life. Oh, God, please let me die!" I sit with Mashenka for about half an hour and lecture her. I frighten the daylights out of her. "The righteous go to paradise in the next world, but you'll go to fiery Gehenna with all the other whores . . . Don't defy your husband, prostrate yourself before him!" But she doesn't say a word, doesn't bat an eyelid, just as if I were talking to a brick wall. Next day Vasya is taken ill – something like cholera – and I hear towards evening that he's dead. They bury him. Mashenka doesn't go to the funeral, not wanting to parade her shameless face or her bruises in public. Soon it's rumoured in town that Vasya didn't die from natural causes and that Mashenka did away with him. The authorities get to hear about it. They dig Vasya up, slit him open and find arsenic in his belly. It was murder, sure as eggs is eggs. The police come and take Mashenka away – and that innocent little Kuzka as well – and they put them in prison. That woman had gone too far and God was punishing her. Eight months later she's tried. I remember her sitting in the dock with her white kerchief and grey convict's smock, looking so thin, pale and sharp-eyed it was a sorry sight. A soldier with a rifle stood behind her. She wouldn't confess. Some of the people at the trial said she'd poisoned her husband, others claimed her husband had poisoned himself, from grief. I was one of the witnesses. When they questioned me I did not hide a thing from them. "She's guilty, she sinned," I tell them. "There's no hiding the fact, she didn't love her husband and she always wanted things her own way."

'The trial began in the morning, and that night they reached the verdict: thirteen years' hard labour in Siberia. After being sentenced Mashenka was kept three months in the local gaol. I would go and visit her and, like any human being would, took her tea and sugar. When she sees me she starts shaking all over, waving her arms and muttering, "Go away, go away!" And she presses Kuzka close to her as if scared I might take him away. "So *this* is what you've come to!" I say. "Oh, Mashenka, Mashenka, you lost soul! You wouldn't listen when I tried to teach you some sense, now you're suffering for it. It's your own fault, you've only yourself to blame." I give her a good lecturing, but she keeps saying, "Go away, go away!", huddles against the wall with Kuzka and shakes all over. When they take her to the main town in the province I go to see her off at the station and push a rouble into her bundle, for the good of my soul. But she never reached Siberia. She caught a fever in that town and died in gaol.'

'She only got what she deserved,' Dyudya said.

'Kuzka was brought home. I thought about it for a long time, then I decided to take him to live with me. And why shouldn't I? Convict's spawn he may be, but he's a living soul, a Christian . . . I was sorry for him. I'll make a salesman out of him and if I don't have any children of my own, I'll make him a merchant. I take him with me wherever I go, so that he can learn things.'

The whole time Matvey Savvich was telling his story Kuzka sat on a small stone near the gate, gazing at the sky, his head propped on his hands. In the dark, from a distance, he resembled a tree stump.

'Kuzka, go to bed!' Matvey shouted.

'Yes, it's time,' Dyudya said, getting up. With a loud yawn he added, 'They all like to go their own way nowadays, they won't listen. In the end they get what they deserve.'

The moon was already sailing in the sky over the yard. It was swiftly moving to one side, while the clouds beneath raced in the other direction. The clouds moved away, but the moon was still visible over the yard. Matvey Savvich turned towards the church, said a prayer, wished everyone goodnight and lay on the ground near the cart. Kuzka prayed too, lay in the cart and covered himself with his coat. To make himself comfortable, he hollowed out a little place for himself in the hay and curled up, so that his elbows touched his knees. From the yard Dyudya could be seen lighting a candle downstairs, putting on his spectacles and standing in a corner. For a long time he read and bowed.

The visitors fell asleep. Afanasyevna and Sofya went over to the cart to look at Kuzka.

'The little orphan's asleep,' the old woman said. 'He's so frail and thin, all skin and bones. He's got no mother and there's no one to feed him properly.'

'My Grishutka must be about two years older, I reckon,' Sofya said. 'He's treated like a slave in that factory without his mother. I'm sure his master beats him. When I looked at this little boy a moment ago I was reminded of my Grishutka and my blood curdled.'

A minute passed in silence.

'He wouldn't remember his mother, would he?' the old woman said.

'How could he?'

Large tears flowed from Sofya's eyes.

'He's rolled himself into a ball,' she said, sobbing and laughing with deeply felt compassion. 'My poor little orphan!'

Kuzka shuddered and opened his eyes. He saw an ugly, wrinkled, tear-stained face and next to it another – an old woman's, toothless, sharp-chinned and hook-nosed. Above them was the fathomless sky and scudding clouds and moon. The boy screamed in terror and Sofya screamed too. Their echoes answered them and alarm spread through the stifling air. A watchman nearby started banging, a dog barked. Matvey Savvich muttered something in his sleep and turned over.

Late that night, when Dyudya, the old woman and the neighbouring watchman were asleep, Sofya went through the gates and sat down on a bench. She felt hot and had a headache from crying. The street was broad and long. To the right were two verst posts and two more on the left – the road seemed endless. The moon had left the yard now and was behind the church. One side of the street was flooded with moonlight, the other was black with shadows. The long shadows of poplars and starling-boxes stretched right across the street and the black, forbidding shadow of the church lay in a broad band, holding Dyudya's gate and half his house in its grasp. All was quiet and deserted. Now and again faint sounds of music drifted over from the end of the street – it was Alyoshka, no doubt, playing his accordion.

Something was walking about in the shadows near the church

fence and it was impossible to see if it was a man or a cow. Perhaps it was no one at all, just a large bird rustling in the trees. But at that moment a figure emerged from the shadows, stopped and spoke in a man's voice. Then it disappeared down the lane by the side of the church. Shortly afterwards another figure appeared about five yards from the gate. It was moving straight from the church to the gate and stopped when it saw Sofya on the bench.

'Barbara, is that you?' Sofya asked.

'Well, what of it?'

It was Barbara. She stood there for a minute, then came over and sat on the bench.

'Where were you?' Sofya asked.

Barbara didn't reply.

'Now, don't get yourself into trouble. A young married girl like you larking around!' Sofya said. 'Did you hear how Mashenka was trodden on and whipped with reins? Watch out, it could happen to you.'

'I don't care.' Barbara laughed into her handkerchief. 'I've just been enjoying myself with the priest's son,' she whispered.

'You're joking.'

'I swear it.'

'But it's a sin,' Sofya whispered.

'So it's a sin. Why should I feel sorry? Sin or no sin, it's better to be struck by lightning than live this kind of life. I'm young and healthy, but I have a hateful, hunchbacked husband. He's so strict with me – he's worse than that wretched Dyudya. As a girl I always went hungry and I had to go around barefoot. I escaped from those wicked devils, tempted as I was by Alyoshka's wealth, and I became a slave, just like a fish caught in a net. I'd rather sleep with a viper than that lousy Alyoshka. What about your life? It's too terrible for words. Your Fyodor drove you out of the factory and made you go to his father's, then he set up with another woman. They took your boy away and turned him into a slave. You yourself work like a horse and you never hear a kind word from anyone. Better pine as an old maid all your life, better take fifty-copeck pieces from priests' sons, better go around begging, better throw yourself head first down a well ...'

'That's a sin!' Sofya whispered again.

'So what!'

Somewhere beyond the church those same three voices – the two tenors and the bass – started a sad song again. And once again it was impossible to make out the words.

'Those nightbirds!' Barbara laughed.

She started whispering about the great time she had at night with the priest's son – what he said to her, what his friends were like and about the fun she had with officials and merchants who stayed overnight with them. The mournful song had the breath of freedom about it. Sofya began to laugh. It was all so sinful, so frightening, so sweet to hear. She was jealous of Barbara and was sorry that she herself had not sinned while she was still young and beautiful. Midnight struck in the old church cemetery.

'Time we were in bed,' Sofya said, getting up. 'Dyudya might start wondering where we are.'

Quietly, they both entered the yard.

'I went away, so I didn't hear the rest of the story about Mashenka,' Barbara said, laying out her bedclothes under the window.

'She died in gaol, they say. She poisoned her husband.'

Barbara lay next to Sofya, pondered a little and then said softly, 'I could do that Alyoshka of mine in and not feel at all sorry.'

'Don't talk such nonsense, for God's sake!'

When Sofya was dozing off, Barbara huddled close and whispered in her ear, 'Let's kill Dyudya and Alyoshka!'

Sofya shuddered and said nothing. Then she opened her eyes and gazed at the sky for a long time without blinking.

'People would find out,' she said.

'They wouldn't. Dyudya's old, it's time he was gone. And they'd say Alyoshka died of drink.'

'That's terrible . . . God would kill us.'

Neither slept and they lay there in silence, thinking.

'It's cold,' Sofya said, beginning to shiver all over. 'It must be nearly morning . . . Are you asleep?'

'No . . . Don't take any notice of what I said, dear,' Barbara whispered. 'I'm so furious with those bastards I don't know what I'm saying. Sleep, it'll soon be dawn. Go to sleep.'

Both said nothing more, calmed down and were soon asleep.

The old woman was the first to wake up. She roused Sofya and both went to the shed to milk the cows. Hunchbacked Alyoshka arrived, dead drunk and without his accordion. His chest and knees were covered in dust and straw – he must have fallen down on the way. Reeling, he went into the shed, slumped on to a sledge without undressing and immediately started snoring. When the crosses on the church and then the windows gleamed like bright flames in the rising sun, when the shadows of trees and well-sweep spread across the dewy grass in the yard, Matvey Savvich leapt up and busied himself. 'Get up, Kuzka!' he shouted. 'Time to harness the horse. Look lively, then!'

The morning bustle began. A young Jewess, in a brown, flounced dress, brought her horse into the yard for watering. A plaintive creak came from the well-sweep, the bucket rattled. Sleepy, sluggish and covered in dew, Kuzka sat in the cart lazily putting on his coat and listening to the water splash from the bucket in the well. He was shivering with cold.

'Hey, Ma,' Matvey shouted to Sofya. 'Give that boy of mine a prod to make him harness the horse!'

Just then Dyudya shouted from a window, 'Sofya, charge that Jewess a copeck for the water – they've made a habit of it, filthy Jews!'

Sheep ran up and down the street bleating. Women shouted at the shepherd, but he kept playing his pipe, cracking his whip or answering them in a heavy, hoarse, deep voice. Three sheep ran into the yard – they couldn't find the gate, so they butted the fence. The noise woke Barbara and she grabbed her bedding in her arms and walked towards the house.

'You might at least have driven the sheep out!' the old woman shouted at her. 'Think you're the proper little lady, don't you!'

'There she goes again. Do I have to work for you monsters?' Barbara grumbled as she went into the house.

They greased the cart and harnessed the horses. Dyudya emerged from the house with an abacus and sat in the porch working out how much to charge the traveller for the night's lodging, oats and water.

'That's a lot of money for oats, old man,' Matvey Savvich said.

'Then don't take them. We won't force you – you *merchant*.' When the travellers were about to drive off in their cart they were held up for a moment: Kuzka's cap was missing.

'Where did you put it, you little swine?' Matvey Savvich shouted angrily. 'Where is it?'

Kuzka's face was twisted in terror as he rushed around by the cart. Not finding his cap there, he ran to the gate, then to the shed. The old woman and Sofya helped him look for it.

'I'll tear your ears off!' Matvey Savvich shouted. 'You little devil!'

They found the cap at the bottom of the cart. Kuzka brushed the hay off, put it on and gingerly climbed into the cart, still looking terrified, as if scared he might be clouted from behind. Matvey Savvich crossed himself, the lad tugged the reins and the cart slowly rolled out of the yard.

Three Years

ᴊᴏᴊ

I

It was dark, but in some houses lights had already been lit, and at the end of the street, behind the barracks, a pale moon was rising. Laptev was sitting on a bench by the gate waiting for evening service to finish at St Peter and St Paul's. He reckoned that Julia Belavin would pass him on her way home from church, and then he could talk to her and perhaps spend the rest of the evening with her.

He had been sitting there an hour and a half, picturing in his mind his Moscow flat, his Moscow friends, Peter his valet, his writing-desk. He looked in bewilderment at the dark, motionless trees and thought it peculiar that he wasn't living in his villa at Sokolniki any more, but in a provincial town, in a house past which a large herd of cattle was driven every morning and evening, raising dreadful clouds of dust – to the accompaniment of blowing horns. He remembered those long conversations in Moscow in which he had taken part not so very long ago, about the possibility of life without love, about passionate love being a psychosis and, finally, about love not existing at all, being only physical attraction, and so on. As he recalled all this he sadly reflected that if someone had asked him now what love really was, he would have been at a loss for an answer.

The service was over now and the congregation appeared. Laptev looked intently at the dark figures. The Bishop had driven past in his carriage, the bells had stopped ringing, the red and green lights on the belfry had been put out, one after the other – these were the illuminations in celebration of the patronal festival – and people were in no hurry, stopping to talk under the windows. But at last Laptev heard familiar voices, his heart started pounding and he was gripped by despair, since Julia wasn't alone, but with two other ladies.

'That's terrible, really terrible!' he whispered jealously. 'That's terrible!'

At the corner of a small side-street Julia stopped to say goodbye to the ladies, and then she glanced at Laptev.

'I'm going to your place,' he said. 'To talk to your father. Is he at home?'

'Probably,' she replied. 'It's too early for the club.'

The side-street had an abundance of gardens. Lime trees grew by the fences, casting broad shadows in the moonlight, so that the fences and gates on one side were completely enveloped in darkness, from which came the sound of women, restrained laughter and someone quietly playing the balalaika. It smelt of lime trees and hay. The whispers of those invisible women and the smell excited Laptev. Suddenly he felt a strong urge to embrace his companion, to shower her face, arms and shoulders with kisses, to fall at her feet and tell her how long he had been waiting for her. There was a faint, barely perceptible smell of incense about her, which reminded him of the time when he too had believed in God, had gone to evening service, had dreamed a great deal about pure, poetic love. Because this girl did not love him he felt that any possibility of the kind of love he had dreamt of then had faded for ever.

She sounded very concerned about his sister Nina's health — two months ago she had had an operation for cancer and everyone was expecting a relapse now.

'I was with her this morning,' Julia said, 'and it struck me that she hasn't only grown thinner this past week, she's simply lost all her colour.'

'Yes, yes,' Laptev agreed. 'There hasn't actually been a relapse, but I can see that she's growing weaker every day – she seems to be wasting away before my eyes. I can't understand what the trouble is.'

'Heavens, how healthy, buxom and rosy-cheeked she used to be!' Julia said after a brief silence. 'Everyone here used to call her "The Moscow Girl". The way she used to laugh! On holidays she'd wear simple peasant costume and it really suited her.'

77

Dr Sergey Belavin was at home. A stout, red-faced man, with a long frock-coat that stretched below his knees and made him appear short-legged, he was pacing the study, hands in pockets, humming softly and pensively. His grey side-whiskers were dishevelled and his hair wasn't combed, as if he'd just got out of bed. And his study, with those cushions on the couches, piles of old papers in the corners and an unhealthy looking, dirty poodle under the table, produced the same scruffy, slovenly impression as the master.

'Monsieur Laptev would like to see you,' his daughter said, entering the study.

He hummed louder, offered Laptev his hand as he came into the drawing-room and asked, 'Well, what's new?'

It was dark in the drawing-room. Laptev did not sit down. Still holding his hat he started apologizing for disturbing him. He asked what could be done to help his sister to sleep at night and why she was growing so terribly thin. He felt embarrassed, as he thought that he had already asked the identical questions when he had called that morning.

'Tell me,' he asked, 'shouldn't we call in some specialist in internal diseases from Moscow? What do you think?'

The doctor sighed, shrugged his shoulders and made some vague gesture with both hands.

He was clearly offended. This doctor was an exceptionally touchy, suspicious person, permanently convinced that no one trusted him, recognized him or respected him enough, that he was being generally exploited and that his colleagues were all hostile towards him. He was always ridiculing himself, maintaining that idiots like himself had been created only for everyone else to trample on.

Julia lit a lamp. Her pale, languid face and sluggish walk showed how tired she was after the church service. She felt like resting and sat on the couch, put her hands on her lap and became lost in thought. Laptev knew that he wasn't handsome and now he was physically conscious of his own ugliness. He was short and thin, with flushed cheeks, and his hair had thinned out so much his head felt cold. His expression had none of that natural grace which makes even coarse, ugly faces likeable. In women's company he was awkward, over-talkative and affected – now he was almost despising himself for this. To stop Julia from being bored he had to talk about something. But about what? About his sister's illness again?

He produced some platitudes about medicine, praising hygiene. He said that it had long been his wish to establish a hostel for the poor in Moscow and that he already had estimates for the work. According to this scheme of his, workmen coming to the hostel in the evenings would get (for five or six copecks) a portion of hot cabbage soup, bread, a warm dry bed with blankets and a place to dry their clothes and footwear.

Julia usually kept silent in his presence and, in some strange way – perhaps it was a man in love's intuition – he was able to guess her thoughts and intentions. Now he concluded that as she hadn't gone to her room to change and have tea after the service she must be going out to visit someone that evening.

'But I'm in no rush with the hostel,' he continued and he felt annoyed and irritated as he turned towards the doctor, who was giving him vague, bewildered looks, evidently unable to see why he needed to talk about hygiene and medicine. 'It will probably be some time before I put it all into motion. I'm frightened the hostel might fall into the hands of those prigs and lady do-gooders in Moscow who wreck any new undertaking.'

Julia stood up and offered Laptev her hand. 'Do excuse me,' she said, 'but I must be going. Remember me to your sister.'

The doctor started humming pensively again.

Julia left and not long afterwards Laptev said goodbye to the doctor and went home. When one feels unhappy and disgruntled, how vulgar lime trees, shadows and clouds seem – all these smug, indifferent beauties of nature! The moon was high, clouds scurried beneath it. 'What a stupid provincial moon!' Laptev thought. 'What pathetic, scraggy clouds!'

He was ashamed of having mentioned medicine and working men's hostels and was horrified at the thought that he wouldn't be able to resist trying to see her and talk to her tomorrow: once again he would learn that he was like a complete stranger to her. It would be exactly the same the day after tomorrow. What was the point of it all? When and how would it all finish?

When he was home he went to see his sister. Nina still looked strong and appeared to be a well-built, powerful woman. But that pronounced pallor made her look like a ~~dead body~~ now as she lay on her back with her eyes clo~~sed~~. Her ~~eleven-year~~-old elder daughter Sasha was sitting reading t~~o her from a school~~ book.

'Alexei is here,' the sick woman said softly to herse~~lf~~.

A tacit agreement had long been in effect between Sa~~sha an~~d her uncle and they had organized a rota. Sasha now closed her reader and left the room quietly, without a word. Laptev took a historical novel from the chest of drawers, found the page and started reading to her.

Nina Panaurov was from Moscow. She and her two brothers had spent their childhood and youth in the family house (they were merchants) on Pyatnitsky Street, and what a long, boring childhood it had been. Their father was a strict man and had birched her on three occasions. Her mother had died after a long illness. The servants had been dirty, coarse and hypocritical. Priests and monks often called at the house and they too were coarse and hypocritical. They drank, ate their fill and crudely flattered her father, whom they did not like. The boys were lucky enough to go to high school, but Nina had no formal education, had written in a scrawly hand all her life and had read nothing but historical novels. Seventeen years ago, when she was twenty-two, she had met her present husband Panaurov – he came from a landowning family – at a villa in Khimki, had fallen in love and was married in secret, against her father's wishes. Panaurov, a handsome and rather arrogant person, who liked lighting cigarettes from icon-lamps and who was a habitual whistler, struck her father as a complete and utter nobody. Later on, when the son-in-law started demanding a dowry in his letters, the old man had written to tell his daughter that he was sending some fur coats to her place in the country, some silver and odds and ends left by her mother, together with thirty thousand roubles in cash, but without his paternal blessing. Afterwards he had sent a further twenty thousand. The money and dowry were all squandered and Panaurov and family moved to town, where he had taken a job in local government. In town he started another family, which caused many tongues to wag since this illegitimate family didn't bother to conceal itself at all.

Nina Panaurov adored her husband. As she listened to the historical novel she thought about how much she had gone through and suffered all this time and what a pathetic narrative her life would make. Since the tumour was in the breast, she was convinced that the cause of her illness was love and family life, and that jealousy and tears had made her bedridden.

Shutting the book, Alexei said, 'That's the end, thank God. We'll start another tomorrow.'

Nina laughed. She had always been easily amused, but Laptev had begun to notice that sometimes her judgement was affected by her illness and she would laugh at the slightest nonsense, for no reason.

'Julia called just before dinner, while you were out,' she said. 'I can see that she doesn't trust her father very much. "All right, let my father treat you," she says, "yet you still write, without anyone knowing, to an elderly monk and ask him to pray for you." It's some wise old man they know who lives locally.' After a brief pause she continued, 'Julia left her umbrella behind. Send it over tomorrow ... No, if this is the end neither doctors nor holy sages will be any use.'

'Nina, why don't you sleep at night?' Laptev asked, to change the subject.

'Oh, I just can't, that's all. I lie thinking.'

'What about, my dear?'

'The children ... you ... my own life. After all, I've been through a lot, haven't I? When you start remembering ... when you ... Good heavens!' She burst out laughing. 'It's no joke having five children and burying three. I'd be about to have a baby and my Grigory would be with another woman and there'd be nobody I could send to fetch the midwife, or someone. If you went into the hall or kitchen for the servants you'd find only Jews, tradesmen and moneylenders waiting for him to come home. It quite made my head go round. He didn't love me, although he never said so. Now I'm reconciled to it, though, and I feel as if a weight has been lifted from me. But it did hurt me when I was younger, it hurt me terribly! Once – we were still living in the country – I caught him in the garden with some woman and I walked away, not caring where I was going, until I found myself in the church porch. There I fell on my knees and repeated "Holy Mother". It was night, the moon was shining . . .'

Exhausted, she started gasping for breath. After a little rest she caught hold of her brother's arm and continued in a faint, almost inaudible voice, 'How kind you are, Alexei! You're so clever . . . What a fine man you've become!'

At midnight Laptev wished her goodnight and on his way out took the umbrella that Julia had forgotten. Despite the late hour, the servants, male and female, were drinking tea in the dining-room. What chaos! The children hadn't gone to bed – they were in the dining-room too. Everyone there was softly talking, whispering, and no one noticed that the lamp was growing dim and would soon go out. All these people, large and small, were worried by a whole series of unfavourable omens and they felt very miserable. The mirror in the hall had been broken, the samovar hummed every day and was humming away now as if to annoy them. A mouse had jumped out of Mrs Panaurov's shoe while she was dressing, so they said. The dreadful significance of these portents was already known to the children. The elder daughter, Sasha, a thin little girl with dark hair, was sitting still at the table with a frightened, mournful look, while seven-year-old Lida, the younger girl, plump and fair-haired, stood by her sister, scowling at the light.

Laptev went down to his low-ceilinged, stuffy rooms on the ground floor – they always smelt of geraniums. Panaurov, Nina's husband, was sitting reading the newspaper in his dining-room. Laptev nodded and sat opposite. Neither said a word. They often spent entire evenings like this, unembarrassed by the mutual silence.

The girls came down to say goodnight. Silently, without hurrying, Panaurov made the sign of the cross over both of them several times and let them kiss his hand. This kissing and curtseying ceremony took place every evening.

When the girls had left, Panaurov laid his paper to one side and said, 'This blessed town is so boring!' Sighing, he went on, 'I must confess, my dear man, I'm delighted you've at last found some entertainment.'

'What do you mean?' Laptev said.

'Just now I saw you leaving Dr Belavin's house. I hope you didn't go there on Daddy's account.'

'Of course I did,' Laptev replied, blushing.

'Well, *of course*. By the way, you'd have a job finding another old mule like that Daddy in a month of Sundays. What a filthy, inept, clumsy oaf he is. Words fail me! You Muscovites have only a kind of poetic interest in provincial landscapes, in the wretched existence of yokels whom our writers wax lyrical about. But you can take it from me, old man, there's nothing lyrical about this place. There's only savagery, meanness and vileness – that's all. Just look at our local high priests of learning, the intelligentsia, so to speak. Can you imagine, we have twenty-eight doctors here, they've all become very rich, they've bought themselves houses, while the rest of the inhabitants are in the same hopeless situation as they've always been. For example, Nina needed an operation, really a very minor one, but we had to send to Moscow for a surgeon because no one here would do it. You can't imagine what it's like. They know nothing, understand nothing and are interested in nothing. Just ask them what cancer is, for example, what causes it.'

Panaurov started explaining cancer. He was a specialist in every branch of learning and had a scientific explanation for anything you could think of. His way of solving problems was something quite unique to himself. He had his own special theory of the circulation of the blood, his own chemistry and astronomy. He spoke slowly, softly, convincingly, pronouncing the words 'you just have no idea about it' as if he were pleading with you. He screwed his eyes up, sighed languidly and smiled graciously like an emperor: he was evidently highly satisfied with himself and quite untroubled at being fifty years old.

'I could do with a bite to eat,' Laptev said. 'Something nice and spicy.'

'That's no problem. I can fix you up right away.'

Shortly afterwards, Laptev was upstairs in the dining-room,

having supper with his brother-in-law. Laptev drank a glass of vodka and then changed to wine. Panaurov drank nothing. He never drank, never played cards, but in spite of this had managed to run through his own and his wife's property and accumulate a whole pile of debts. To fritter so much money away in so short a time, something besides sexual craving was needed – some special talent. Panaurov loved tasty food, fine table appointments, music with dinner, bowing waiters to whom he could casually toss ten- or even twenty-rouble tips. He took part in all subscription schemes and lotteries, sent bouquets to ladies he knew on their name-days, bought cups, glass-holders, cuff-links, ties, canes, perfume, cigarette-holders, pipes, dogs, parrots, Japanese goods and antiques. He wore silk nightshirts, his bed was of ebony, inlaid with mother-of-pearl, he had a genuine Bokhara dressing-gown, and so on. Every day he spent 'heaps of money', as he put it, on these things.

During supper he kept sighing and shaking his head. 'Yes, everything in this world comes to an end,' he said softly, screwing up his dark eyes. 'You'll fall in love, fall out of love. You'll be deceived, because faithful women don't exist. You'll become desperate and do some deceiving yourself. But the time will come when all this will be only a memory and you'll coolly reflect that it was all absolutely trivial.'

Laptev was tired and slightly drunk. As he looked at the other man's fine head, his trimmed beard, he felt that he could understand why women loved that spoilt, self-assured, physically attractive man.

After supper Panaurov didn't stay at home but went off to his other flat. Laptev accompanied him. Panaurov was the only man in the entire town who wore a top hat, and against a background of grey fences, pathetic three-windowed little houses and nettle clumps his elegant, smart figure, top hat and orange gloves never failed to produce a strange, sad impression.

After saying goodnight, Laptev started off home, without hurrying. The moon shone brightly, making every scrap of straw on the ground visible, and Laptev felt that the moonlight was caressing his uncovered head – it was just as though someone were running feathers over his hair.

'I'm in love!' he said out loud and he had a sudden urge to run after Panaurov and embrace him, forgive him and present him with a lot of money – and then dash off into the fields or a copse, forever running, without looking back.

Back home, on a chair, he saw the umbrella that Julia had forgotten. He seized it and hungrily kissed it. It was made of silk, was not new and had a piece of old elastic tied round it. The handle was of cheap bone. Laptev opened it over his head and it seemed that the sweet scent of happiness was all around.

He settled himself more comfortably in his chair and started writing a letter to one of his Moscow friends, still holding the umbrella.

My dearest Kostya,

Here's some news for you: I'm in love again. I say 'again', because six years ago I was in love with a Moscow actress whom I never even met and over the past eighteen months I've been living with a 'personage' who is familiar to you, a woman who is neither young nor beautiful. My dear friend, how unlucky I've been in love! I've never had any success with women and if I say 'again', it's only because it's so sad, it hurts me so much to have to acknowledge that my youth has passed by without any love at all, and that I'm only really in love now for the first time, at the age of thirty-four. So, may I write that I'm in love 'again'?

If you only knew the kind of girl she is. One wouldn't call her a beauty – she has a broad face, she's terribly thin. But what a wonderfully kind expression, what a smile! Her voice is so resonant, she seems to be singing when she speaks. She never starts a conversation when she's with me, I don't really know her, but when I'm close to her I sense she is a rare, unusual person, imbued with intelligence and lofty ideals. She's religious and you just can't imagine how deeply this moves me, how much it raises her in my estimation. I'm ready to argue with you endlessly on this point, You're right, you can think what you like, but I still love her going to church. She's from the provinces, but she went to school in Moscow – she loves our Moscow – and she dresses in true Muscovite style. For that I love her, love her, love her.

I can see you frowning and getting up to read me a long lecture about the nature of love, whom one may or may not love, and so on. But before I fell in love I too knew exactly what love is, my dear Kostya!

My sister thanks you for your good wishes. She often remembers once taking Kostya Kochevoy to preparatory class. She still calls you 'poor', since she still remembers you as the little orphan. So, my poor orphan, I'm in love. It's a secret for the time being – don't say anything *there* to the familiar 'personage'. That will all come right in the end – or as the servant says in Tolstoy, 'everything will sort itself out . . .'

Having finished the letter, Laptev went to bed. He was so tired, his eyes closed of their own accord, but for some reason he couldn't sleep – the street noises seemed to be disturbing him. The herd of cattle was driven past and the horn blown, and soon after that the bells rang for early mass. A cart would creak past, then he would hear the voice of a woman going to market. And the sparrows never stopped chirping.

II

It was a cheerful, festive morning. At about ten o'clock Nina, in a brown dress, hair combed, was led into the drawing-room and there she walked up and down. Then she stood by the open window with a broad innocent smile on her face. Looking at her, you were reminded of a local artist, a drunkard, who had called her face a 'countenance' and had wanted to include her in a painting of a Russian Shrovetide. Everyone, the children, servants and even her brother Alexei, even she herself, was suddenly convinced that she was bound to recover. The little girls screamed with laughter as they pursued their uncle and tried to catch him, and the house grew noisy.

People from outside came to inquire about her health. They brought communion bread and said that prayers were being offered for her today in almost every church. She had done a great deal of good in that town and the people loved her. She dispensed charity with the same lack of fuss as her brother, who gave away money very readily, without stopping to consider whether he should or not. Nina paid poor schoolboys' fees, took tea, sugar and jam to old ladies, gave indigent brides dresses, and if she happened to see a newspaper she would first look for appeals or stories about anyone in dire straits.

Now she was holding a bundle of chits with which various

impecunious petitioners had obtained goods at the grocer's. This grocer had sent these to her yesterday, requesting eighty-two roubles.

'Heavens, they've been taking so much, they really have no shame!' she said, barely recognizing her own ugly handwriting. 'That's no joke, eighty-two roubles! I don't feel like paying!'

'I'll pay it today,' Laptev said.

'But what on earth for?' Nina said anxiously. 'It's really enough for me, those two hundred and fifty roubles I get every month from you and our brother. God bless you,' she added in a soft voice, so that the servants wouldn't hear.

'Well, I spend two thousand five hundred a month,' he said. 'Let me tell you again, my dear, you're just as entitled to spend money as Fyodor and myself. Never forget that. Father has three children, so one in every three copecks belongs to you.'

But Nina didn't understand and she looked as if she was trying to do a very complicated piece of mental arithmetic. This obtuseness in financial matters always worried and embarrassed Laptev. Moreover, he suspected that she had some personal debts which she was too ashamed to tell him about and which were distressing her.

They heard footsteps and heavy breathing. It was the doctor coming upstairs, as scruffy and unkempt as ever. He was humming away as usual.

To avoid meeting him, Laptev went into the dining-room, then down to his own rooms. It was quite clear to him that getting on more intimate terms with the doctor and calling informally was impossible. Any encounter with that 'old mule', as Panaurov called him, was unpleasant. This was why he saw Julia so seldom. He reckoned that if he took the umbrella back now, when her father was out, he would catch her alone in the house, and his heart leapt with joy. He must hurry, hurry!

Greatly excited, he took the umbrella and flew off on the wings of love. It was hot in the street. At the doctor's house, in the huge courtyard overgrown with tall weeds and nettles, about twenty boys were playing ball. They were all children of the tenants – working people who lived in the three old, unsightly outbuildings which the doctor was meaning to repair every year, but was always putting off. Healthy voices rang out. Far to one side, near her front porch, stood Julia, her arms behind her back as she watched the game.

'Good morning!' Laptev called out.

Julia turned round. Usually she looked cool and indifferent when he saw her, or tired, as yesterday. But now she seemed as lively and playful as those boys at their game. 'Just look at them,' she said, going over to him. 'They don't enjoy themselves like that in Moscow. But they don't have such large yards there, so there's no room for running about. Father's just gone over to your place,' she added.

'I know, but it's you I've come to see, not him,' Laptev said, admiring her youthfulness, which he hadn't noticed before, apparently seeing it only for the first time today. And he felt that he was looking at her delicate white neck, with its little golden chain, for the very first time.

'I've come to see *you*,' he repeated. 'My sister's sent this umbrella you forgot yesterday.'

She stretched out her hand to take it, but he pressed the umbrella to his chest and said in a passionate, uncontrolled voice, as he surrendered once again to the exquisite delight experienced the previous night beneath the umbrella, 'I beg you, give it to me. I shall keep it in memory of you, of our friendship. It's a really wonderful umbrella!'

'Keep it,' she said, blushing. 'I don't think it's so wonderful.'

He looked at her in speechless ecstasy.

'Why am I making you stand in this heat?' she said after a short silence, laughing. 'Let's go inside.'

'I hope I'm not disturbing you.'

They entered the hall. Julia ran upstairs, rustling her white dress with its blue flower pattern.

'You can't disturb *me*,' she replied, stopping on the stairs. 'After all, I never do a thing. Every day's a holiday for me, from morning to night.'

'That's something I can't understand,' he said, going up to her. 'I grew up in surroundings where everyone without exception – men and women – had to slave away, every single day.'

'But supposing there's nothing to do?' she asked.

'Then you must organize your life so that you just can't avoid working. Without work life can never be honest and happy.'

He pressed the umbrella to his chest again and said in a soft voice that didn't sound like his, 'If you would agree to be my wife I would give anything. Just *anything*. There's no price I wouldn't pay, no sacrifice I wouldn't make.'

She shuddered and looked at him in surprise and fear.

'What are you saying!' she exclaimed, turning pale. 'It's out of the question, I do assure you. I'm sorry.'

Still rustling her dress as before, she dashed upstairs and vanished through a door.

Laptev understood what this meant and his mood changed abruptly, as if the light had suddenly gone out in his soul. Suffering the shame and humiliation of someone who had been rejected, who wasn't loved, who was thought unattractive, repulsive and perhaps even hateful, and whom everyone avoided, he walked out of the house. 'I'd give *anything*,' he said, mimicking himself as he walked home in the heat and recalled the details of his declaration. '"Give *anything*" – why, that's how shopkeepers talk! A fat lot of good your *anything* is!'

All the things he had said just now struck him as sickeningly stupid. Why had he lied to her about growing up in surroundings where everyone worked 'without exception'? Why had he adopted that didactic tone about the 'honest, happy life'? It was silly, boring, hypocritical – typical Moscow pomposity. But gradually he lapsed into the indifference felt by criminals after a harsh sentence. Now, thank God, it was all over, he thought, no longer was there that dreadful uncertainty, no longer would he have to wait day after day, suffer, forever thinking about the same thing. Everything was clear now. He must abandon all hope of personal happiness and live without desire or hope; he must never have yearnings or expectations any more. If he wanted to dispel the boredom that he was so sick and tired of, he could start caring about what other people did, about their happiness. Old age would then creep up on him unnoticed, his life would come to an end – and that was the long and short of it. Now he didn't care about a thing, he wanted nothing and he could reflect coolly. But he felt a certain heaviness in his face, especially under the eyes. His forehead was as taut as stretched elastic and it seemed that tears would spurt at any moment. Feeling weak all over, he climbed into bed and in five minutes he was fast asleep.

III

Julia was plunged into despair by Laptev's proposal, which had been so unexpected.

She didn't know him very well and they had met by chance. He was rich, a director of the well-known Moscow firm of Fyodor Laptev & Sons. He was always very serious, obviously highly intelligent and preoccupied with his sister's health. She had thought that he had been completely ignoring her, and on her part she had treated him with the utmost indifference. But suddenly there was that sudden declaration on the stairs, that pathetic, enraptured face . . .

His proposal had disturbed her by its very suddenness, and she was upset at his using the word 'wife' and that she had had to refuse him. She had forgotten what she actually told Laptev, but vestiges of that impetuous, unpleasant feeling she had experienced when refusing him still lingered. She did not like him. He looked like a shop assistant, he was boring, and the only possible reply was *no*. All the same, she felt awkward, as if she had behaved badly. 'My God, not even in the flat. Right there, on the stairs,' she said despairingly, turning towards the small icon above the bed-head. 'And he never paid me any attention before. It's all rather unusual, strange . . .'

In her loneliness she felt more uneasy by the hour, unable to cope unaided with those oppressive feelings. She needed someone to listen to her and tell her that she had behaved correctly. But there was no one to talk to. Her mother had died long ago, and she looked on her father as some kind of eccentric with whom she couldn't have a serious conversation. He embarrassed her with his whims, his excessive touchiness and vague gestures. The moment you started a discussion with him he would start talking about himself. Even in her prayers she hadn't been completely frank, since she wasn't sure exactly what she should ask of God.

The samovar was brought in. Very pale and tired, with a helpless-looking face, Julia entered the dining-room, made the tea – this was her responsibility – and poured her father a glass. In that long frock-coat that reached below the knees, with his red face, uncombed hair, hands in pockets, the doctor paced the dining-room – not from corner to corner, but haphazardly, like a beast in a cage. He would stop by the table, drink with relish from his glass and then pensively pace the room again.

'Laptev proposed to me today,' Julia said, blushing.

The doctor looked at her and didn't seem to understand. 'Laptev?' he asked. 'Nina Panaurov's brother?'

He loved his daughter. She would most probably marry sooner or later and leave him, but he tried not to think about it. He was scared at the prospect of loneliness and (for some reason) he felt he might have a stroke if he were left alone in that large house, but he didn't like to say it outright.

'I'm really very pleased,' he said, shrugging his shoulders. 'My heartiest congratulations! Now you have an excellent chance of abandoning me and *that* must give you great pleasure. I understand you very well. Living with a senile, sick, half-demented father must be rotten for someone of your age. I understand you perfectly. If only I were to peg out soon, if only the devil would cart me off, everyone would be so delighted. I congratulate you most heartily.'

'I turned him down.'

The doctor felt relieved, but now he couldn't stop talking and he continued, 'I'm amazed. I've been asking myself this for a long time now, why haven't they put me in a lunatic asylum? Why am I wearing this frock-coat, instead of a straitjacket? I still believe in truth, goodness, I'm a stupid old idealist – surely that's madness in this day and age? And what do I get for my love of truth, for being honest with people? I'm almost stoned in the streets, everyone rides roughshod over me. Even my nearest and dearest walk all over me. So to hell with me, stupid old fool!'

'It's impossible to have a proper talk with you!' Julia said. Abruptly, she stood up from the table and furiously went to her room. She well remembered how often her father had been unfair to her. But after a little while she began to feel sorry for him, and when he left for his club she went downstairs with him and shut the door after him. The weather was bad, very blustery. The door shook from the force of the wind and in the hall there were draughts everywhere which nearly blew the candle out. Julia went all through her rooms upstairs and made the sign of the cross over all windows and doors. The wind howled and someone seemed to be walking about on the roof. Never had she felt so low, never had she felt so lonely.

She wondered if she had behaved badly in refusing a man just because she didn't care for his looks. She didn't love him – that was true – and marrying him would have meant saying farewell to her dreams and ideas of a happy married life. But would she ever meet the man of her dreams and fall in love? She was already twenty-one. There were no eligible bachelors in town. She thought of all the men she knew – civil servants, teachers, officers. Some of them were already married and their family life was staggeringly empty and boring. Others were dull, colourless, stupid and immoral. Whatever you said about Laptev, he was a Muscovite, he'd been to university, he spoke French. He lived in Moscow, the capital, where there were so many clever, idealistic, remarkable people, where everything was so lively, with magnificent theatres, musical evenings, first-class dressmakers and patisseries. The Bible says that a wife must love her husband and love is of prime importance in novels. But wasn't all that going too far? Surely family life *without* love was somehow possible? Wasn't it said that love soon passes, that it becomes a mere habit and that the purpose of family life isn't love and happiness, but responsibility – bringing up children, looking after the house and so on. Perhaps what the Bible meant was loving one's husband in the same way as one's neighbour, having respect, making allowances . . .

That night Julia attentively read her evening prayers, then she knelt down, clasped her hands to her breast and looked at the icon-lamp. 'Teach me to understand, Holy Mother. Teach me, O Lord!' she said, with deep feeling.

In the course of her life she had met poor, pathetic old maids who bitterly regretted having turned down their suitors at some time. Wouldn't the same thing happen to her? Shouldn't she enter a convent or become a nurse?

She undressed and got into bed, crossing herself and the air around. Suddenly a bell rang sharply, plaintively, in the corridor. 'Good God!' she said, feeling intense irritation all over her body at this sound. She lay there thinking about provincial life, so uneventful and monotonous, yet so disturbing at times: you were always being forced to shudder, to feel angry and guilty and in the end your nerves became so shattered you were too frightened to look out from under the blankets.

Half an hour later the bell rang again, just as sharply. The servants were most probably asleep and didn't hear it. Annoyed with them and shivering, Julia lit a candle and started dressing. When she had finished and gone out into the corridor the maid was bolting the downstairs door. 'I thought it was the master, but it was somebody one of the patients sent over,' she said.

Julia returned to her room. She took a pack of cards from her chest-of-drawers and decided that if, after shuffling them well and cutting them, the bottom card turned out red, that would mean *yes*, that is, she had to accept Laptev. If it was black she must say *no*. The card was the ten of spades.

This had a calming effect and she fell asleep. But in the morning it was neither 'yes' nor 'no' again. She realized that she could change her whole life now if she so wanted. These thoughts wearied her – she felt exhausted and ill. However, just after eleven o'clock, she dressed and went to visit Nina. She wanted to see Laptev – he might strike her as more attractive now and perhaps she had been making a mistake.

Fighting one's way against that wind was hard work. She hardly made any progress, and she held her hat with both hands, seeing nothing for dust.

IV

When he entered his sister's room and unexpectedly saw Julia there, Laptev again felt the humiliation of someone who has been snubbed. He concluded that if, after yesterday, she had no qualms about visiting his sister and meeting him, then either he didn't exist as far as she was concerned, or he was considered a complete nonentity. But when he greeted her and she looked at him sadly and guiltily with a pale face and dust under her eyes, he could see that she too was suffering.

She was not feeling well. After sitting there for a very short time – about ten minutes – she made her farewell. 'Please take me home, Mr Laptev,' she said on her way out. They walked in silence down the street, holding on to their hats; he kept behind her, trying to shield her from the wind. It was calmer in a side-street and here they walked side by side.

'Please forgive me if I was unkind yesterday,' she began and her voice shook, as if she were about to cry. 'It's sheer torture! I haven't slept all night.'

'I had an excellent night,' Laptev replied without looking at her, 'but that doesn't mean I feel all right. My life is in shreds, I'm deeply unhappy after your turning me down yesterday, I feel as if I've taken poison. The most painful things were said yesterday, but today I don't feel at all inhibited and can speak quite frankly. I love you more than my sister, more than my late mother. I could – and I did – live without my sister and mother, but life without you makes no sense. I just can't . . .'

As usual, he had guessed her intentions. He saw that she wanted to continue yesterday's conversation: it was only for this that she had asked him to accompany her and now she was taking him to her house. But what could she add to her refusal? Was there any more to say? Her glance, her smile, even the way she held her head and shoulders as she walked with him – everything indicated that she still did not love him, that he was a stranger to her. So what else was there for her to say?

Dr Belavin was at home. 'Welcome! Delighted to see you, Fyodor,' he said, getting the name wrong. 'Delighted, absolutely delighted.'

He had never been so friendly before and Laptev concluded that the doctor already knew about the proposal – and he found this unpleasant to think about. He was sitting in the drawing-room now: it produced a strange impression, with its cheap vulgar furniture and poor pictures. Although there were armchairs and a huge lamp with a shade, it looked unlived-in, rather like a spacious barn. Obviously, only someone like the doctor could feel at home in such a room. Another room, almost twice as big, was called 'The Ballroom' – here there were only chairs, as at a dancing-class. And something suspicious began to worry Laptev as he sat in the drawing-room talking to the doctor about his sister. Had Julia been to see his sister Nina and then brought him here to announce that she had accepted his proposal? This was bad enough, but even worse was having a nature that was prey to such suspicions. He imagined father and daughter having lengthy deliberations yesterday evening and night, long arguments perhaps, and then agreeing that Julia had behaved recklessly in refusing a rich man. Even the words spoken by parents on such occasions – 'It's true, you don't love him, but on the other hand think of the good deeds you'll be able to perform!' – rang in his ears.

The doctor prepared to leave on his rounds. Laptev wanted to go with him but Julia said, 'Please stay, I beg you.'

She had been suffering from dreadful depression and now she was trying to reassure herself that to refuse a respectable, kind man who loved her just because he didn't attract her, especially when this marriage provided the opportunity of changing her life, so cheerless, monotonous and idle, when her youth was passing and the future held no hope of anything brighter – to refuse him in these circumstances was insane, irresponsible and perverse, and God might even punish her for it.

Her father left the house. When his footsteps had died away she suddenly stopped in front of Laptev.

'I spent a long time thinking it over yesterday, Mr Laptev, and I accept your proposal,' she said decisively, turning pale.

He bent down and kissed her hand. Awkwardly, she kissed his head with cold lips. He felt that the essential thing, her love, was absent from this amorous declaration, which none the less stated what was superfluous. He felt like shouting, running away, setting off for Moscow immediately. But she was standing close to him and she seemed so beautiful that he was suddenly gripped with desire. He saw that it was too late now for further discussion, embraced her passionately, pressed her to his chest, muttered something, addressed her intimately, kissed her neck, cheek and head . . .

She retreated to the window, frightened by these caresses.

Now they both regretted their declarations. 'Why did this happen?' they asked themselves in their embarrassment.

'If only you knew how unhappy I feel!' she said, wringing her hands.

'What's wrong?' he asked, going up to her and wringing his hands too. 'My dear, tell me what's wrong, for God's sake! But only the truth. I beg you, only the truth!'

'Don't take any notice,' she said, forcing a smile. 'I promise to be a faithful, devoted wife. Come over this evening.'

Later, as he sat reading the historical novel to his sister, he remembered all this and felt insulted that his admirable, pure and generous feelings had elicited such a trivial response. He was *not* loved, but his proposal had been accepted, probably only because he was rich. In other words, they valued that part of him he valued least. The pure, devout Julia had never given any thought to money – he granted her that – but she didn't love him, did she? No, she did not, and obviously there had been some sort of calculation here – even though it was somewhat vague and not wholly intentional perhaps, it was calculation none the less. The doctor's house, with its vulgar décor, repelled him and the doctor himself resembled some fat, pathetic miser, rather like the buffoon Gaspard in *The Bells of Corneville*.* The very name Julia sounded common. He imagined Julia and himself during the wedding, essentially complete strangers and without a scrap of feeling on her part, as if it were an arranged marriage. And now his only consolation (as banal as the marriage itself) was that he wasn't the first and wouldn't be the last and that thousands of men had made similar marriages and that, in time, when she knew him better, Julia might perhaps come to love him.

'Romeo and Julia!' he said, closing the book and laughing. 'I'm Romeo, Nina. You may congratulate me. I proposed to Julia Belavin today.'

Nina first thought that he was joking, then she believed him and burst into tears. The news didn't please her. 'All right, congratulations,' she said. 'But why so sudden?'

'It's not, it's been going on since March, only you never notice

*Operetta by the French composer R. Planquet.

a thing. I've been in love since March, when I first met her here in your room.'

'But I thought you'd marry someone we know, from Moscow,' Nina said after a brief silence. 'The girls from our little circle are not so complicated. But the main thing, Alexei, is for you to be happy, that's what's important. My Grigory never loved me, and you can see how we live – it's an open secret. Of course, any woman would love you for your kindness and intellect. But Julia went to a boarding-school, she's out of the top drawer. Intellect and kindness don't mean much to her. She's young. As for you, Alexei, you're neither young nor handsome.'

To soften these last words she stroked his cheek and said, 'You're not handsome, but you're a wonderful person.'

She was so excited her cheeks flushed slightly and she talked enthusiastically about whether it would be correct to bless Alexei with an icon. All said and done, she was his elder sister and was like a mother to him. And she kept trying to convince her despondent brother that the wedding should be celebrated correctly, cheerfully and with great ceremony, so that people didn't start criticizing.

Then the husband-to-be started calling on the Belavins three or four times a day and he was no longer able to take Sasha's place reading the historical novel. Julia received him in her own two rooms, away from the drawing-room and her father's study, and he liked them very much. There were dark walls and a full icon-case in one corner; and there was a smell of fine perfume and lamp oil. She lived in the remotest rooms, her bed and dressing-table were surrounded by screens and her book-case doors were curtained inside with a green material. She had carpets, so that she couldn't be heard walking about, and all this led him to believe that hers was a secretive nature, that she loved a quiet, peaceful, enclosed life. Legally, she was only a minor in that house. She had no money of her own: during their walks she was sometimes embarrassed at not having a single copeck on her. Her father gave her a little money for dresses and books, not more than a hundred roubles a year. And the doctor himself had hardly any money, despite his first-class practice: every evening he played cards at the club and always lost. Besides that, he bought houses on mortgage through a mutual credit society and rented them out. His tenants were always behind with their payments, but he was confident that the property deals were highly profitable. He had mortgaged his own house, where he lived with his daughter, and had bought a plot of waste ground with the money. He was already building a large, two-storey house there, with the intention of mortgaging it.

Laptev now seemed to be living in some kind of haze, as if replaced by his double, and he was doing many things he would never have attempted before. Three times he accompanied the doctor to the club, had supper with him and volunteered money for the house-building. He even visited Panaurov in his other flat. One day Panaurov invited him to dinner and, without thinking, Laptev accepted. He was greeted by a lady of about thirty-five, tall and thin, slightly greying and with black eyebrows. She was obviously not Russian. She had white powder blotches on her face and a sickly smile, and she shook his hand brusquely, making the bracelets jingle on her white arm. Laptev thought that she smiled that way to hide the fact she was unhappy from others and from herself. He saw two little girls there too, five and three years old, who looked like Sasha. For dinner they had milk soup, cold veal and carrots, and then chocolate. It was all sickly-sweet and not very tasty, but on the table were gleaming gold forks, bottles of soya sauce and cayenne pepper, an exceptionally ornate sauce-boat and a golden pepper pot.

Only after he had finished his soup did Laptev realize the mistake he had made in coming here for dinner. The lady was embarrassed and kept smiling and showing him her teeth the whole time. Panaurov offered a scientific explanation of falling in love and its origins.

'Here we are dealing with an electrical phenomenon,' he said in French, addressing the lady. 'Everyone's skin has microscopic glands with currents running through them. If you meet someone whose currents are parallel to yours – there's love for you!'

Back home, when his sister asked where he had been, Laptev felt awkward and didn't answer.

Right up to the wedding he had felt in a false position. With every day his love for Julia grew – she seemed ethereal, sublime.

All the same, she didn't return this love: basically, he was buying her, she was selling herself. Sometimes, after much reflection, he simply grew desperate and wondered whether he should run away from it all. Night after night he didn't sleep, all he did was think of meeting that lady in Moscow after the wedding – that lady he had called a 'personage' in letters to friends. And he wondered how his father and brother, both difficult characters, would react to his marriage and to Julia. He was afraid his father might say something rude to Julia at the first meeting. And his brother Fyodor had been acting very strangely lately. In his lengthy letters he wrote about the importance of health, about the influence of illness on one's state of mind, about the nature of religion, but not one word about Moscow and business. These letters irritated Laptev and he thought that his brother's character had taken a turn for the worse.

The wedding was in September. The actual ceremony was held after morning service at the Church of St Peter and St Paul and that same day the couple left for Moscow. When Laptev and his wife (she wore a black dress and train and now resembled a grown woman instead of a girl) were saying goodbye to Nina, the invalid's whole face twisted, but not one tear flowed from her dry eyes.

'If I should die, God forbid,' she said, 'take care of my little girls.'

'Oh, I promise!' Julia replied, her lips and eyelids twitching nervously too.

'I'll come and see you in October,' Laptev said, deeply moved. 'Get better now, my dearest.'

They had a railway compartment to themselves. Both felt sad and embarrassed. She sat in one corner without taking her hat off, pretending to be dozing, while he lay on the couchette opposite, troubled by various thoughts: about his father, about the 'personage', about whether Julia would like his Moscow flat. As he glanced at his wife who didn't love him he gloomily asked himself 'How did all this happen?'

V

In Moscow the Laptevs ran a wholesale haberdashery business, selling fringes, ribbons, braid, knitting items, buttons and so on. The gross receipts amounted to two million roubles a year. What the net profit was no one knew except the old man. The sons and assistants put it at about three hundred thousand and said that it could have been a hundred thousand more if the old man hadn't 'frittered profits away' by giving credit indiscriminately. Over the past ten years they had accumulated nearly a million worthless bills of exchange alone, and when the matter was discussed the senior assistant would produce a crafty wink and use language that many couldn't understand: 'It's the psychological aftermath of the age.'

The main business was carried on in the city's commercial quarter, in a building called the warehouse. This was entered from a perpetually gloomy yard that smelt of matting, where hooves of dray-horses clattered over asphalt. A very modest-looking, iron-bound door led from this yard into a room whose walls, brown from the damp, were covered in charcoal scribbles. This room was lit by a narrow, iron-grilled window. To the left was another room, a little larger and cleaner, with a cast-iron stove and two tables, but with a prison-like window too. This was the office and from it a narrow stone staircase led up to the first floor, where the main business was carried on. This was a fairly large room but, because of the perpetual twilight, low ceiling and lack of space caused by crates, packages and people rushing about, it struck newcomers as just as unprepossessing as the two rooms down below. Up on this floor, and on the office shelves too, goods lay in stacks, bales and cardboard boxes. They were all displayed any old how, with no attempt at order or creating a nice show. If it hadn't been for the crimson threads, tassels and pieces of fringe sticking out of paper-wrapped parcels here and there, no one could have guessed, at first glance, what kind of business was being carried on here. Looking at those crumpled paper parcels and boxes it was hard to believe that millions of roubles were spent on these trifles and that fifty men – excluding buyers – were busy in that warehouse every day.

When Laptev appeared at the warehouse at noon, the day after arriving in Moscow, men were packing goods and making such a racket with the crates no one in the first room or office heard him come in. A postman he knew was going downstairs with a bundle of letters in his hand – he was frowning at the noise and didn't notice him either. The first person to welcome him upstairs was his brother Fyodor, who was so like him people thought that they were twins. This similarity kept reminding Laptev of his appearance and now, seeing before him a short man with flushed cheeks, thinning on top, with lean thighs of poor pedigree, so dull and unbusinesslike, he asked himself: 'Surely *I* don't look like that?'

'I'm so glad to see you!' Fyodor exclaimed, exchanging kisses with his brother and firmly shaking his hand. 'I've been waiting impatiently every day, my dear brother. When you wrote that you were getting married I was racked with curiosity. I've really missed you, old man. Just think, we haven't seen each other for about six months. Well now, what's new? How's Nina? Is she *very* bad?'

'Yes.'

'It's God's will,' Fyodor sighed. 'Well, how's the wife? I dare say she's a beauty. I love her already. After all, she's the same as a little sister to me. We'll spoil her, the two of us.'

Just then Laptev spotted the long familiar, broad, bent back of his father, also called Fyodor. The old man was sitting on a stool by the counter, talking to a customer.

'Father, God has sent us joy today!' Fyodor cried. 'My brother's arrived!'

Laptev senior was tall and so very powerfully built that despite his wrinkles and eighty years he still looked like a strong, healthy man. He spoke in a deep, heavy, booming voice that came thundering from his broad chest as if from a barrel. He shaved his beard, sported an army-style trimmed moustache and smoked cigars. Since he was always feeling warm, he wore a loose-fitting canvas jacket in the warehouse and at home, at all seasons. Recently he'd had a cataract removed, his sight was poor and he no longer took an active part in the business, merely chatting to people and drinking tea with jam.

Laptev bent down and kissed his hand, then his lips.

'It's been such a long time since we saw each other, my dear sir,' the old man said. 'Yes, such a long time. Well, I suppose I must congratulate you on your marriage? All right. Congratulations.'

He offered his lips to receive a kiss. Laptev bent down and kissed them.

'Well now, have you brought the young lady with you?' the old man asked and without waiting for an answer turned to the customer and said, '"I hereby inform you, dear Dad, that I'm marrying Miss So-and-So." Yes. But asking for Dad's blessing and advice isn't in the rules. They just do what they like now. I was over forty when I married and I fell down at my father's feet and asked his advice. They don't do that sort of thing these days.'

The old man was delighted to see his son, but thought it improper to display any affection or show that he was pleased. His voice, his manner of speaking and that 'young lady' expression put Laptev in the bad mood which invariably came over him in that warehouse. Every little detail here reminded him of the past, when he had been whipped and given plain, lenten food. He knew that boys were still whipped and punched on the nose until it bled, and that when these boys grew up they would do the punching. Only five minutes in that warehouse, so it seemed, was enough for him to expect abuse or a punch on the nose at any moment.

Fyodor slapped the customer on the shoulder and said to his brother, 'Alexei, let me introduce Grigory Timofeyevich, the firm's right arm in Tambov. He's a shining example to the youth of today. He's in his sixth decade, yet he has children still at their mother's breast.'

The clerks laughed – and so did the customer, a skinny, pale-faced old man.

'It's contrary to the course of nature,' observed the senior clerk, who was also standing behind the counter. 'Whatever goes in must come out the same.'

This senior clerk, a tall man of about fifty, with a dark beard, spectacles and a pencil behind the ear, usually expressed his thoughts ambiguously, in far-fetched allusions, and it was plain from his cunning smile that he attached some special, subtle meaning to his words. He loved obscuring what he said with bookish expressions that he interpreted in his own peculiar way, often giving common words – 'furthermore', for example – a different meaning from their original one. Whenever he said something categorically and didn't want to be contradicted, he would stretch out his right arm and say 'Furthermore!'

Most surprising of all, the other clerks and the customers understood him perfectly. His name was Ivan Pochatkin and he came from Kashira. Congratulating Laptev, he expressed himself as follows: 'It is a valiant service on your part, for a woman's heart is bold and warlike!'

Another person of consequence in the warehouse was the clerk Makeichev, a stout, fair-haired pillar of the community, with a bald patch on top and side-whiskers. He went over to Laptev and congratulated him respectfully, in a low voice: 'I have the honour, sir ... The Lord has listened to your good father's prayers, sir. The Lord be praised, sir.'

Then the others came over to congratulate him on his marriage. They were all smartly dressed and all seemed impeccably honest, educated men. They spoke with provincial accents and as they said 'sir' after every other word their rapidly delivered congratulations – 'I wish you, sir, all the best, sir' – sounded like whiplashes in the air.

Laptev soon grew bored with all this and wanted to go home. But leaving was awkward. For propriety's sake, he must spend at least two hours in the warehouse. He walked away from the counter and asked Makeichev if they had had a good summer and if there was any news. Makeichev replied politely, without looking him in the eye. A boy with close-cropped hair, in a grey blouse, handed Laptev a glass of tea without a saucer. Soon afterwards another boy stumbled on a crate as he went past and nearly fell over. The stolid Makeichev suddenly pulled a terrifying, vicious, monster-like face and shouted at him, 'Look where you're going!'

The clerks were glad that the young master was married now and had finally returned. They gave him inquisitive, welcoming looks, each considering it his duty to make some pleasant, polite remark as he went past. But Laptev was certain that all this was insincere and that the flattery came from fear. He just couldn't forget how, fifteen years before, a mentally ill clerk had run into the street in his underclothes, barefoot, had waved his fist menacingly at the windows in the boss's office and shouted that they were tormenting the life out of him. People kept laughing at the poor devil for a long time after he had been cured, reminding him how he had called the bosses 'explanters' instead of 'exploiters'. On the whole, life was very hard for the Laptev employees and this had long been the main topic for discussion in the whole commercial quarter. Worst of all was the oriental deviousness with which old Laptev treated them. Because of this, no one knew what salary his favourites Pochatkin and Makeichev received – actually they got no more than three thousand a year, including bonuses, but he pretended he was paying them seven. The bonuses were paid every year to all the clerks, but in secret, so that those who didn't get much were forced by pride to say they'd received a lot. Not one of the junior boys knew when he would be promoted to clerk, and none of the staff ever knew whether the boss was satisfied with him or not. Nothing was categorically forbidden the clerks, so they didn't know what was allowed and what wasn't. They were not in fact forbidden to marry, but they didn't marry for fear of displeasing the boss and losing their job. They were allowed to have friends and to pay visits, but the gates were locked at nine in the evening and every morning the boss would eye his staff suspiciously and test them to see if they smelt of vodka: 'You there, let's smell your breath!'

Every church holiday the staff had to go to early service and stand in church so the boss could see them all. The fasts were strictly observed. On special occasions – the boss's or his family's name-days, for example – the clerks had to club together and buy a cake from Fley's, or an album. They lived on the ground floor of the house on Pyatnitsky Street, as well as in the out-building, three or four to a room, and they ate from a common bowl, although each had his own plate in front of him. If any of the boss's family came in during a meal they would all stand up.

Laptev realized that only those ruined by receiving their education through the old man could seriously consider him their benefactor – the remainder saw him as an enemy and 'explanter'. Now, after a six-month absence, he saw that nothing had improved and that a change had taken place which didn't augur well. His brother Fyodor, who used to be quiet, thoughtful and exceptionally sensitive, was rushing around the place now, looking extremely efficient and businesslike, pencil behind ear, slapping buyers on the shoulder and calling the clerks 'My friends!' Evidently he was acting a part, one in which Alexei didn't recognize him at all.

The old man's voice droned on non-stop. As he had nothing else to do, Laptev senior was instructing a clerk in decent living and the best way to conduct his affairs, setting himself as a good example the whole time.

Laptev had heard that boasting, authoritarian, crushing tone of voice ten, fifteen, twenty years ago. The old man adored himself. What he said invariably gave the impression that he had made his late wife and her family happy, had encouraged his children with rewards, had been a benefactor to his clerks and the rest of the staff, and had made the whole street and all who knew him eternally grateful. Whatever he did was absolutely perfect, and if other men's business went badly this was only because they hadn't followed his advice, without which *no* business enterprise could ever hope to succeed. In church he always stood right in front of the congregation and even rebuked the priests when, according to him, they made mistakes in the ritual. This would please God, he thought, since God loved him.

By two o'clock everyone in the warehouse was busy, except the old man, who was still going on in that thunderous voice. To give himself something to do, Laptev took some braid from a female worker and then sent her away. Then he listened to a buyer – a Vologda merchant – and instructed a clerk to look after him.

The prices and serial numbers of goods were denoted by letters and cries of T–V–A and R–I–T rang out from all sides.

When he left Laptev said goodbye only to his brother.

'I'm coming to Pyatnitsky Street with the wife tomorrow,' he said. 'But I'm warning you, if Father says one rude word to her I won't stay one minute.'

'Just the same as ever!' Fyodor sighed. 'Marriage hasn't

changed you. You must be kind to the old man, dear chap. All right then, see you there tomorrow at eleven. We look forward to it – come straight after church.'

'I don't go to church.'

'Well, it doesn't matter. The main thing is, don't be later than eleven – we have to pray to the Lord before we have lunch. Regards to my little sister-in-law, please kiss her hand for me. I have the feeling I'm going to like her very much.' Fyodor added in complete sincerity. 'I envy you, my dear brother!' he shouted as Alexei was on his way downstairs.

'Why all that cringing, that shyness, as if he felt naked?' Laptev wondered as he walked down Nikolsky Street trying to fathom the reason for the change in Fyodor. 'And this new way of speaking – "dear brother", "old chap", "God's mercy", "Let's pray to the Lord" – what sanctimonious nonsense!'

VI

At eleven the next day – a Sunday – Laptev drove down Pyatnitsky Street with his wife in a one-horse carriage. He was afraid his father might have tantrums and he felt anxious even before arriving. After two nights in her father's house, Julia considered her marriage a mistake, a disaster even. If she'd gone to live anywhere but Moscow with her husband she would not have survived such horrors, she thought. But Moscow did have its diversions. She loved the streets, houses and churches: had it been possible to drive around Moscow in this magnificent sledge with expensive horses, drive all day, from morning till night, at high speed, breathing in the cool, autumn air, she might perhaps have felt a little happier.

The coachman halted the horse near a white, newly plastered two-storey house, then turned right. Here everyone was waiting. A house porter stood at the gate in his new tunic, high boots and galoshes, together with two police constables. The whole area, from the middle of the street to the gate and then across the yard to the porch, was strewn with fresh sand. The house porter doffed his cap, the constables saluted. His brother Fyodor greeted them at the porch with a grave expression.

'Delighted to meet you, my dear sister-in-law,' he said, kissing Julia's hand. 'Welcome.'

He led her upstairs by the arm, then along a corridor, through a crowd of men and women. The vestibule was packed with people too, and there was a smell of incense.

'I'm going to introduce you to Father now,' Fyodor whispered amid that solemn, funereal silence. 'A venerable old man, a true *pater familias*.'

In the large hall, near a table prepared for divine service, stood Fyodor Laptev senior, a priest with his high hat, and a deacon, all evidently expecting them. The old man offered Julia his hand without a word. Everyone was quiet. Julia felt awkward.

The priest and deacon began robing themselves. A censer, scattering sparks and smelling of incense and charcoal, was brought in. Candles were lit. Clerks entered the hall on tiptoe and stood by the wall, in two rows. It was quiet – no one even coughed.

'Bless us, oh Lord,' the deacon began.

The service was performed solemnly, with nothing omitted, and two special prayers, 'Sweetest Jesus' and 'Holy Mother', were chanted. Laptev noticed how embarrassed his wife had just been. While the prayers were being chanted and the choristers sang a triple 'God have mercy', in varying harmonies, he felt dreadfully tense, expecting the old man to look round any minute and rebuke him with something like 'You don't know how to make the sign of the cross properly.' And he felt annoyed: what was the point of all that crowd, ceremony, priests, choir? It reeked too much of the old merchant style. But when Julia joined the old man in allowing the Gospel to be held over her head and then genuflected several times, he understood that it was all to her liking and he felt relieved. At the end of the service, during the prayers for long life, the priest gave the old man and Alexei the cross to kiss, but when Julia came up to him he covered it with one hand and apparently wanted to say a few words to her. They waved to the choristers to keep quiet.

'The Prophet Samuel came to Bethlehem at the Lord's command,' the priest began, 'and the elders of that town besought him, trembling: "Comest thou peaceably, O prophet?" And the Prophet said, "Peaceably. I am come to make sacrifice unto the

Lord! Sanctify yourselves and rejoice this day with me." Shall we question thee, Julia, servant of the Lord, if thou comest peaceably to this house?'

Julia was deeply moved and she blushed. After he had finished, the priest handed her the cross to kiss and then continued in a completely different tone of voice, 'The young Mr Laptev should get married, it's high time.'

The choir began to sing again, the congregation moved about and it became noisy. The old man was deeply touched and his eyes were full of tears as he kissed Julia three times and made the sign of the cross before her face. 'This is your house,' he said. 'I'm an old man, I don't need anything.'

The clerks offered their congratulations and added a few words, but the choir sang so loud it was impossible to hear anything. Then they had lunch and drank champagne. Julia sat next to the old man, who told her that living apart was not good, that one should live together, in the same house, and that divisions and disagreements led to ruin.

'I made my fortune, all my children can do is spend it,' he said. 'Now you must live in the same house as me and make money. I'm an old man, time I had a rest.'

Julia kept glimpsing Fyodor, who was very much like her husband, but more fidgety and more reserved. He fussed around nearby, repeatedly kissing her hand.

'My dear sister-in-law!' he exclaimed, 'we're just ordinary people,' and as he spoke red blotches broke out all over his face. 'We lead simple Russian, Christian lives, dear sister.'

On the way home Laptev felt very pleased everything had gone so well and that, contrary to what he had been expecting, nothing disastrous had happened.

'You seem surprised,' he told his wife, 'that such a strong, broad-shouldered father should have such undersized, weak-chested children like myself and Fyodor. That's easy to explain! Father married Mother when he was forty-five and she was only seventeen. She used to turn pale and tremble in his presence. Nina was first to be born and Mother was comparatively healthy at the time, so she turned out stronger, better than us. But Fyodor and myself were conceived and born when Mother was worn-out from being in a perpetual state of terror. I remember Father started giving me lessons – putting it bluntly, he started beating me – before I was five even. He birched me, boxed my ears, hit me on the head. The first thing I did when I woke up every morning was wonder whether I'd be beaten that day. Fyodor and I were forbidden to play games or have any fun. We had to go to matins and early service, kiss the priests' and monks' hands, read special prayers at home. Now, you're religious and you like that kind of thing, but I'm scared of religion and when I pass a church I remember my childhood and I'm frightened. When I was eight they made me start work at the warehouse. I was just a simple factory hand and this was rotten, as I was beaten almost every day. Then, after I'd started high school, I'd sit and do my home-work before dinner and from then until very late I'd have to stay in that same warehouse. This went on until I was twenty-two and met Yartsev at university. He persuaded me to leave my father's house. This Yartsev has done me a lot of good. Do you know what?' Laptev said, cheerfully laughing. 'Let's go and see Yartsev right now. He's a terribly decent person, he'll be so touched!'

VII

One Saturday in November, Anton Rubinstein was conducting at the Conservatoire. The concert hall was extremely crowded and hot. Laptev stood behind some pillars, while his wife and Kostya Kochevoy sat far off, in the front, in the third or fourth row. Right at the beginning of the interval the 'personage', Polina Rassudin, came by, quite out of the blue. Since the wedding he had often worried at the thought of meeting her. As she looked at him, openly and frankly, he remembered that he had so far made no attempt to patch things up or write a couple of friendly lines – it was just as if he were hiding from her. He felt ashamed and he blushed. She shook his hand firmly and impulsively, and asked, 'Have you seen Yartsev?'

Without waiting for a reply she moved swiftly on, with long strides, as if someone were pushing her from behind.

She was extremely thin and ugly, with a long nose, and she looked constantly tired and worn-out: apparently she was always having great difficulty in keeping her eyes open and not falling over. She had beautiful, dark eyes and a clever, kind, sincere expression, but her movements were jerky and brusque. She wasn't easy to talk to since she was incapable of listening or speaking calmly. Loving her had been a difficult proposition. When she stayed with Laptev she used to have long, loud fits of laughter, covering her face with her hands and maintaining that her life didn't revolve around love. She was as coy as a seventeen-year-old and all the candles had to be extinguished before someone kissed her. She was thirty and had married a teacher, but had long lived apart from her husband. She earned her living from music lessons and playing in quartets.

During the Ninth Symphony she once again went past, as if by accident, but a large group of men standing behind some pillars barred her way and she stopped. Laptev noticed that she was wearing the same velvet blouse she had worn for last year's concerts, and the year before that. Her gloves were new – and so was her fan, but cheap. She wanted to be smartly dressed, but she had no flair for it and grudged spending money. As a result, she was so badly and scruffily turned out that she could easily be mistaken for a young monk as she strode hurriedly down the street on her way to a lesson.

The audience applauded and demanded an encore.

'You're spending this evening with me,' Polina said, going up to Laptev and eyeing him severely. 'We'll go and have tea together when the concert's finished. Do you hear? I insist on it. You owe me a lot and you have no moral right to refuse me this little trifle.'

'All right, let's go then,' Laptev agreed.

After the symphony there were endless encores. The audience rose and left extremely slowly. But Laptev couldn't leave without telling his wife, so he had to stand at the door and wait.

'I'm just dying for a cup of tea,' Polina Rassudin complained. 'I'm simply burning inside.'

'We can get some tea here,' Laptev said. 'Let's go to the bar.'

'No, I don't have the money to throw away on barmen. *I'm* not a businessman's wife!'

He offered her his arm, but she refused, producing that long, tedious sentence he had heard from her so often before, to the effect that she didn't consider herself one of the weaker or fair sex and could dispense with the services of gentlemen.

As she talked to him she kept looking at the audience and greeting friends – fellow-students from Guerrier's courses and the Conservatoire, and her male and female pupils too. She shook their hands firmly, impulsively, with a jerky movement. But then she started twitching her shoulders and trembling as if she were feverish. Finally she looked at Laptev in horror and said softly, 'Who's *this* you've married? Where were your eyes, you madman? What did you see in that stupid, insignificant little cow? Didn't I love you for your mind, for what's deep down inside you? All that china doll wants is your money!'

'That's enough, Polina,' he pleaded. 'Everything you might say about my marriage I've already told myself dozens of times. Don't cause me any unnecessary pain.'

Julia appeared in a black dress with a large diamond brooch that her father-in-law had sent her after the prayer service. She was followed by her retinue: Kochevoy, two doctor friends, an officer and a stout young man in student uniform by the name of Kish.

'You go with Kostya,' Laptev told his wife. 'I'll join you later.'

Julia nodded and moved on. Trembling all over and twitching nervously, Polina followed her with a look of revulsion, hatred and anguish.

Laptev was scared of going to her room as he anticipated some nasty show-down, harsh words and tears, so he suggested having tea in a restaurant. But she said, 'No, no, come to my place. Don't you dare mention restaurants to me!'

She didn't like restaurants, because the air in them seemed poisoned by tobacco and men's breath. She was peculiarly pre-judiced towards strange men, considering them all libertines, capable of pouncing on her at any moment. Besides, the music in restaurants irritated her and gave her headaches.

After leaving the Gentry Club they took a cab to Savelovsky Street, off Ostozhenka Street, where Polina lived. Laptev thought about her the whole way. In actual fact, he did owe her a great deal. He had met her at his friend Yartsev's, whom she was teaching theory. She had fallen deeply in love with him, without ulterior motives, and after becoming his mistress she continued giving lessons and working until she dropped. Thanks to her he began to understand and love music, to which he had been almost completely indifferent.

'Half my kingdom for a glass of tea!' she said in a hollowish voice, covering her mouth with her muff to avoid catching cold. 'I've given five lessons today, damn it. My pupils are such clots and blockheads I nearly died of anger. I just don't know when this hard labour will end. I'm absolutely flaked. The moment I've saved three hundred roubles I shall give everything up and go to the Crimea. I shall lie on the beach and gulp oxygen. How I love the sea, how I love it!'

'You won't go anywhere,' Laptev said. 'Firstly, you won't save a thing and secondly, you're mean. Forgive me, but I must say it again: your amassing three hundred roubles, a few copecks at a time, from those idlers who only take lessons from you because they have nothing to do – is that any less degrading than borrowing it from your friends?'

'I have no friends,' she said, irritably. 'And I would ask you not to talk such rubbish. The working class, to which I belong, has one privilege – consciousness of its own incorruptibility, plus the right to despise shopkeepers and not be beholden to them. No, you can't buy *me*, I'm not a Julia!'

Laptev didn't pay the cab-driver, knowing that this would provoke that all too familiar torrent of words. She paid herself.

She was renting a small furnished room with board, in a flat that belonged to a single lady. Her Becker grand piano was kept at Yartsev's place in Great Nikitsky Street for the time being and she went there every day to play. In her room were armchairs with covers, a bed with a white summer quilt, and flowers put there by the landlady. On the walls were oleographs, and there was nothing to suggest that a university woman was living in that room. There was no dressing-table, no books, not even a desk. It was obvious that she went to bed immediately she came home and left the house the moment she got up in the morning.

The cook brought in the samovar and Polina made tea. Still trembling – it was cold in her room – she started criticizing the choir which had sung in the Ninth Symphony. Her eyes closed from weariness and she drank one glass of tea, then another, then a third.

'So, you're married,' she said. 'Don't worry, though, I shan't start moping. I'll manage to tear you out of my heart. But I'm annoyed. It hurts me to discover you're a lousy rotter like everyone else, that it's not a woman's mind and intellect you need, but her body, her beauty, her youth ... Youth, youth!' she said through her nose as if mimicking someone, and she laughed. 'You need purity, *Reinheit*!' she added amid loud peals of laughter, leaning back in her chair. '*Reinheit*!'

When she had finished laughing her eyes were full of tears. 'Are you happy at least?' she asked.

'No.'

'Does she love you?'

'No.'

Upset and miserable, Laptev got up and paced the room. 'No,' he repeated. 'If you really want to know, Polina, I'm very unhappy. But what can I do? That was a silly thing I did and I can't repair the damage now. I must be philosophical about it. She didn't marry for love. It was stupid of her, perhaps. She married me for my money, but without thinking. Now she clearly realizes how wrong she was and she's suffering for it. That's painfully obvious. At night we sleep together, but during the day she's scared of staying alone with me for five minutes. She's looking for entertainment, some social life. She's ashamed and scared when she's with me.'

'But she takes your money all the same, doesn't she?'

'Don't be silly, Polina,' Laptev shouted. 'She takes money because she couldn't care less whether she has any or not. She's an honest, high-principled person. She married me simply to get away from her father, that's all.'

'But are you sure that she would have married you if you hadn't been rich?' Polina asked.

'I'm not sure about anything,' Laptev replied wearily. 'I don't understand a thing. For God's sake, Polina, let's not talk about it.'

'Do you love her?'

'Madly.'

Silence followed. She drank a fourth glass, while he kept pacing the room, thinking that his wife was probably, at that moment, having supper at the Doctors' Club.

'But is it possible to love not knowing why?' Polina asked, shrugging her shoulders. 'No, it's the animal passion in you. You're intoxicated, you're poisoned by that beautiful body, by that *Reinheit*! Leave me, you're filthy! Go to her!'

She waved him away, picked up his hat and threw it at him. Silently, he put on his fur coat and left, but she ran into the hall, feverishly grabbed hold of the upper part of his arm and burst into sobs.

'Stop it, Polina, that's enough!' he said, unable to unclench her fingers. 'Please calm down!'

She closed her eyes and turned pale; her long nose took on the nasty waxen colour of a corpse. And still Laptev couldn't unclench her fingers. She had fainted. Carefully, he lifted her, laid her on the bed and sat by her side for about ten minutes until she came round. Her hands were cold, her pulse weak and irregular.

'Go home,' she said, opening her eyes. 'Go home, or I'll start howling again. I must take a grip on myself.'

After leaving her he did not go to the Doctors' Club, where they were expecting him, but straight home. All the way he kept reproaching himself with the question: why had he settled down with another woman instead of this one, who loved him so much, who was his real wife and true friend? She was the only person at all attached to him. And besides, wouldn't it have been a rewarding, worthy undertaking to bring happiness and quiet sanctuary to this clever, proud, overworked woman? That longing for beauty, youth and impossible happiness which seemed to be punishing or mocking him by keeping him in a dreadful state of depression for three months – was that in character? The honeymoon was long over and he still didn't know what kind of person his wife really was, which was quite ludicrous. She penned long letters, on five sheets of paper, to her old boarding-school friends and her father, so there was plenty to write about, in fact. But all she could find to talk to him about was the weather, that it was time for lunch or supper. When she took a long time over her prayers before going to bed and then kissed her nasty little crosses and icons, he would look at her with loathing and think: 'There she is praying, but what, what is she praying about?' He was insulting the two of them by telling himself – when he went to bed with her and took her in his arms – that he was only getting what he was paying for. That was a shocking thought. If she'd been a healthy, uninhibited, loose woman it wouldn't have mattered. But here was youth, religious devotion, gentleness, those pure, innocent eyes. When they had become engaged he had been touched by her religious faith, but now the conventional, definitive nature of her views and convictions was a barrier between him and the truth. His whole domestic life was sheer hell now. When his wife sighed or laughed heartily as she sat by him in the theatre, he was embittered by her enjoying herself on her own, by her reluctance to share her pleasure with him. Remarkably, she had got on well with all his friends. All of them knew the kind of person she was, whereas he did not. All he could do was mope and feel jealous without saying anything about it.

When he arrived home Laptev put on his dressing-gown and slippers and sat down in his study to read a novel. His wife was out, but barely half an hour passed before he heard the bell ring in the hall, and then the hollow patter of Peter's footsteps as he ran to open the door. It was Julia. She entered the study in her fur coat and her cheeks were red from the frost.

'There's a big fire at Presnya,' she said, gasping for breath. 'The glow is really enormous. I'm going there with Kostya Kochevoy.'

'Good luck, then.'

Her fresh, healthy look and the childlike fear in her eyes calmed Laptev. He read for another half hour and then went to bed.

Next day Polina sent two books she had once borrowed from him to the warehouse, and all his letters and photographs, together with a note consisting of one word: *basta*.

VIII

At the end of October, Nina had a pronounced relapse. She was rapidly losing weight and her face was changing. Despite the severe pain she imagined that she was recovering and every morning she dressed herself as if she was well and then lay in bed the whole day in her clothes. Towards the end she had become very talkative. She would lie on her back and after a great effort managed to talk quietly, gasping the whole time.

She died suddenly, in the following circumstances.

It was a bright, moonlit night. Out in the street people were riding in sleighs over the fresh snow, and the noises from outside drifted into the room. Nina was lying in bed, on her back, while Sasha, who had no one to take her place, was sitting nearby dozing.

'I can't remember his second name,' Nina said softly, 'but his Christian name was Ivan and his surname Kochevoy. He was a poor clerk, a terrible drunkard, God rest his soul. He used to call on us and every month we'd give him a pound of sugar and a few ounces of tea. Of course, we gave him money too. Yes . . . Well now, this is what happened after that. Kochevoy hit the bottle really hard and he popped off – it was vodka that finished him. He left a son, a little seven-year-old. That poor little orphan! We took him in and hid him in the clerks' place and he managed to get by a whole year without Father finding out. But the moment Father saw him he dismissed him with a wave of the arm and said nothing. When this poor little orphan was eight – I was engaged then – I tried to get him into high school. I took him here, there and everywhere, but they just wouldn't accept him. He wouldn't stop crying. "You silly little boy, why are you crying?" I asked. I took him to the Second High School on Razgulyay Square and there, God bless them, they accepted him. Every day the little lad would walk from Pyatnitsky Street to Razgulyay Square and back. Alexei paid his fees. Thank God, the boy was good at his work, very quick to learn, so everything turned out all right in the end. Now he's a lawyer in Moscow and a friend of Alexei's. They're both of them very bright. We didn't turn our noses up at him, we took him in, and now he's surely mentioning us in his prayers. Oh, yes . . .'

Nina began to speak more and more softly, with long pauses. Then, after one brief silence, she suddenly lifted herself up in bed. 'Mm . . . I don't feel so good,' she said. 'Oh God, I just can't breathe!'

Sasha knew that her mother was soon going to die. When she

saw how her face had sunk she guessed that this was the end and she panicked.

'Mama, please don't!' she sobbed. 'Please don't!'

'Run into the kitchen and tell them to send for your father. I feel really shocking.'

Sasha tore through every room in the house calling out, but not one of the servants was in. Only Lida was there, and she was sleeping in her clothes, without any pillow, on a chest in the dining-room. Just as she was, without galoshes, Sasha ran into the yard, then out into the street. Her nanny was sitting on a bench outside the gate watching the sleighs drive past. From the river, where there was a skating-rink, came the sound of a military band.

'Nanny, Mama's dying!' sobbed Sasha. 'We must fetch Father.' Nanny went upstairs to the bedroom, took one look at the sick woman and thrust a lighted wax candle into her hand. Sasha was horrified and rushed around begging someone – anyone – to go and fetch Father. Then she put on her coat and scarf and ran into the street. The servants had told her that her father had another wife and two little children with whom he was living in Market Street. At the gate she ran to the left, weeping and terrified of the strange people. Soon she was sinking into the snow and shivering with cold.

An empty cab came along but she didn't take it. Perhaps the driver would take her right out of town, rob her and throw her into the cemetery – the servants had spoken of such things over tea. She walked on and on, exhausted, gasping for breath and sobbing. When she came out on to Market Street she asked where Mr Panaurov lived. Some woman she didn't know gave her lengthy directions, but seeing that she didn't understand a thing took her by the hand and led her to a one-storeyed house with a porch. The door wasn't locked. Sasha ran through the hall, across a corridor, until finally she found herself in a bright warm room where her father was sitting by a samovar with a lady and two little girls. But by now she was unable to produce one word and all she did was sob. Panaurov understood.

'Mother's ill, isn't she?' he asked. 'Tell me, Mother's not well then?'

He grew alarmed and sent for a cab.

When they reached the house Nina was sitting surrounded by pillows, candle in hand. Her face had grown dark, her eyes were closed. Nanny, cook, the chambermaid, the peasant Prokofy and some other ordinary working folk she didn't know crowded at the door. Nanny was whispering some orders which no one understood. Looking pale and sleepy, Lida was standing at the other end of the room by the window, grimly eyeing her mother.

Panaurov took the candle from Nina's hands, frowned disgustedly and flung it behind the chest-of-drawers.

'This is dreadful!' he said, his shoulders trembling. 'Nina, you must lie down,' he said tenderly. 'Please lie down, dear.'

She looked at him without recognizing him. They laid her back on the bed. When the priest and Dr Belavin arrived, the servants were devoutly crossing themselves and saying prayers for the dead.

'A fine thing!' the doctor remarked thoughtfully as he came out into the drawing-room. 'She was so young, not yet forty.'

The loud sobbing of the little girls was heard. Pale-faced, with moist eyes, Panaurov went up to the doctor and said in a weak, lifeless voice, 'My dear man, please do me a favour and send a telegram to Moscow. I'm just not up to it at the moment.'

The doctor obtained some ink and wrote the following telegram to his daughter: NINA PANAUROV DIED 8 PM TELL HUSBAND HOUSE ON DVORYANSKY STREET FOR SALE WITH TRANSFERABLE MORTGAGE STOP BALANCE NINE THOUSAND TO PAY AUCTION ON TWELFTH ADVISE NOT TO MISS OPPORTUNITY.

IX

Laptev lived on one of the side-streets off Little Dmitrovka Street, not far from Old St Pimen's Church. Besides that large house facing the street, he rented a two-storeyed lodge in the courtyard for his friend Kochevoy, a junior barrister called simply Kostya by the Laptevs, as they had all seen him grow up. Opposite the lodge was another, also with two storeys, where a French family lived – husband, wife and five daughters.

It was twenty degrees below freezing and the windows were frosted over. When he woke up in the mornings, Kostya would drink fifteen drops of medicine with an anxious look, then he would take two dumb-bells from a book-case and do his exercises. He was tall and very thin, with a large reddish moustache, but the most striking thing about him was the exceptional length of his legs.

Peter, a middle-aged handyman, in a jacket and with cotton trousers tucked into his high boots, brought in the samovar and made the tea.

'Very fine weather it is we're 'aving, Mr Kochevoy,' he said.

'Yes, very fine it is, only it's a pity you and I aren't coping too well, old chap.'

Peter sighed out of politeness.

'What are the girls doing?' Kochevoy asked.

'The priest 'asn't come. Mr Laptev's teaching them 'imself.'

Kostya found a part of the window free of ice and looked through his binoculars, directing them at the French family's windows.

'Can't see them,' he said.

Just then Laptev was giving Sasha and Lida a scripture lesson downstairs. They had been living in Moscow for about six weeks with their governess, on the ground floor of the lodge, and three times a week a priest and a teacher from a municipal school came to give them lessons. Sasha was studying the New Testament, while Lida had recently started the Old. At the last lesson Lida had been asked to revise everything up to Abraham.

'So, Adam and Eve had two sons,' Laptev said. 'Good, but what were their names? Please try and remember.'

Grim-faced as ever, Lida gazed silently at the table and just moved her lips. But her elder sister Sasha peered into her face and suffered torments.

'You know it very well, only you mustn't be so nervous,' Laptev said. 'Well now, what were Adam's sons called?'

'Abel and Cabel,' Lida whispered.

'Cain and Abel,' Laptev corrected.

A large tear trickled down Lida's cheek and dropped on to the book. Sasha looked down and blushed, on the verge of tears too. Laptev didn't have the heart to say anything and he gulped back the tears. He got up from the table and lit a cigarette. Just then

Kochevoy came down with a newspaper. The little girls stood up and curtsied without looking at him.

'For heaven's sake, Kostya, *you* try and teach them,' Laptev said. 'I'm afraid I'll burst out crying as well and I must call at the warehouse before lunch.'

'All right.'

Laptev left. Frowning, with a very serious expression, Kostya sat at the table and drew the Bible over to him. 'Well,' he asked, 'what are you doing now?'

'She knows all about the Flood,' Sasha said.

'The Flood? Good, we'll give that a good bash then. Let's do the Flood.'

Kostya ran through the brief account of the Flood in the Bible and said, 'I must point out that no flood like this ever took place. And there wasn't any Noah. Several thousand years before Christ was born there was an extraordinary inundation of the earth which is mentioned not only in the Hebrew Bible, but also in the books of other ancient peoples such as the Greeks, Chaldees and Hindus. No matter what kind of inundation this may have been, it couldn't have flooded the whole earth. Okay, the plains were flooded, but the mountains remained, you can be sure of that. Carry on reading your little book if you like, but don't put too much faith in it.'

Lida's tears flowed again. She turned away and suddenly started sobbing so loudly that Kostya shuddered and rose from his chair in great confusion.

'I want to go home,' she said. 'To Daddy and Nanny.'

Sasha cried too. Kostya went up to his room and telephoned Julia. 'The girls are crying again, my dear. It's quite impossible!'

Julia came running across from the main house, just in her dress and with a knitted scarf. Half-frozen, she comforted the girls.

'Believe me, you must believe me,' she pleaded, pressing first one, then the other to her. 'Your Daddy *is* coming today, he's sent a telegram. You're sad about your Mummy. So am I. My heart is breaking. But what can one do? You can't go against what God has willed!'

When they had stopped crying, she wrapped them up and took them for a cab-ride. First they drove down Little Dmitrovka Street, then past Strastnoy Boulevard to the Tver Road. They stopped at the Iversky Chapel and each of them placed a candle there and knelt in prayer. On the way back they called at Filippov's and bought some lenten poppy-seed rolls.

The Laptevs usually had lunch between two and three, with Peter serving at table. During the day this same Peter would run errands to the post office, then to the warehouse, or the local court for Kostya, and helped out with lots of jobs. In the evening he packed cigarettes, at night he would run back and forwards to open the door, and after four o'clock in the morning would see to the stoves: no one knew when he actually slept. He loved opening bottles of soda water, which he did easily, noiselessly, without spilling a drop.

'Cheers!' Kostya said, drinking a glass of vodka before his soup.

Julia had at first taken a dislike to Kostya, his deep voice, the crude expressions he would come out with, such as 'clear off', 'sock on the jaw', 'dregs of humanity, 'ginger up the samovar', as well as his habit of waxing sentimental after vodka. All of it seemed so trite. But after she knew him better she began to feel much more at ease with him. He was quite open with her, loved a quiet talk in the evenings, and even let her borrow novels that he had written himself and which up to now had been kept a complete secret – even from friends like Laptev and Yartsev. She would read and praise them in order not to upset him, which pleased him, since he had aspirations of becoming a famous writer – sooner or later. He wrote only about the countryside and manor houses, although he saw the country very seldom, when he was visiting friends in their holiday villas. Only once in his life had he stayed on a country estate, when he had gone to Volokolamsk on some legal business. Avoiding any love interest, as if ashamed of it, he filled his novels with nature descriptions and showed a great partiality for expressions such as 'the hills' intricate outlines', 'quaint shapes of clouds' and 'chord of mysterious harmonies'. No one published his novels, for which he blamed the censorship.

He liked being a barrister, but he considered novels, not legal work, his true vocation in life. He felt that he possessed a subtle, artistic make-up and constantly felt drawn to the fine arts. He didn't sing, nor did he play an instrument, and he had no ear at all for music. However, he went to all the symphonic and philharmonic concerts, organized charity performances and kept company with singers.

During lunch they talked. 'It's really amazing,' Laptev said. 'My brother Fyodor's completely stumped me again! He says we must find out when our firm's going to celebrate its centenary, so that we can apply to become gentlefolk. He's really serious! What's happening to him? To be honest, it worries me.'

They discussed Fyodor and the current fashion for self-dramatization. Fyodor, for example, was trying to act the simple merchant, although he wasn't one any more, and when the teacher came from the school (where old Mr Laptev was a governor) for his salary, he would even alter his walk and speech, behaving as if he were the teacher's superior officer.

After lunch there was nothing to do, so they went into the study. They discussed the Decadent Movement and the *Maid of Orleans*. Kostya delivered a whole monologue and felt that he gave a very good imitation of Marya Yermolov.* Then they sat down to cards. The little girls didn't return to the lodge. Instead, they sat there, pale-faced and sad, in the same armchair, listening to the street noises and trying to hear if their father was coming. They felt miserable in the dark evenings, when candles were alight. The conversation over cards, Peter's footsteps, the crackle in the fireplace – all this irritated them and they didn't want to look at the fire. In the evenings they didn't even feel like crying, and were uneasy and heavy at heart. They couldn't understand how people could talk and laugh when Mother had died.

'What did you see today through your binoculars?' Julia asked Kostya.

'Nothing. But yesterday the old Frenchman himself took a bath.'

At seven o'clock Julia and Kostya went off to the Maly Theatre. Laptev stayed behind with the girls.

'It's time your father was here,' he said, glancing at his watch. 'The train must be late.'

The girls sat silently in the chair, snuggling close to each other like tiny animals feeling the cold, while Laptev kept pacing the

* Marya Yermolov (1853–1928), a well-known actress of the time.

rooms, looking impatiently at his watch. The house was quiet, but just before nine someone rang the bell. Peter went to open the door.

When they heard that familiar voice the girls shrieked, burst out sobbing and ran into the hall. Panaurov was wearing a splendid fur coat and his beard and moustache were white with frost.

'Just a moment, just a moment,' he muttered while Sasha and Lida, sobbing and laughing, kissed his cold hands, his cap, his fur coat.

A handsome, languid sort of man who had been spoilt by love, he unhurriedly caressed the girls and went into the study. Rubbing his hands he said, 'It's only a brief visit, my dear friends. Tomorrow I'm off to St Petersburg. I've been promised a transfer to another city.'

He was staying at the Dresden Hotel.

X

Ivan Yartsev was a frequent visitor at the Laptevs'. He was a sturdy, strongly built, black-haired man with a clever, pleasant face. People thought him handsome, but recently he'd put on weight, which spoilt his face and figure, as did the way he had his hair cut very short, almost to the scalp. At one time his fellow-students at university called him 'Muscle Man', on account of his strength and powerful build.

He had graduated from the arts faculty together with the Laptev brothers and had then changed to science; he had a master's degree in chemistry. Without any aspirations to a professorship, he had never been a laboratory assistant even, but taught physics and zoology at a boy's secondary school and at two high schools for girls. Thrilled with his students – especially the girls – he used to say that a remarkable generation was growing up. Besides chemistry, he also studied sociology and Russian history at home and his short papers were sometimes published in newspapers and learned journals under the signature 'Ya'. Whenever he talked about botany or zoology, he resembled a historian; when he was trying to settle some historical problem, he looked like a scientist.

Kish, who was nicknamed the 'eternal student', was also a close friend of the Laptevs. He had studied medicine for three years, then had changed to mathematics, taking two years for each year of the course. His father, a provincial pharmacist, sent him forty roubles a month, and his mother (unbeknown to the father) sent him ten. This money sufficed for everyday expenses and was even enough for luxuries such as an overcoat with Polish beaver trimmings, gloves, scent and photography – he often had his portrait done and sent copies around to his friends. Neat, slightly balding, with golden whiskers around the ears, he was a modest man, who always seemed ready to oblige. He was forever helping others, running round collecting subscriptions, freezing at dawn outside a theatre box-office to buy a ticket for a lady friend. Or he would go and order a wreath or bouquet at someone's command. All one heard about him was: 'Kish will fetch it,' or 'Kish will do it,' or 'Kish will buy it.' He usually made a mess of the errands, for which he was showered with reproaches. People often forgot to pay him for purchases. But he never said a word, and in particularly ticklish situations all he would do was sigh. He was never very pleased, never annoyed and he was always telling long, boring stories: his jokes invariably made people laugh, but only because they weren't at all funny. Once, for example, trying to be witty, he told Peter, 'You are not a sturgeon.' Everyone burst out laughing and he himself couldn't stop laughing, so pleased he was with his highly successful joke. At professors' funerals he liked walking in front, with the torch-bearers.

Yartsev and Kish usually came over for tea in the afternoon. If the master and mistress weren't going out to the theatre or a concert the tea would drag on until supper-time. One evening in February the following conversation took place in the dining-room:

'Works of art are only significant and useful when they are concerned with some serious social problem,' Kostya said, angrily looking at Yartsev.

'If there's some protest against serfdom in a book, or if the author takes up arms against high society and all its vulgarity, then that work is significant and useful. But novels and short stories which contain nothing but moaning and groaning, about her falling in love with him, or him falling out of love with her – I maintain those types of work are worthless and to hell with them.'

'I agree with you, Mr Kochevoy,' Julia said. 'One writer will describe a lover's assignation, another a betrayal, another a meeting after separation. Surely there's other things to write about, isn't there? There's lots of sick, unhappy, wretchedly poor people who must feel revolted when they read all that stuff.'

Laptev didn't like it when his wife, a young woman, not yet twenty-two, argued so seriously, so coolly, about love. But he guessed the reason for it.

'If poetry doesn't solve problems that strike you as important,' Yartsev said, 'then you'd better turn to technical books, to criminal and financial law. You should read scientific papers. There's no point at all in *Romeo and Juliet* containing discussions about freedom of education or disinfecting prisons if you can find it all in specialized articles or reference books.'

'But that's going too far, old chap,' Kostya interrupted. 'We're not discussing giants like Shakespeare or Goethe, we're talking about a hundred or so talented or less talented writers who'd be a lot more use if they steered clear of love and concentrated on bringing knowledge and humane ideals to the masses.'

Talking slightly through his nose and burring his 'r's, Kish began to relate the plot of a story he had recently read. He gave a detailed account and took his time. Three minutes passed, then five, then ten, but he rambled on and on, and no one had the faintest idea what he was talking about. His face became more and more apathetic, his eyes grew dim.

Julia could stand it no longer and said, 'Come on, Kish, make it short! It's sheer torment!'

'Pack it in, Kish,' Kostya shouted.

Everyone laughed – including Kish.

In came Fyodor. He had red blotches on his face. Hurriedly, he greeted them all and led his brother into the study. Recently he had been avoiding large gatherings, preferring the company of just one person.

'Let those young people laugh, you and I must have a heart-to-heart,' he said, settling into a deep armchair away from the lamp. 'When were you last in the warehouse? I should think it must be a week now.'

'Yes, there's nothing for me to do and I must confess I'm sick and tired of the old man.'

'Of course, they can cope without you and me in the warehouse, but you must have some sort of occupation. "In the sweat of thy brow shalt thou eat bread" as it is said. God likes hardworking people.'

Peter brought in a glass of tea on a tray. Fyodor drank it without sugar and asked for some more. He liked to drink a lot of tea and could polish off ten glasses in an evening.

'Do you know what, old man?' he said, getting up and going over to his brother. 'Why don't you just stand as candidate for the City Council? We'll gradually get you on to the Board and after that you'll be Deputy Mayor. The further you go, the bigger you'll be. You're an intelligent, educated man. They'll take notice of you, they'll invite you to St Petersburg. Local and municipal officials are in fashion there now. Before you know it you'll be a Privy Councillor with a ribbon over your shoulder – before you're fifty.'

Laptev didn't reply. He realized that Fyodor himself had set his heart on promotion to Privy Councillor, on wearing a ribbon, and he was at a loss for an answer.

The brothers sat in silence. Fyodor opened his watch and scrutinized it for an interminably long time, as if he wanted to check that the hands were moving correctly. His expression struck Laptev as peculiar.

They were called in to supper. Laptev entered the dining-room, while Fyodor remained in the study. The argument had finished and Yartsev was speaking like a professor delivering a lecture.

'Because of differences of climate, energy, tastes and age, equality among people is a physical impossibility. But civilized man can render this inequality harmless, just as he has done with swamps and bears. One scientist has succeeded in getting a cat, a mouse, a falcon and a sparrow to eat from the same bowl. So we can only hope that education can achieve the same with human beings. Life is forever marching on, we are witnesses to the great progress that culture is making, and obviously the time will come when the present condition of factory workers, for example, will strike us as just as absurd as serfdom – when girls were exchanged for dogs – does now.'

'That won't be soon, all that's a long way off,' Kostya laughed. 'It'll be a long time before Rothschild will think that his vaults with all their gold are absurd and until then the worker will have to bend his back and starve till his belly swells. No, old man, we mustn't stand doing nothing, we must fight. If a cat eats from the same saucer as a mouse would you say it does it from a sense of community? Never. Because it was *forced* to.'

'Fyodor and I are rich, our father's a capitalist, a millionaire, so it's *us* you have to fight!' Laptev said, wiping his forehead with his palm. 'A battle against myself – that's what I find so hard to accept! I'm rich, but what has money given me up to now? What has this power brought me? In what way am I happier than you? My childhood was sheer purgatory and money never saved me from birching. Money didn't help Nina when she fell ill and was dying. If I'm not loved I can't force anyone to love me, even if I were to spend a hundred million.'

'On the other hand you can do a lot of good,' Kish said.

'What do you mean by *good*? Yesterday you asked me to help some musician looking for work. Believe me, I can do as little for him as you can. I can give him money, but that's not what he's after, is it? Once I asked a well-known musician to find a position for an impecunious violinist and all he said was, "You only turned to *me* for help because you're not a musician yourself." So I'm offering you the same answer: you feel so confident when you ask me for help precisely because you've never known what it's like to be rich yourself.'

'But why this comparison with a famous musician?' Julia said, blushing. 'What's a famous musician got to do with it?'

Her face quivered with rage and she lowered her eyes to hide her feelings. However, her expression was understood not only by her husband, but by everyone sitting at the table.

'What's a famous musician got to do with it?' she repeated softly. 'There's nothing easier than helping the poor.'

Silence followed. Peter served hazel-grouse. No one ate any, however – they just had some salad. Now Laptev couldn't remember what he'd said, but he saw quite clearly that it wasn't his words that made her hate him, but the mere fact that he had joined in the conversation.

After supper he went to his study. His heart pounded as he listened – very tensely – to what was happening in the drawing-room, and he anticipated fresh humiliations. Another argument started. Then Yartsev sat at the piano and sang a sentimental song. He was Jack-of-all-trades – he could sing, play and even do conjuring tricks.

'Please yourself what you do, gentlemen, but I don't want to stay at home,' Julia said. 'Let's go for a drive.'

They decided to drive out of town and sent Kish to the Merchants' Club for a troika. Laptev wasn't invited, as he hardly ever went on such trips and because he had his brother with him. But he took it that they found him boring and that he was completely out of place among that cheerful, young crowd. He was so annoyed and bitter he almost wept. He even felt pleased that they were being so nasty to him, that he was despised, that he was looked upon as a stupid, boring husband, as an old moneybags. He would have been even more pleased, he felt, if his wife were to betray him that night with his best friend and admit it with loathing in her eyes . . . He was jealous of the students, actors and singers she knew, of Yartsev – even of chance acquaintances – and he dearly longed for her to be unfaithful now. He wanted to surprise her with someone, then poison himself to rid himself of the nightmare for good.

Fyodor gulped his tea noisily and then he too started leaving.

'There's something wrong with the old man,' he said, putting on his fur coat. 'His eyesight's very poor.'

Laptev put on his coat too and left. After seeing his brother as far as Strastnoy Boulevard he took a cab to Yar's restaurant.

'And they call this domestic bliss!' he said, laughing at himself. 'This is supposed to be love.'

His teeth were chattering – whether from jealousy or something else he didn't know. At Yar's he walked up and down by the tables and listened to a ballad singer in the ballroom. He didn't have one sentence ready in case he should meet his wife or friends and was convinced in advance that if she did happen to turn up he would only smile pathetically and stupidly – then everyone would understand what kind of feeling had compelled him to come here. The electric lights, the loud music, the smell of powder, those staring women – all this made his head go round. He stopped by the doors, trying to spy and overhear what was going on in the private rooms; he felt that he was acting in concert with that singer and those women, playing some vile, despicable role. Then he went on to the Strelna, but met none of his friends there either. Only when he was on his way home and approaching Yar's restaurant again did a troika noisily overtake him – the drunken coachman was shouting and he could hear Yartsev's loud guffaws.

Laptev returned home after three in the morning. Julia was in bed, but when he saw that she wasn't sleeping he went over and snapped,

'I can understand your revulsion, your hatred. But you might have spared me before strangers, you might have tried to hide your feelings.'

She sat up in bed, her legs dangling. In the lamplight her eyes were large and black.

'Please forgive me,' she said.

He couldn't say one word for agitation and trembling, and he stood silently in front of her. She too was trembling and she sat there like a criminal waiting to be charged.

'This is sheer torture!' he said at last, clutching his head. 'I seem to be in hell. I feel I've gone mad!'

'And do you think it's easy for *me*?' she asked, her voice shaking. 'God only knows how *I* feel.'

'You've been my wife for six months, but there's no spark of love in your heart, no hope of any – not even a glimmer! Why did you marry me?' Laptev continued despairingly. 'Why? What demon drove you into my arms? What were you hoping for? What did you want?'

She looked at him in horror, as if frightened he might kill her.

'Did you ever like me? Did you ever love me?' he gasped. 'No! Then what was it? Tell me, *what*?' he shouted. 'Yes, it was that damned money!'

'I swear to God it wasn't!' she cried and crossed herself. The insult made her wince and for the first time he heard her cry. 'I swear to God it wasn't!' she repeated. 'I wasn't thinking about money, I don't need any. I simply thought that it would be nasty of me to refuse you. I was afraid of spoiling your life and mine. And now I'm suffering for my mistake, suffering unbearably!'

She sobbed bitterly. Not knowing what to say and realizing how painful everything was for her, he sank before her on the carpet.

'Please don't. Please don't!' he muttered. 'I insulted you because I love you madly.' Suddenly he kissed her foot and passionately embraced her. 'All I want is just one spark of love!' he said. 'Well, tell me lies! Don't say it was a mistake!'

But she went on crying and he felt that she was only putting up with his caresses because they were the unavoidable consequence of her mistake. Like a bird she drew in beneath her that foot he had kissed. He felt sorry for her.

She lay down and covered herself with the blanket. He undressed and lay down as well. In the morning they both felt awkward – neither knew what to talk about. He even had the impression that she was treading unsteadily with the foot he had kissed.

Before lunch Panaurov dropped in to say goodbye. Julia had an irresistible urge to go back home to her native town. It would be nice to leave, she thought, to have a rest from married life, from all this embarrassment, from the ever-present awareness of having behaved badly. Over lunch they decided that she should leave with Panaurov and stay with her father for two or three weeks, until she got bored.

XI

Panaurov and Julia travelled in a private railway compartment. He was wearing a rather odd lambskin cap.

'Yes, St Petersburg was a let-down,' he sighed, speaking slowly and deliberately. 'They promise you a lot, but nothing definite. Yes, my dear, I've been Justice of the Peace, a Permanent Secretary, President of the Court of Appeal and finally adviser to the

District Council. I think I've served the fatherland and have a right to some attention. But would you believe it, there's just no way I can get a transfer to another town.'

Panaurov closed his eyes and shook his head. 'They won't recognize me,' he continued and he seemed to be dozing off. 'Of course, I'm no administrative genius, but on the other hand I'm a respectable, honest man and even that's quite rare these days. I must admit I've deceived women just a little, but I've always been a perfect gentleman in my relations with the Russian government. But enough of that,' he added, opening his eyes. 'Let's talk about you. What made you suddenly want to go and visit your dear papa?'

'I'm not getting on very well with my husband,' Julia said, glancing at his cap.

'Yes, he's a queer fish. All the Laptevs are weird. Your husband's not so bad really, he'll pass. But that brother of his, Fyodor, is a real idiot.'

Panaurov sighed and asked seriously, 'And do you have a lover?'

Julia looked at him in astonishment and laughed. 'Good God, what a thing to ask!'

After ten, at some large station, they both got out and had supper. When the train moved off Panaurov took off his coat and cap and sat next to Julia.

'You're very nice, I must say,' he began. 'Pardon the pub simile, but you put me in mind of a freshly salted gherkin. It still has the smell of the hothouse, so to speak, but it's already a bit salty and smells of dill. You're gradually developing into a wonderful woman, so marvellous and refined. If this journey had taken place about five years ago,' he sighed, 'then I'd have considered it my pleasant duty to join the ranks of your admirers. But now, alas, I'm just an old pensioner.'

He gave her a smile that was at once sad and kind, and he put his arm around her waist.

'You're out of your mind!' she said, blushing. She was so frightened that her hands and feet went cold. 'Stop it, Grigory!'

'Why are you so scared, my dear?' he asked softly. 'What's so dreadful about it? You're just not used to this sort of thing.'

If a woman happened to protest, then for him that only meant that he had made a good impression and that she liked him. Holding Julia around the waist, he kissed her firmly on the cheek, then the lips, quite certain he was giving her great pleasure. Then Julia recovered from her fright and embarrassment and started laughing. He kissed her again and as he donned his comical cap he said, 'That's all an old campaigner can give you. There was a Turkish Pasha, a kind old man, who was once presented with – possibly as an inheritance – a whole harem. When his beautiful young wives paraded before him, he inspected them, saying as he kissed each one, "That's all I'm able to give you now." That's what I'm saying too.'

She thought all this stupid but unusual, and it cheered her up. Feeling rather playful, she stood on the seat humming, took a box of sweets from the luggage rack and shouted, 'Catch' as she threw him one.

He caught it. Laughing out loud, she threw him another, then a third, and he caught them all, popping them in his mouth and looking at her with imploring eyes.

She felt that there was much that was feminine and childlike about his face, features and expression. When she sat down, out of breath, and kept looking at him and laughing, he touched her cheek with two fingers and said in mock annoyance,

'You naughty little girl!'

'Take it,' she said, handing him the box. 'I don't like sweets.'

He ate the whole lot and then locked the empty box in his trunk – he loved boxes with pictures on them.

'Enough of this larking about,' he said. 'Time for bye-byes, for the old campaigner!'

He took his Bokhara dressing-gown and a cushion from a hold-all, lay down and covered himself with the dressing-gown.

'Goodnight, my sweet!' he said softly, sighing as if his whole body were aching.

The sound of his snoring soon followed. Without feeling in the least inhibited she lay down too and was soon fast asleep.

Next morning, as she was driving home from the station in her native town, the streets seemed deserted and empty, the snow grey and the houses small, with a squashed look about them. She met a funeral procession – the body was in an open coffin, with banners.

'They say a funeral brings good luck,' she thought.

The windows of the house where Nina had once lived had white posters stuck all over them.

Her heart sank as she drove into the yard and rang the door-bell. A strange, sleepy-looking maid in a warm quilted jacket opened the door. As she went upstairs Julia remembered that Laptev had declared his love there. But now the stairs were unwashed, with footmarks all over them. In the cold corridor on the first floor patients in fur coats were waiting. For some reason her heart pounded and she could barely walk for agitation.

The doctor – stouter than ever, red as a brick, his hair dishevelled – was drinking tea. He was delighted to see his daughter and even shed a few tears. She was his only joy, she thought. Deeply moved, she firmly embraced him and told him she would be staying for a long time, until Easter. After she had changed in her room she went into the dining-room to have tea with him. He kept pacing up and down, hands in pockets, humming away – this meant he was annoyed about something.

'You're having quite a gay time in Moscow,' he remarked. 'I'm so pleased for you, but an old man like me doesn't need anything. I'll soon peg out and free the lot of you. Aren't you amazed that I've such a tough skin, that I'm still in the land of the living! It's really amazing!'

He said that he was a robust old beast of burden, whom everyone liked to ride. He had been lumbered with Nina's treatment, with looking after her children and taking care of the funeral: that dandified Panaurov just didn't want to know and had even borrowed a hundred roubles from him which, up to now, he hadn't returned.

'Take me to Moscow and put me in a lunatic asylum,' the doctor said. 'You must think I'm mad, a simple child, believing as I do in truth and justice!'

Then he reproached her husband with lack of foresight – he had failed to buy houses that were being offered at very favourable prices. And now Julia realized that she was no longer the old man's only joy. While he was receiving patients or on his rounds she roamed through the house, not knowing what to do or think. She had become a stranger in her home town, in her own house. She felt no urge to go out into the street, to call on old friends, and when she remembered her former girl friends and her life as a young girl she did not feel sad, nor did she regret the past.

In the evening she put on a smart dress and went to late service. But there was no one of importance in the church and her magnificent fur coat and hat were wasted there. She thought that both she and the church had undergone a transformation. In the past she had been fond of hearing the canon read out at vespers, when the choirboys sang hymns such as 'I shall open my lips'. Once she had loved slowly moving with the congregation towards the priest who stood in the middle of the church and then feeling the holy oil on her forehead. But now she couldn't wait for the service to finish. As she left the church she felt frightened that beggars might approach her for money – rummaging through her pockets would have been a nuisance. In any case, she had no small change, only roubles.

She went early to bed but fell asleep very late, constantly dreaming of certain portraits and the funeral procession she had seen that morning. The open coffin with the corpse was borne into the yard, the bearers stopped at a door, rocked the coffin on some sheets for some time and then swung it against the door as hard as they could. Julia woke and jumped up in terror. Someone was in fact knocking on the downstairs door and the bell-wire was rustling along the wall, although she hadn't heard anyone ring.

The doctor coughed. After this she heard the maid going downstairs and coming back.

'Madam!' she exclaimed, knocking at the door.

'What is it?' Julia asked.

'It's a telegram!'

Julia went out with a candle. Behind the maid stood the doctor, his coat over his underclothes. He was also holding a candle.

'The bell's broken,' he yawned, half-asleep. 'It should have been repaired ages ago.'

Julia opened the telegram and read it.

WE DRINK YOUR HEALTH. YARTSEV, KOCHEVOY

'Oh, the idiots!' she said, laughing out loud.

She began to feel relaxed and cheerful.

Back in her room she quietly washed and dressed, and then spent a long time packing – right until dawn broke. At noon she set off for Moscow.

XII

During Easter week the Laptevs went to a painting exhibition at the School of Art. The whole household went – in Moscow style – and both little girls, the governess and Kostya were taken along.

Laptev knew the names of all the famous artists and never missed an exhibition. During the summers at his country villa he sometimes painted landscapes himself, believing that he had superb taste and that he would have made an excellent painter had he studied. When abroad he sometimes dropped into antique shops, inspected their contents and expressed his opinion with the air of an expert. He would buy some object and the dealer would charge him as much as he liked. Subsequently, the piece would be stuffed into a box and lie in the coach-house until it disappeared no one knew where. Or he would call at a print shop, spend a long time carefully inspecting the prints and bronzes, make various remarks and then suddenly buy some cheap frame or box of worthless paper. All the pictures at home were of ample dimensions, but poorly painted. Those that were any good were badly hung. More than once he had paid dearly for what afterwards turned out to be crude forgeries. Strangely enough, although a timid person on the whole, he was particularly bumptious and outspoken at exhibitions. Why?

Julia looked at the paintings in the same way as her husband, through parted fingers or opera glasses, and she was amazed that the people in them seemed so alive, the trees so real. But she didn't understand them and thought that many paintings at the exhibition were really identical and that the whole aim of art was making people and objects appear real when viewed through the fingers.

'This wood is a Shishkin,' her husband explained. 'He always paints the same old thing . . . Just look, you'll never find snow as violet as that. And that boy's left arm is shorter than his right.'

When everyone was exhausted and Laptev had gone to look for Kostya, so that they could all go home, Julia stopped by a small landscape and looked at it rather indifferently. In the foreground was a small stream with a wooden bridge across it and a path disappearing into dark grass on the far bank. There were fields and a strip of wood on the right with a bonfire near it – horses were probably being pastured for the night over there. In the distance the sunset glow was dying . . .

Julia imagined herself crossing the bridge, then walking further and further down the path. It was quiet all around, sleepy landrails cried and a distant fire flickered. Suddenly she had the feeling that many times, long ago, she had seen those clouds stretching across the red sky, that wood, those fields. She felt lonely and wanted to go on and on, down that path. And there, near the sunset glow, lay the reflection of something unearthly and eternal.

'How well painted!' she exclaimed, amazed that she suddenly understood the picture. 'Look, Alexei! See how calm it is!'

She tried to explain why she liked that landscape so much, but neither her husband nor Kostya understood. She continued looking at the painting, sadly smiling: she was upset at the others seeing nothing special in it. Then she went through the rooms again and looked at the paintings. She wanted to understand them. There no longer seemed to be so many identical pictures at the exhibition. When she was home she turned her attention (for the first time ever) to the large picture above the grand piano in the hall. It made her feel hostile.

'How can anybody want that sort of picture!' she said.

On top of that, the golden cornices, the Venetian mirrors with flowers, paintings like the one over the piano – all this, plus her husband's and Kostya's arguments about art, made her feel bored, irritable and sometimes even full of loathing.

Life ran its normal course, from day to day, and promised nothing special. The theatre season was over and warm days had arrived – the weather was always fine now. One morning the Laptevs went off to the local assizes to hear Kostya, who had been appointed by the court, defend someone. They had taken their time before leaving and arrived when the cross-examination of witnesses had already started. A soldier from the reserves was accused of burglary. Many of the witnesses were laundresses, who testified that the accused often visited their employer, the laundry proprietress. Late on the eve of the Exaltation of the Cross this soldier had come to ask for money to buy himself a drink for the 'morning-after', but no one gave him any. Then he had left, but returned an hour later with some beer and peppermint cakes for the girls. They drank and sang almost till dawn, but in the morning they noticed that the lock to the loft entrance had been broken and some linen was missing – three men's night-shirts, a skirt and two sheets. Kostya sarcastically asked each witness if she had drunk any of the beer that the accused had brought that night. He was obviously trying to make it look as if the laundresses had robbed their own laundry. He delivered his speech coolly, angrily eyeing the jury.

He explained burglary and petty larceny. He spoke in great detail and with conviction, displaying an outstanding talent for expatiating long and solemnly about what was common know-ledge to everyone. And it was difficult to make out what precisely he *was* getting at. The jurors were able to draw only the following conclusion from his lengthy speech: either there had been a burglary, but no petty larceny, since the money from the sale of the linen was spent by the laundresses on drink; or that there had been larceny, but no burglary. But Kostya was evidently on the right tack, since his speech deeply moved the jury and public and pleased everyone. Julia nodded to Kostya when an acquittal was brought and afterwards shook him firmly by the hand.

In May the Laptevs went to their villa at Sokolniki, as Julia was pregnant.

XIII

More than a year passed. At Sokolniki, not far from the main Yaroslavl railway line, Julia and Yartsev were sitting on the grass. Kochevoy was lying nearby, his hands under his head, gazing up at the sky. All three had had enough of walking and were waiting for the six o'clock suburban train so that they could go home for tea.

'Mothers always think their children are exceptional, Nature's arranged it that way,' Julia said. 'A mother will stand by the cot for hours on end looking rapturously at her baby's tiny ears, eyes and nose. If some stranger kisses her baby the poor woman thinks this gives him the utmost pleasure. And mothers can talk of nothing but babies. I know that mothers tend to have this weakness and I'm guarding against it myself. But my Olga really *is* exceptional, honestly! The way she looks at me when she's feeding, the way she laughs! She's only eight months old, but I swear to you I've never seen such clever eyes, even in a three-year-old.'

'Incidentally, whom do you love more?' asked Yartsev. 'Your husband or your baby?'

Julia shrugged her shoulders. 'I don't know,' she said. 'I never felt deep affection for my husband and Olga's really my first love. You know I didn't marry Alexei for love. I used to be stupid, I went through absolute hell and I couldn't stop thinking that I had ruined his life and mine. But I realize now that one doesn't need love, it's a lot of nonsense.'

'So, if it isn't love, then what kind of feeling attaches you to your husband? Why do you stay with him?'

'I don't know . . . Must be force of habit, I think. I respect him, I miss him when he's away for a long time, but that's not love. He's a clever, honest man and that's enough to make me happy. He's very kind and unpretentious . . .'

'Alexei's clever, Alexei's kind,' Kostya said, lazily raising his head. 'But you need to know him for ages before you ever find out that he's intelligent, kind and fascinating, my dear. And what's the use of his kindness or his brains? He'll stump up as much money as you want – he's capable of *that*. But when it comes to showing strength of character, seeing off some cheeky devil or smart aleck, then he fights shy and loses heart. Men like your dear Alexei may be fine people, but they're absolutely useless in battle. Yes, they're actually fit for absolutely nothing.'

At last the train came into sight. Bright pink steam poured

from its funnel and rose over the small patch of forest. Two windows in the last carriage suddenly flashed so brilliantly in the sun it hurt one's eyes.

'Teatime!' Julia said, standing up.

She had recently put on weight and now she walked rather lazily, like a middle-aged lady.

'All the same, it's not much of a life without love,' Yartsev said, following her. 'We're always talking and reading about love, but we don't put it into practice – and that's a bad thing, I must say.'

'That's not important, Ivan,' Julia said. 'You won't find happiness there.'

They drank tea in the little garden, where mignonette, stocks and tobacco plants were in flower and early gladioli were opening out. From the expression on Julia's face, Yartsev and Kochevoy could tell that this was a happy time of spiritual calm and equilibrium for her and that she needed nothing besides what she already possessed; they too began to feel relaxed, tranquil at heart. Whatever one might think, things were turning out very well – just right, in fact. The pines were beautiful, the smell of resin was more wonderful than ever, the cream was delicious. Sasha was a clever, fine girl.

After tea Yartsev sang some sentimental songs, accompanying himself on the piano, while Julia and Kochevoy listened in silence – only Julia got up now and then and quietly left the room to have a look at the baby, and at Lida, who had had a temperature for two days and wasn't eating.

'My dear, tender love,' Yartsev sang. Then he shook his head and said, 'By the life of me I can't understand what you have against love. If I weren't busy fifteen hours a day I'd fall in love myself – no question about it.'

Supper was laid on the terrace. It was warm and quiet, but Julia wrapped herself in her shawl and complained of the damp. When it was dark she grew rather restless, kept shivering and asked her guests to stay on. She regaled them with wine and after supper had them served with brandy to stop them leaving. She didn't want to be on her own with the children and servants.

'We lady villa-dwellers are organizing a show for the children,' she said. 'We already have everything – theatre, actors. All that's missing is a play. We've been sent a score of different ones, but none is any good.' Turning to Yartsev she said, 'Now, you love the theatre and you're a history expert. Why don't you write a historical play for us?'

'All right.'

The guests finished all the brandy and prepared to leave. It was past ten, which was late for people in holiday villas.

'It's so dark, it's pitch black,' Julia said, seeing them through the gate. 'I don't know how you'll find the way back, my friends. It's really *very* cold!'

She wrapped herself more tightly and went back to the porch.

'My Alexei must be playing cards somewhere!' she exclaimed. 'Goodnight!'

After the bright lights in the house they couldn't see a thing. Yartsev and Kostya groped along like blind men until they reached the railway line, which they crossed.

'Can't see a damned thing!' Kostya said in a deep voice, stopping to gaze at the sky. 'Look at those stars – like new fifteen-copeck pieces! Yartsev!!'

'What?' came back Yartsev's voice.

'I said I can't see a thing. Where are you?'

Whistling, Yartsev went up to him and took his arm.

'Hey, all you holiday-makers!' Kostya suddenly shouted at the top of his voice. 'We've caught a socialist!'

Whenever he'd had a few drinks he was boisterous, shouting and picking quarrels with policemen and cabbies, singing and laughing furiously.

'To hell with Nature!' he shouted.

'Now now,' Yartsev said, trying to calm him down. 'That's enough. *Please!*'

The friends soon grew used to the dark and began to make out the silhouettes of lofty pines and telegraph poles. Now and then whistles could be heard from railway stations in Moscow, and telegraph wires hummed mournfully. But no sound came from that patch of forest and there was something proud, strong and mysterious about the silence. And now, at night, the tops of the pines seemed almost to touch the sky. The friends found the correct cutting and went down it. Here it was pitch black and only the long strip of star-strewn sky and the well-trodden earth beneath their feet told them that they were on the path. Silently they walked, side by side, both imagining that people were coming towards them. Yartsev had the idea that souls of Muscovite Tsars, boyars and patriarchs might be wandering around the forest. He wanted to tell Kostya, but stopped himself.

When they reached the city gate dawn was just glimmering. Still without a word, Yartsev and Kochevoy walked down a road past cheap holiday villas, pubs and timber yards. Under the branch-line railway bridge they suddenly experienced a pleasant dampness, smelling of lime trees. Then a long, broad street opened up without a soul or light on it. When they reached Krasny Prud, dawn was breaking.

'Moscow's a city that will have to go through a lot more suffering in the future!' Yartsev said, looking at the Alekseyev Monastery.

'What makes you think that?'

'I just do. I love Moscow.'

Both Yartsev and Kostya were born in Moscow and they adored it – for some reason they felt hostile towards other cities. They were convinced that Moscow was a remarkable city, and Russia a remarkable country. Away in the Crimea or the Caucasus, or abroad, they felt bored, uncomfortable, out of place, and their beloved Moscow's dreary grey weather was the most pleasant and healthy of all, they thought. Days when the cold rain beats on windows and dusk comes on early, when walls of houses and churches take on a sombre, brownish colour, when you don't know what to wear when you go out into the street – days like these pleasantly stimulated them. In the end they took a cab near the station.

'Actually, I'd like to write a historical play,' Yartsev said, 'but without all those Lyapunovs and Godunovs. I'd write about the times of Yaroslav or Monomakh. I hate all Russian historical plays, except for Pimen's soliloquy.* When you're dealing with some historical source or reading text books on Russian history, everything Russian appears so incredibly talented, competent and interesting. But when I see a historical play at the theatre, Russian life strikes me as inept, morbid and uninspiring.'

*A famous speech from Pushkin's Boris Godunov.

141

The friends parted at Dmitrovka Street and Yartsev drove on to his rooms in Nikitsky Street. He rocked to and fro, dozing, his whole mind on that play. Suddenly he imagined a terrible noise, clanging, shouts in some incomprehensible language – Kalmuck, most likely. There was a village engulfed in flames, and the nearby woods, covered in hoar frost and faint pink in the conflagration, could be so clearly seen for miles around that every little fir tree was distinguishable. Some wild savages, on horse and on foot, tore through the village: both they and their steeds were as crimson as the glow in the sky.

'They're Polovtsians,' thought Yartsev.

One of them – old, bloody-faced and covered all over with burns – was tying a young, white-faced Russian girl to his saddle. The old man was ranting and raving, while the girl looked on with sad, intelligent eyes.

Yartsev shook his head and woke up.

'"My dear, tender love,"' he chanted.

He paid the cab-driver and went up to his room, but he just couldn't return to reality and saw the flames spreading to the trees. The forest crackled and began to smoke. An enormous wild boar, maddened with fear, charged through the village. And the girl who was tied to the saddle was still watching.

It was light when Yartsev entered his room. Two candles were burning low on the piano, near some open music books. In a dark dress with a sash, a newspaper in her hands, Polina lay fast asleep on the couch. She must have been playing for some time waiting for Yartsev and fallen asleep.

'God, she looks worn-out!' he thought.

Carefully removing the paper from her hands, he covered her with a rug, snuffed the candles and went to his bedroom. As he lay down he thought of that historical play and couldn't get that line – 'My dear, tender love' – out of his head.

Two days later Laptev dropped in for a moment to say that Lida had diphtheria and that Julia and the baby had caught it from her. Five days later came the news that Lida and Julia were recovering, but that the baby had died and the Laptevs had dashed back to town from the villa at Sokolniki.

XIV

Laptev didn't like spending much time at home now. His wife often went over to the lodge, saying that she had to see to the girls' lessons. However, she didn't go there for that, but to cry at Kostya's. The ninth, twentieth, fortieth day passed and still he had to go to the St Alexis Cemetery for requiem mass, after which he had a hellish twenty-four hours thinking only of that unfortunate baby and uttering various platitudes to console his wife. He seldom went to the warehouse now and busied himself solely with charitable work, inventing sundry little jobs or worries for himself, and he was delighted when he had to ride around the whole day on some trivial matter.

Recently he had been intending to go abroad to learn about organization of hostels for the poor and now this idea provided some diversion.

It was one day in autumn. Julia had just gone to the lodge to cry, while Laptev was lying on his study couch wondering where to go. Then Peter announced that Polina had arrived. Absolutely delighted, Laptev leapt up and went to greet his unexpected visitor, that former friend he had almost forgotten now. Since that evening when he had seen her last she hadn't changed at all.

'Polina!' he said, stretching out both hands. 'It's been so long! You just can't imagine how glad I am to see you. Welcome!'

Polina greeted him by tugging at his hand, entered the study and sat down without taking off her coat or hat.

'I've only dropped in for a minute, I've no time for chit-chat. Please sit down and listen. I couldn't care less whether you're pleased or not to see me, as I don't give a damn for the gracious attentions of members of the male sex. The reason I'm here now is that I've already called at five places today and was refused in every one of them. It's an urgent matter. Now, listen,' she added, looking him in the eye. 'Five students I know, all with limited brain-power, but indubitably poor, haven't paid their fees and have been expelled. Your wealth makes it incumbent on you to go to the university immediately and pay their fees for them.'

'With pleasure, Polina.'

'Here are their names,' Polina said, handing Laptev a note.

'You must go this minute, you can wallow in domestic bliss later.'

Just then came a vague rustling sound from behind the door into the drawing-room – it was most probably the dog scratching itself. Polina blushed and leapt to her feet. 'Your little Dulcinea's trying to eavesdrop,' she said. 'That's a rotten trick!'

Laptev felt insulted on Julia's behalf.

'She's not here, she's at the lodge,' he said. 'And don't talk about her like that. We've lost our baby and she's terribly depressed.'

'You can set her mind at rest,' Polina laughed, sitting down again. 'She'll have another dozen of them. You don't need brains to have babies!'

Laptev remembered hearing this, or something similar, many times before, long ago, and he recaptured that idyllic past, his free bachelor life when he had felt young and capable of anything, when love for a wife and memories of a child just didn't exist for him.

'Let's go together,' he said, stretching himself.

When they reached the university Polina waited at the gates, while Laptev went to the bursar's office. After a short time he returned and handed Polina five receipts.

'Where are you off to now?' he asked.

'To see Yartsev.'

'I'm coming with you.'

'But you'll interrupt him in his work.'

'I won't, I assure you!' he replied, looking at her imploringly.

She was wearing a black mourning hat with crêpe trimmings, and a very short, shabby coat with bulging pockets. Her nose seemed longer than ever and her face had no colour, in spite of the cold. Laptev liked following and obeying her, and listening to her grumbling. On the way he reflected on the inner strength she must have if, despite her ugliness, clumsiness and restlessness, despite her lack of dress sense, despite her hair always being dishevelled and despite her rather ungainly figure, she was still a woman of great charm.

They made their way into Yartsev's rooms by the back door – through the kitchen, where they were welcomed by the cook, a neat old woman with grey curls. Deeply embarrassed, she smiled sweetly at them and this made her small face look like a piece of puff pastry.

'Please come in,' she said.

Yartsev was out. Polina sat at the piano and started some boring, difficult exercises, having instructed Laptev not to interrupt. He didn't distract her with conversation, but sat to one side leafing through the *European Herald*. After practising for two hours – that was her daily stint – she ate something in the kitchen and went off to give some lessons. Laptev read an instalment of some novel, then sat there for some time, neither reading nor feeling bored, but pleased that he was already late for dinner at home.

'Ha, ha, ha!' he heard Yartsev laugh – and then the man himself came in. He was healthy, hearty, red-cheeked, and wore a new tailcoat with shiny buttons. 'Ha, ha, ha!'

The friends dined together. Then Laptev lay on the couch, while Yartsev sat near him and lit a cigar. Twilight fell.

'I must be getting old,' Laptev said. 'Since my sister Nina died I've taken to thinking about death, for some reason.'

They talked of death and immortality, about how lovely it would be if they were resurrected and then flew off to Mars or somewhere to enjoy eternal idleness and happiness – and, most of all, if they could think in some special, non-terrestrial way.

'But I don't want to die,' Yartsev said softly. 'No philosophy can reconcile me to death and I look upon it simply as destruction. I want to live.'

'Do you love life, old man?'

'Yes, I love life.'

'Well, in that respect I just can't make myself out. Gloomy moods alternate with apathetic ones. I'm timid, I've no self-confidence, I'm cowardly in matters of conscience, I cannot adapt to life at all or become master of it. Other people talk rubbish or behave like rogues – and with such gusto! As for me, sometimes I consciously perform good deeds, but in the event I experience only anxiety or complete indifference. My explanation for all this is that I'm a slave – a serf's grandson. Many of us rank and file will fall in battle before we find the right path.'

'That's all very well, dear man,' Yartsev sighed. 'It only goes to show yet again how rich and varied Russian life is. Yes, very rich! Do you know, every day I'm more convinced that we're on the threshold of some fantastic triumph. I'd like to survive till then and take part in it myself. Believe it or not, in my opinion a remarkable generation is growing up now. It's a pleasure teaching children, especially girls. Wonderful children!'

Yartsev went over to the piano and struck a chord.

'I'm a chemist,' he continued. 'I think like a chemist and I'll die a chemist. But I'm greedy, I'm afraid I'll die without having gorged myself. Chemistry alone isn't enough for me. I clutch at Russian history, at the history of art, at educational theory, music. Your wife told me this summer to write a historical play and now I want to write, write, write. I feel I could sit down and write for three days and nights, without ever getting up. Images have exhausted me, my head is crammed with them, I feel a pulse beating in my brain. I don't want to make anything special out of myself or achieve something really great. All I want is to live, dream, hope, to be everywhere at the same time. Life, my dear man, is short and we must live it as best we can.'

After this friendly chat, which finished only at midnight, Laptev began calling at Yartsev's almost every day. He felt drawn to the place. He usually arrived just before evening, lay down and waited impatiently for Yartsev to arrive, not feeling bored in the least. When he had returned from the office and eaten, Yartsev would sit down to work. But Laptev would ask him something, a conversation would start, work would be forgotten and the friends would part at midnight feeling very pleased with each other.

But this didn't last long. Once, after arriving at Yartsev's, Laptev found only Polina there, sitting practising at the piano. She gave him a cold, almost hostile look. Without shaking hands she asked, 'Please tell me when all this will end?'

'All *what*?'

'You come here every day and stop Yartsev working. Yartsev's no lousy little shopkeeper, he's a scholar – every minute of his life is precious. Try and understand that, show some consideration at least!'

'If you think I'm interfering,' Laptev replied curtly, somewhat embarrassed, 'then I'll put a stop to these visits.'

'That's all right by me. Leave now or he might come and find you here.'

The tone in which Polina said this, her apathetic look, was the finishing touch to his embarrassment. She had no feeling at all for him, all she wanted was for him to leave as soon as possible – what a difference from their former love! He left without shaking hands, thinking she might call him back. But he heard the scales again and as he slowly made his way downstairs he realized that he was a stranger to her now.

Three days later Yartsev came over to spend the evening with him.

'I've news for you,' he laughed. 'Polina has moved in with me.' He became rather embarrassed and added in a low voice, 'Well now, we're not in love of course but ... hm ... that doesn't matter. I'm glad I can offer her a quiet sanctuary and the chance to stop working if she becomes ill. Well, she thinks there'll be a lot more order in my life now that she's living with me and that I'll become a great scholar under her influence. If that's what she thinks, then let her. There's a saying down south: Idle thoughts give wings to fools. Ha, ha, ha!'

Laptev said nothing. Yartsev paced the study, glanced at the paintings he had seen many times before and heaved a sigh as he said, 'Yes, my friend. I'm three years older than you and it's too late for me to start thinking about true love. Really, a woman like Polina is a godsend and I'll live happily with her until old age, of course. But to hell with it, I have regrets and I'm always hankering after something and imagining that I'm lying in a valley in Daghestan, dreaming I'm at a ball.* In short, one's never satisfied with what one has.'

He went into the drawing-room and sang some songs, as if he had no worries at all, while Laptev stayed in the study, eyes closed, trying to fathom why Polina had moved in with Yartsev. Then he kept mourning the fact that there was no such thing as a firm, lasting attachment. He was annoyed about Polina having an affair with Yartsev and he was annoyed with himself for feeling quite differently towards his wife now.

*A reference to Lermontov's famous poem *The Dream* (1841).

XV

Laptev was sitting in his armchair, rocking himself as he read. Julia was also in the study reading. Apparently there was nothing to discuss and neither had said a word since morning. Now and then he looked at her over his book and wondered if it made any difference if one married from passionate love or without any love at all. That time of jealousy, great agitation and suffering seemed remote now. He had already managed a trip abroad and was now recovering from the journey, hoping to return to England, which he had liked very much, at the beginning of spring.

Julia had grown inured to her grief and no longer went to the lodge to cry. That winter she didn't visit the shops, or go to the theatre or concerts, but stayed at home. She didn't like large rooms and was always either in her husband's study or in her own room, where she had some icon-cases that were part of her dowry and where the landscape painting she had admired so much at the exhibition hung on the wall. She spent no money on herself and got through as little as in her father's house.

Winter passed cheerlessly. All over Moscow people were playing cards, but whenever some other entertainment was devised – singing, reciting, sketching, for example – this made life even more boring. Because there were so few talented people in Moscow and because the same old singers and reciters were to be found at every soirée, enjoyment of the arts gradually palled and for many was transformed into a boring, monotonous duty.

Besides this, not one day passed at the Laptevs without some upset. Old Mr Laptev's eyesight was very poor, he no longer went to the warehouse and the eye surgeons said he would soon go blind. For some reason Fyodor stopped going there too, staying at home the whole time to write. Panaurov had obtained his transfer – he had been promoted to Councillor of State – and he was living at the Dresden Hotel now. Almost every day he called on Laptev to borrow money. Kish had finally left university and while he was waiting for the Laptevs to find him a job would hang around for days on end, regaling them with long, boring stories. All this was very irritating and wearisome, and made everyday life most unpleasant.

Peter entered the study to announce the arrival of a lady they didn't know: the name on her visiting card was 'Josephine Milan'. Julia lazily stood up and went out, limping slightly from pins and needles in one leg. A thin, very pale lady with dark eyebrows, dressed completely in black, appeared at the door. She clasped her breast and said pleadingly, 'Monsieur Laptev, please save my children!'

Laptev was familiar with the clink of those bracelets and that powder-blotched face. He recognized her as the lady at whose house he had been so stupid to dine just before the wedding. She was Panaurov's second wife.

'Save my children!' she repeated and her face trembled and suddenly looked old and pathetic. Her eyes reddened. 'Only you can save us and I've spent my last rouble to come and see you in Moscow. My children will starve!'

She made as if to go down on her knees. This scared Laptev and he gripped her arms above the elbows.

'Please sit down, I beg you,' he muttered as he gave her a chair.

'We have no money for food now,' she said. 'Grigory is leaving to take up his new position but he doesn't want to take me or the children, and that money you were so generous to send us he only spends on himself. What on earth can we do? I'm asking you. Those poor, unfortunate children!'

'Please calm yourself! I'll tell the people at the office to send the money direct to *you*.'

She burst out sobbing, then calmed down, and he noticed that the tears had made little channels on her powdered cheeks and that she had a little moustache.

'You're *infinitely* generous, Monsieur Laptev. But please be our guardian angel, our good fairy. Persuade Grigory not to leave me, to take me with him. I do love him, I'm mad about him. He's the light of my life.'

Laptev gave her a hundred roubles and promised he would have a talk with Panaurov. As he saw her into the hall he became frightened she might start sobbing again or fall on her knees.

Kish was next to arrive. Then in came Kostya, with a camera. Recently he'd become keen on photography and would take snaps of everyone in the house several times a day. This new hobby was causing him a great deal of distress and he'd even lost weight.

Fyodor arrived before afternoon tea. He sat down in a corner of the study, opened a book and stared at the same page for ages, obviously not reading. Then he lingered over his tea; his face was red. Laptev felt depressed in his presence and even found his silence unpleasant.

'You can congratulate Russia on her new pamphleteer,' Fyodor remarked. 'Joking aside, old man, it's to put my pen to the test, so to speak, and I've come here to show you it. Please read it, dear chap, and tell me what you think. Only please be quite frank.'

He took an exercise-book from his pocket and handed it to his brother. The article was called 'The Russian Soul' and it was written in that dull flat style usually employed by untalented people who are secretly conceited. Its main idea was as follows: intellectuals have the right not to believe in the supernatural, but they are obliged to conceal their lack of belief so as not to lead others astray or shake them in their faith. Without faith there is no idealism, and idealism is destined to save Europe and show humanity the true path.

'But you don't say from *what* Europe must be saved,' Laptev commented.

'That's self-evident.'

'No it's not,' Laptev said, walking up and down excitedly. 'It's not at all clear why you wrote it. However, that's your affair.'

'I want to have it published as a pamphlet.'

'That's your affair.'

For a minute they didn't speak, then Fyodor sighed and said, 'I deeply, infinitely regret that we see things differently. Oh, Alexei, my dear brother Alexei! We're both Russians, we belong to the Orthodox Church, we have breadth of vision. Those rotten German and Jewish ideas – do they really suit us? We're not a pair of blackguards, are we? We're representatives of a distinguished family.'

'Distinguished my foot!' Laptev exclaimed, trying to keep back his irritation. 'Distinguished family! Our grandfather was knocked around by rich landowners, the most miserable little clerk used to hit him in the face. Grandfather beat Father, Father beat you and me. What ever did this "distinguished family" of yours give you or me? What kind of nerves and blood did we inherit? For close on three years you've been blethering away like some wretched parish priest, spouting no end of drivel. And now this thing you've penned – why, it's the ravings of a lackey! And what about *me*? Just take a look. I'm quite unadaptable, I've no spirit or moral fibre.

'For every step I take I'm scared of being flogged. I cringe before nonentities, idiots, swine who are immeasurably inferior to me both intellectually and morally. I'm afraid of house porters, janitors, city police. I'm scared of everyone because I was born of a persecuted mother – from childhood I've been beaten and bullied. We'd both do well not to have children. Let's hope, God willing, that this distinguished merchant house comes to an end with us!'

Julia entered the study and sat by the desk.

'Were you having an argument?' she asked. 'I'm not interrupting, am I?'

'No, my dear sister-in-law,' Fyodor replied. 'We're discussing questions of principle. So, you were saying,' he went on, turning to his brother, 'that our family is this and that. But this family built up a million-rouble business. That's something!'

'Blast your million-rouble business! A man without any special intelligence or ability becomes a merchant by accident, makes his fortune and does his business day in day out without any method or purpose – without even any craving for wealth. He carries on like a machine and the money just pours in, without him lifting a finger. His whole life is business and he likes it only because he can lord it over his clerks and make fun of customers. He's a churchwarden only because he can bully the choir and keep them under his thumb. He's a school governor because he likes to see the schoolmaster as his subordinate and can order him around. It's not business you merchants care for, it's being the boss. That warehouse of yours is no business premises, it's a torture-chamber! Yes, for your sort of business you need clerks with no personality, deprived of any material share in it, and you train them to be that way. From childhood you force them to prostrate themselves before you for every crust of bread, from childhood you bring them up to believe that you are their benefactors. I could never imagine you having university men in your warehouse – no question about that!'

'Graduates are no good in our kind of business.'

'That's not true!' Laptev shouted. 'That's a lie!'

'I'm sorry, but you seem to be fouling your own water,' Fyodor said, getting up. 'You find our business hateful, yet you still enjoy the profits!'

'Aha, so now we've come to the point!' Laptev laughed and gave his brother an angry look. 'Yes, if I didn't belong to your distinguished family, if I had one iota of will-power and courage, I'd have chucked away all these profits of yours years ago and gone out to earn my own living. But you in your warehouse have been stripping me of all individuality since I was a child. I'm yours now!'

Fyodor glanced at his watch and hurriedly made his farewell. He kissed Julia's hand and left the room. But instead of going into the hall he went into the drawing-room, then into a bedroom.

'I've forgotten which rooms are which here,' he said, deeply embarrassed. 'It's a strange house, don't you think? Most peculiar.'

While he was putting on his fur coat he seemed stunned by something and his face was full of pain. Laptev no longer felt angry: he was afraid and at the same time he felt sorry for Fyodor. That fine, heartfelt love for his brother that had seemingly died within him during those past three years awoke now and he felt a strong urge to express it.

'Fyodor, come and have lunch tomorrow,' he said, stroking his brother's shoulder. 'Will you come?'

'Oh, all right. But please fetch me some water.'

Laptev dashed into the dining-room himself, picked up the first thing he found on the sideboard – a tall beer jug – poured some water and took it to his brother. Fyodor started drinking thirstily, but suddenly he bit on the jug and then the gnashing of teeth could be heard, followed by sobbing. The water spilt on to his fur coat and frock-coat. Laptev, who had never seen a man weep before, stood there embarrassed and frightened, at a loss what to do. In his bewilderment he watched Julia and the maid remove Fyodor's fur coat and take him back into the house. He followed them, feeling that he was to blame.

Julia helped Fyodor lie down and sank to her knees before him. 'It's nothing, it's only nerves,' she said comfortingly.

'My dear, I feel so low,' he said. 'I'm so unhappy, but I've been trying to keep it a secret the whole time.'

He put his arms round her neck and whispered in her ear, 'Every night I dream of my sister Nina. She comes and sits in the armchair by my bed.'

An hour later, when he was putting on his fur coat again in the hall, he was smiling and he felt ashamed because of the maid. Laptev drove with him to Pyatnitsky Street.

'Please come and have lunch tomorrow,' he said on the way, holding his arm, 'and let's go abroad together at Easter. You must get some fresh air – you've really let yourself go.'

'Yes, of course I'll come. And we'll take sister-in-law Julia with us.'

Back home Laptev found his wife terribly overwrought. That incident with Fyodor had shocked her and she just wouldn't calm down. She wasn't crying, but she looked very pale, tossing and turning in bed and clutching at the quilt, pillow and her husband's hands with cold fingers. Her eyes were dilated with fear.

'Don't leave me, please don't leave me,' she said to her husband. 'Tell me, Alexei, why have I stopped saying my prayers? Where is my faith? Oh, why did you have to talk about religion in my presence? You and those friends of yours have muddled me. I don't pray any more.'

He put compresses on her forehead, warmed her hands and made her drink tea, while she clung to him in terror . . .

By morning she was exhausted and fell asleep with Laptev sitting by her holding her hand. So *he* didn't get any sleep. All next day he felt shattered and listless, his mind a blank as he sluggishly wandered round the house.

XVI

The doctors said that Fyodor was mentally ill. Laptev didn't know what was happening at Pyatnitsky Street, but that dark warehouse, where neither the old man nor Fyodor appeared any more, reminded him of a crypt. Whenever his wife told him that he should visit the warehouse and Pyatnitsky Street every day, he either said nothing or talked irritably about his childhood, about his inability to forgive his father the past, about his hatred for Pyatnitsky Street and the warehouse, and so on.

One Sunday morning Julia went to Pyatnitsky Street herself. She found old Mr Laptev in the same room where the service to celebrate her arrival had once been held. Without any tie, in canvas jacket and slippers, he was sitting motionless in an armchair, blinking his blind eyes.

'It's me, your daughter-in-law,' she said, going over to him. 'I've come to see how you are.'

He was breathing heavily from excitement. Touched by his unhappiness and loneliness, she kissed his hand, while he felt her face and head. Then, as if having convinced himself that it really was her, he made the sign of the cross over her.

'Thank you so much,' he said. 'I've lost my sight, I can hardly see a thing. I can just make out the window and the light too, but not people and things. Yes, I'm going blind and Fyodor's ill. It's really bad without the boss's eye on them – if there's trouble and no one to take charge they'll just run wild. And what's wrong with Fyodor? Got a cold, has he? As for me, I've never been ill, never been to the doctor's. No, can't say I've had anything to do with doctors.'

As usual, the old man started boasting. Meanwhile the servants hurriedly began laying the table in that large room, placing savouries and bottles of wine on it. They brought in about a dozen bottles, one of which was the same shape as the Eiffel Tower. Then they brought a whole plateful of hot pies that smelt of boiled rice and fish.

'Please have something, my dear,' the old man said.

She took his arm, led him to the table and poured him some vodka. 'I'll come again tomorrow,' she said, 'and I'll bring your granddaughters Sasha and Lida. They'll pamper and comfort you.'

'Oh, no, don't go bringing them here, they're not legitimate.'

'What? Not legitimate? Surely their father and mother were married?'

'Yes, but without my permission. I never blessed them and I don't want anything to do with them, blast them.'

'What a strange way to speak, Father,' Julia sighed. 'According to the Gospels children must honour and fear their parents.'

'Nothing of the sort. The Gospels say that we must forgive even our enemies.'

'In our kind of business you can't forgive anyone. If you started forgiving everyone you'd go bust within three years.'

'But forgiving, saying a kind, friendly word to someone – even if he's done wrong – that's better than business and wealth!'

Julia wanted to mollify the old man, to inspire him with compassion and make him feel repentant, but he listened to what she had to say condescendingly, like a parent listening to a child.

'Father, you're an old man,' Julia said decisively. 'God will soon be calling you to Him. He won't ask what kind of business you had, or if you made a profit. He'll ask whether you've been kind to others. Haven't you been hard on those weaker than yourself – your servants or clerks, for example?'

'I've always been generous to my staff. They should always mention me in their prayers,' the old man said with great conviction. However, he was touched by Julia's sincere tone of voice and, to please her, he added, 'Good, bring my little granddaughters tomorrow. I'll see they get some presents.'

The old man was untidily dressed and there was cigar ash on his chest and lap. Evidently no one cleaned his shoes or clothes. The rice in the pies was under-cooked, the table-cloth smelt of soap, the servants trod noisily. The old man, the whole house on Pyatnitsky Street, had a neglected look. Sensing this, Julia felt ashamed on her own and her husband's account.

'I'll come and see you tomorrow, without fail,' she said.

She walked through the house and ordered the servants to tidy up the old man's bedroom and light his icon-lamp. Fyodor was sitting in his room looking at an open book without reading. Julia spoke to him and ordered his room to be tidied too. Then she went down to the clerks' quarters. In the middle of the room where they ate stood an unpainted wooden column, which propped up the ceiling. The ceilings here were low and the walls cheaply papered, and there was a smell of fumes from the stove and cooking. As it was Sunday, all the clerks were at home, sitting on their beds waiting for their meal. When Julia came in they jumped up, timidly answered her questions, lowering at her like convicts.

'Heavens, what a dreadful place you live in!' she exclaimed, clasping her hands. 'Don't you feel cramped here?'

'Yes, it's cramped all right,' Makeichev said, 'but it don't do us no harm. We're very thankful to you and we lift up our prayers to all-merciful God.'

'Corresponding to the plenitude of the personality,' Pochatkin said.

Noticing that Julia hadn't understood Pochatkin, Makeichev hastened to explain, 'We're humble folk and must live according to our station in life.'

She inspected the boys' quarters and the kitchen, met the housekeeper and was highly dissatisfied.

At home she told her husband, 'We must move to Pyatnitsky Street as soon as possible. And you'll go to the warehouse every day.'

Afterwards they both sat next to each other in the study without speaking. Laptev felt miserable and didn't want to go to Pyatnitsky Street or the warehouse. But he guessed what his wife was thinking and didn't have the strength to offer any opposition.

'I feel as if our life's over and that some dull half-life is just beginning. When I heard that my brother Fyodor is hopelessly ill, I just wept. We spent our childhood and youth together. I once loved him deeply. Now this catastrophe comes along and I feel that losing him is the final break with the past. When you spoke just now about moving to Pyatnitsky Street, to that prison, I began to think that I've no future either.'

He stood up and went over to the window.

'Whatever happens, I can say goodbye to any hope of happiness,' he said, looking into the street. 'It doesn't exist. I've never experienced happiness, so there probably isn't such a thing. However, I *was* happy once in my life, when I sat under your umbrella that night. Do you remember leaving your umbrella at my sister Nina's?' he asked, turning towards his wife. 'I was in love with you then and I remember sitting up the whole night under that umbrella in a state of bliss.'

In the study, by the bookcases, stood a mahogany chest-of-drawers, with bronze handles, where Laptev kept various things that weren't needed, including the umbrella. He took it out and handed it to his wife.

'There you are.'

Julia looked at the umbrella for about a minute and recognized it with a sad smile. 'I remember,' she said. 'You were holding it when you said you loved me.'

When she saw that he was preparing to leave she added, 'Please come home early if you can. I miss you.'

Then she went to her room and stared at the umbrella for a long time.

XVII

Despite the complexity of the business and the enormous turnover, there was no accountant at the warehouse and it was impossible to make any sense of the ledger clerk's books. Every day commission agents – German and English, with whom the clerks discussed politics and religion – called at the warehouse. An alcoholic nobleman (a sick, pathetic man) would come to translate the office's foreign correspondence. The clerks called him 'Midget' and gave him tea with salt in it. On the whole, the business struck Laptev as one vast operation in eccentricity.

Every day he called at the warehouse and tried to introduce a new system. He forbade them to whip the boys or make fun of customers, and he lost his temper whenever the clerks laughed as they cheerfully dispatched useless old stock to the provinces, trying to pass it off as new and fashionable. Now he was in charge at the warehouse, but he still had no idea how much he was worth, whether the business was prospering or what salary his chief clerks received. Pochatkin and Makeichev thought him young and inexperienced, concealed many things from him, and had mysterious whispering sessions with the blind old man every evening.

One day in early June, Laptev and Pochatkin went to Bubnov's inn for a business lunch. Pochatkin had been with the Laptevs for ages, having joined the firm when he was eight. He was really part of the place and was trusted implicitly: when he took all the money from the cash-box on his way out and stuffed his pockets this didn't arouse the least suspicion. He was boss at the warehouse, at home and in church too, where he stood in as warden for the old man. Because of his cruel treatment of his inferiors he had been nicknamed Ivan the Terrible by the clerks and boys.

When they arrived at the inn he nodded to the waiter and said, 'Look here, old chap, bring us half a prodigy and twenty vexations.'

After a short while, the waiter brought them half a bottle of vodka on a tray and various plates of savouries.

'Now look here, old fellow-me-lad,' Pochatkin said, 'bring us a portion of the leading expert in slander and scandal with some mashed potatoes.'

The waiter didn't understand, grew embarrassed and looked as if he wanted to say something. But Pochatkin eyed him sternly and said, 'Furthermore!'

The waiter racked his brains and then went off to consult his colleagues. Finally he guessed correctly and brought a portion of tongue. When they had each drunk two glasses and eaten, Laptev asked, 'Tell me, Pochatkin, is it true our business has been in decline over the past few years?'

'Not at all.'

'Now, be quite straight with me, don't equivocate. Tell me how much profit we used to make, how much we're making now, and how much capital we have. We can't go around like blind men, can we? The warehouse accounts were done not so long ago, but I'm very sceptical, I'm sorry to say. You feel you must hide something from me and you only tell my father the truth. You've been mixed up in shady dealings since you were young and now you can't do without them. But what's the use? Now, I'm asking you. Please be open with me. What's the state of the business?'

'That depends on oscillation of credit,' Pochatkin replied after pausing for thought.

'What do you mean, "oscillation of credit"?'

Pochatkin began explaining, but Laptev understood nothing and sent for Makeichev. He came at once, said a short prayer, ate some savouries and, in his rich, pompous baritone expatiated chiefly on the clerks' duty to pray night and day for their benefactors.

'Fine, but please don't include me among your benefactors,' Laptev said.

'Every man must remember what he is and be conscious of his station in life. By the grace of God you are our father and benefactor and we are your slaves.'

'I'm just about sick and tired of all this!' Laptev fumed. 'Now, *you* be my benefactor for a change and tell me how the business stands. Please stop treating me like a child or I'll close down the warehouse tomorrow. My father's gone blind, my brother's in a mad-house, my nieces are still very young. I hate the business and I'd love to get out of it. But there's no one to replace me, you know that too well. So, enough of your fiddling, for God's sake!'

They went into the warehouse to check the accounts and that evening they were still working on them in the house – the old man himself helped them. As he initiated his son into his business secrets he gave the impression he had been practising black magic, not commerce. It turned out that the profits were increasing yearly by about ten per cent and that the Laptevs' wealth, in cash and securities alone, amounted to six million roubles.

It was about one o'clock in the morning when Laptev went out into the fresh air after doing the accounts, and he felt hypnotized by those figures. It was a calm, moonlit, fragrant night. The white walls of the houses in Moscow's suburbs south of the river, the sight of heavy, locked gates, the silence and those black shadows created the general impression of a fortress – only a sentry with rifle was missing. Laptev went into the little garden and sat on a bench near the fence separating it from next door's garden. The bird-cherry was in bloom. Laptev remembered that this cherry had been just as gnarled and exactly the same height when he was a child – it hadn't changed at all since then. Every corner of the garden and yard reminded him of the remote past. In his childhood, just as now, the whole yard, flooded in moonlight, had been visible through the sparse trees, with shadows that were as mysterious and menacing as before. And just as then, a black dog lay in the middle of the yard and the clerks' windows were all wide open. But all these were sombre memories.

Beyond the fence, the sound of footsteps came from next door.

'My dearest, my darling,' a man's voice whispered – so close to the fence that Laptev could hear breathing.

Then there was a kiss. Laptev was sure that all those millions of roubles, that business he disliked so much, would ruin his life and turn him into a slave in the end. He imagined gradually settling down in his new position, gradually assuming the role of head of a business house, growing dull and old, and finally dying the way mediocrities usually do – shabbily, miserably, depressing all his associates. But what was stopping him abandoning all those millions and the business, and leaving that garden and yard he had hated since he was a boy?

The whispering and kissing on the other side of the fence disturbed him. He went into the middle of the yard, unbuttoned his shirt and looked at the moon: he felt that he wanted to order the gate to be unlocked immediately so that he could leave and never return. His heart thrilled at the prospect of freedom and he laughed with joy as he imagined how wonderful, idyllic and perhaps even saintly that life might be.

But he did not make a move and asked himself, 'What in heaven's name is keeping me here?' He felt annoyed with himself and with that black dog which lay sprawled over the stones instead of running off into fields and forest where it would be free and happy. Obviously, the same thing was preventing both him and the dog from leaving that yard – the habit of bondage, slavery.

Next day, at noon, he went to his wife's and invited Yartsev to come along too, in case he got bored. Julia was living in a villa at Butovo and he hadn't been there for five days. When they arrived at the station the friends entered a carriage and Yartsev waxed lyrical about the wonderful weather the whole way. The villa was in a park, not far from the station. Julia was sitting under a poplar waiting for her guests right at the beginning of the main avenue, about twenty yards from the gate. She was wearing a light, elegant, cream-coloured, lace-trimmed dress and was holding that familiar umbrella. Yartsev greeted her and went towards the villa, from which he could make out Sasha and Lida's voices, while Laptev sat beside her to talk business.

'Why have you been so long?' she asked. 'I've been waiting here for days on end. I really miss you!'

She got up, ran her hand through his hair and looked quizzically at his face, shoulders, hat.

'You know, I do love you,' she said, blushing. 'You're very dear to me. You're here, I can see you now and I'm too happy for words! Well, let's talk. Tell me something.'

As she declared her love he felt as though he had already been married for ten years; and he wanted his lunch. She put her arms round his neck, tickling his cheek with her silk dress. He carefully removed her hand, stood up and went off towards the villa without a word. The girls came running to meet him.

'How they've grown!' he thought. 'There's been so many changes over these three years. But perhaps I've another thirteen, thirty years left. What does the future hold in store? Time will tell.'

He embraced Sasha and Lida, who clung to his neck.

'Grandfather sends his regards,' he said. 'Uncle Fyodor is going to die soon. Uncle Kostya has sent us a letter from America and sends his regards. He's bored with the Exhibition and he'll be back soon. And Uncle Alexei is hungry.'

Afterwards he sat on the terrace and saw his wife strolling down the path towards the villa. She seemed deep in thought and wore an enchantingly sad expression. Tears glistened in her eyes. She wasn't the delicate, fragile, pale-faced girl of before, but a mature, beautiful, strong woman. Laptev noticed how rapturously Yartsev was looking at her and how her fresh, beautiful

With Friends

(A Story)

෨෬

A letter arrived one morning.

Kuzminki, June 7th

Dear Misha,
  You've completely forgotten us, please come and visit us soon, we so want to see you. Come today. We beg you, dear sir, on bended knees! Show us your radiant eyes!

Can't wait to see you,
Ta and Ba

The letter was from Tatyana Losev, who had been called 'Ta' for short when Podgorin was staying at Kuzminki ten or twelve years ago. But who was this 'Ba'? Podgorin recalled the long conversations, the gay laughter, the love affairs, the evening walks and that whole array of girls and young women who had once lived at Kuzminki and in the neighbourhood. And he remembered that open, lively, clever face with freckles that matched chestnut hair so well – this was Barbara, Tatyana's friend. Barbara had taken a degree in medicine and was working at a factory somewhere beyond Tula. Evidently she had come to stay at Kuzminki now.

'Dear Ba!' thought Podgorin, surrendering himself to memories. 'What a wonderful girl!'

Tatyana, Barbara and himself were all about the same age. But he had been a mere student then and they were already marriageable girls – in their eyes he was just a boy. And now, even though he had become a lawyer and had started to go grey, all of them still treated him like a youngster, saying that he had no experience of life yet.

He was very fond of them, but more as a pleasant memory

than in actuality, it seemed. He knew little about their present life, which was strange and alien to him. And this brief, playful letter too was something quite foreign to him and had most probably been written after much time and effort. When Tatyana wrote it her husband Sergey was doubtlessly standing behind her. She had been given Kuzminki as her dowry only six years before, but this same Sergey had already reduced the estate to bankruptcy. Each time a bank or mortgage payment became due they would now turn to Podgorin for legal advice. Moreover, they had twice asked him to lend them money. So it was obvious that they either wanted advice or a loan from him now.

He no longer felt so attracted to Kuzminki as in the past. It was such a miserable place. That laughter and rushing around, those cheerful carefree faces, those rendezvous on quiet moonlit nights – all this had gone. Most important, though, they weren't in the flush of youth any more. Probably it enchanted him only as a memory, nothing else. Besides Ta and Ba, there was someone called 'Na', Tatyana's sister Nadezhda, whom half-joking, half-seriously they had called his fiancée. He had seen her grow up and everyone expected him to marry her. He had loved her once and was going to propose. But there she was, twenty-three now, and he still hadn't married her.

'Strange it should turn out like this,' he mused as he re-read the letter in embarrassment. 'But I can't *not* go, they'd be offended.'

His long absence from the Losevs lay like a heavy weight on his conscience. After pacing his room and reflecting at length, he made a great effort of will and decided to go and visit them for about three days and so discharge his duty. Then he could feel free and relaxed – at least until the following summer. After lunch, as he prepared to leave for the Brest Station, he told his servants that he would be back in three days.

It was two hours by train from Moscow to Kuzminki, then a twenty-minute carriage drive from the station, from which he could see Tatyana's wood and those three tall, narrow holiday villas that Losev (he had entered upon some business enterprise in the first years of his marriage) had started building but had never finished. He had been ruined by these holiday villas, by various business projects, by frequent trips to Moscow, where he used to lunch at the Slav Fair and dine at the Hermitage, ending up in Little Bronny Street or at a gipsy haunt named Knacker's Yard, calling this 'having a fling'. Podgorin liked a drink himself – sometimes quite a lot – and he associated with women indiscriminately, but in a cool, lethargic way, without deriving any pleasure. It sickened him when others gave themselves up to these pleasures with such zest. He didn't understand or like men who could feel more free and easy at the Knacker's Yard than at home with a respectable woman, and he felt that any kind of promiscuity stuck to them like burrs. He didn't care for Losev, considering him a boring, lazy, old bungler and more than once had found his company rather repulsive.

Just past the wood, Sergey and Nadezhda met him.

'My dear fellow, why have you forgotten us?' Sergey Losev asked, kissing him three times and then putting both arms round his waist. 'You don't feel affection for us any more, old chap.'

He had coarse features, a fat nose and a thin, light-brown beard. He combed his hair to one side to make himself look like a typical simple Russian. When he spoke he breathed right into your face and when he wasn't speaking he'd breathe heavily through the nose. He was embarrassed by his plumpness and inordinately replete appearance and would keep thrusting out his chest to breathe more easily, which made him look pompous.

In comparison, his sister-in-law Nadezhda seemed ethereal. She was very fair, pale-faced and slim, with kind, loving eyes. Podgorin couldn't judge as to her beauty, since he'd known her since she was a child and grown used to the way she looked. Now she was wearing a white, open-necked dress and the sight of that long, white bare neck was new to him and not altogether pleasant.

'My sister and I have been waiting for you since morning,' she said. 'Barbara's here and she's been expecting you, too.'

She took his arm and suddenly laughed for no reason, uttering a faint cry of joy as if some thought had unexpectedly cast a spell over her. The fields of flowering rye, motionless in the quiet air, the sunlit wood – they were so beautiful. Nadezhda seemed to notice these things only now, as she walked at Podgorin's side.

'I'll be staying about three days,' he told her. 'I'm sorry, but I just couldn't get away from Moscow any earlier.'

'That's not very nice at all, you've forgotten we exist!' Sergey said, reproaching him good-humouredly. *'Jamais de ma vie!'* he suddenly added, snapping his fingers. He had this habit of suddenly blurting out some irrelevance, snapping his fingers in the process. He was always mimicking someone: if he rolled his eyes, or nonchalantly tossed his hair back, or adopted a dramatic pose, that meant he had been to the theatre the night before, or to some dinner with speeches. Now he took short steps as he walked, like an old gout-ridden man, and without bending his knees – he was most likely imitating someone.

'Do you know, Tanya wouldn't believe you'd come,' Nadezhda said. 'But Barbara and I had a funny feeling about it. I somehow *knew* you'd be on that train.'

'Jamais de ma vie!' Sergey repeated.

The ladies were waiting for them on the garden terrace. Ten years ago Podgorin – then a poor student – had given Nadezhda coaching in maths and history in exchange for board and lodging. Barbara, who was studying medicine at the time, happened to be taking Latin lessons from him. As for Tatyana, already a beautiful mature girl then, she could think of nothing but love. All she had desired was love and happiness and she would yearn for them, forever waiting for the husband she dreamed of night and day. Past thirty now, she was just as beautiful and attractive as ever, in her loose-fitting peignoir and with those plump, white arms. Her only thought was for her husband and two little girls. Although she was talking and smiling now, her expression revealed that she was preoccupied with other matters. She was still guarding her love and her rights to that love and was always on the alert, ready to attack any enemy who might want to take her husband and children away from her. Her love was very strong and she felt that it was reciprocated, but jealousy and fear for her children were a constant torment and prevented her from being happy.

After the noisy reunion on the terrace, everyone except Sergey went to Tatyana's room. The sun's rays did not penetrate the lowered blinds and it was so gloomy there that all the roses in a large bunch looked the same colour. They made Podgorin sit down in an old armchair by the window; Nadezhda sat on a low stool at his feet. Besides the kindly reproaches, the jokes and laughter that reminded him so clearly of the past, he knew he could expect an unpleasant conversation about promissory notes and mortgages. It couldn't be avoided, so he thought that it might be best to get down to business there and then without delaying matters, to get it over and done with and then go out into the garden, into fresh air.

'Shall we discuss business first?' he said. 'What's new here in Kuzminki? Is anything rotten in the state of Denmark?'

'Kuzminki is in a bad way,' Tatyana replied, sadly sighing. 'Things are so bad it's hard to imagine they could be any worse.' She paced the room, highly agitated. 'Our estate's for sale, the auction's on 7 August. Everywhere there's advertisements, and buyers come here – they walk through the house, looking ... Now anyone has the right to go into my room and look round. That may be legal, but it's humiliating for me and deeply insulting. We've no funds – and there's nowhere left to borrow any from. Briefly, it's shocking!'

She stopped in the middle of the room, the tears trickling from her eyes, and her voice trembled as she went on, 'I swear, I swear by all that's holy, by my children's happiness, I can't live without Kuzminki! I was born here, it's my home. If they take it away from me I shall never get over it, I'll die of despair.'

'I think you're rather looking on the black side,' Podgorin said. 'Everything will turn out all right. Your husband will get a job, you'll settle down again, lead a new life ...'

'How *can* you say that!' Tatyana shouted. Now she looked very beautiful and aggressive. She was ready to fall on the enemy who wanted to take her husband, children and home away from her, and this was expressed with particular intensity in her face and whole figure. 'A new life! I ask you! Sergey's been busy applying for jobs and they've promised him a position as tax inspector somewhere near Ufa or Perm – or thereabouts. I'm ready to go anywhere, Siberia even. I'm prepared to live there ten, twenty years, but I must be certain that sooner or later I'll return to Kuzminki. I can't live without Kuzminki. I can't, and I won't!' She shouted and stamped her foot.

'Misha, you're a lawyer,' Barbara said, 'you know all the tricks and it's your job to advise us what to do.'

There was only one fair and reasonable answer to this, that there was nothing anyone could do, but Podgorin could not bring himself to say it outright.

'I'll . . . have a think about it,' he mumbled indecisively. 'I'll have a think about it . . .'

He was really two different persons. As a lawyer he had to deal with some very ugly cases. In court and with clients he behaved arrogantly and always expressed his opinion bluntly and curtly. He was used to crudely living it up with his friends. But in his private, intimate life he displayed uncommon tact with people close to him or with very old friends. He was shy and sensitive and tended to beat about the bush. One tear, one sidelong glance, a lie or even a rude gesture were enough to make him wince and lose his nerve. Now that Nadezhda was sitting at his feet he disliked her bare neck. It palled on him and even made him feel like going home. A year ago he had happened to bump into Sergey Losev at a certain Madame's place in Bronny Street and he now felt awkward in Tatyana's company, as if *he* had been the unfaithful one. And this conversation about Kuzminki put him in the most dreadful difficulties. He was used to having ticklish, unpleasant questions decided by judge or jury, or by some legal clause, but faced with a problem that he personally had to solve he was all at sea.

'You're our friend, Misha. We all love you as if you were one of the family,' Tatyana continued. 'And I'll tell you quite candidly: all our hopes rest in you. For heaven's sake, tell us what to do. Perhaps we could write somewhere for help? Perhaps it's not too late to put the estate in Nadezhda's or Barbara's name? What shall we do?'

'Please save us, Misha, *please*,' Barbara said, lighting a cigarette. 'You were always so clever. You haven't seen much of life, you're not very experienced, but you have a fine brain. You'll help Tatyana, I know you will.'

'I must think about it . . . perhaps I can come up with something.'

They went for a walk in the garden, then in the fields. Sergey went too. He took Podgorin's arm and led him on ahead of the others, evidently intending to discuss something with him – probably the trouble he was in. Walking with Sergey and talking to him were an ordeal too. Sergey kept kissing him – always three kisses at a time – took Podgorin's arm, put his own arm round his waist and breathed into his face. He seemed covered with sweet glue that would stick to you if he came close. And that look in his eyes which showed that he wanted something from Podgorin, that he was about to ask him for it, was really quite distressing – it was like having a revolver aimed at you.

The sun had set and it was growing dark. Green and red lights appeared here and there along the railway line. Barbara stopped and as she looked at the lights she started reciting:

> 'The line runs straight, unswerving,
> Through narrow cuttings,
> Passing posts, crossing bridges,
> While all along the verges,
> Lie buried so many Russian workers!*

'How does it go on? Heavens, I've forgotten!

> 'In scorching heat, in winter's icy blasts,
> We laboured with backs bent low.'

She recited in a magnificent deep voice, with great feeling. Her face flushed brightly, her eyes filled with tears. This was the Barbara that used to be, Barbara the university student, and as he listened Podgorin thought of the past and recalled his student days, when he too knew much fine poetry by heart and loved to recite it.

> 'He still has not bowed his hunched back
> He's gloomily silent as before . . .'

But Barbara could remember no more. She fell silent and smiled weakly, limply. After the recitation those green and red lights seemed sad.

'Oh, I've forgotten it!'

But Podgorin suddenly remembered the lines – somehow they

* From *The Railway* (1865), by N. A. Nekrasov.

had stuck in his memory from student days and he recited in a soft undertone,

> 'The Russian worker has suffered enough,
> In building this railway line.
> He will survive to build himself
> A broad bright highway
> By the sweat of his brow ...
> Only the pity is ...'

' "The pity is," ' Barbara interrupted as she remembered the lines,

> 'that neither you nor I
> Will ever live to see that wonderful day.'

She laughed and slapped him on the shoulder.

They went back to the house and sat down to supper. Sergey nonchalantly stuck a corner of his serviette into his collar, imitating someone or other. 'Let's have a drink,' he said, pouring some vodka for himself and Podgorin. 'In our time, we students could hold our drink, we were fine speakers and men of action. I drink your health, old man. So why don't you drink to a stupid old idealist and wish that he will die an idealist? Can the leopard change his spots?'

Throughout supper Tatyana kept looking tenderly and jealously at her husband, anxious lest he ate or drank something that wasn't good for him. She felt that he had been spoilt by women and exhausted by them, and although this was something that appealed to her, it still distressed her. Barbara and Nadezhda also had a soft spot for him and it was obvious from the worried glances they gave him that they were scared he might suddenly get up and leave them. When he wanted to pour himself a second glass Barbara looked angry and said, 'You're poisoning yourself, Sergey. You're a highly strung, impressionable man – you could easily become an alcoholic. Tatyana, tell him to remove that vodka.'

On the whole Sergey had great success with women. They loved his height, his powerful build, his strong features, his idleness and his tribulations. They said that his extravagance stemmed only from extreme kindness, that he was impractical because he was an idealist. He was honest and high-principled. His inability to adapt to people or circumstances explained why he owned nothing and didn't have a steady job. They trusted him implicitly, idolized him and spoilt him with their adulation, so that he himself came to believe that he really was idealistic, impractical, honest and upright, and that he was head and shoulders above these women.

'Well, don't you have something good to say about my little girls?' Tatyana asked as she looked lovingly at her two daughters – healthy, well-fed and like two fat buns – as she heaped rice on their plates. 'Just take a good look at them. They say all mothers can never speak ill of their children. But I do assure you I'm not at all biased. My little girls are quite remarkable. Especially the elder.'

Podgorin smiled at her and the girls and thought it strange that this healthy, young, intelligent woman, essentially such a strong and complex organism, could waste all her energy, all her strength, on such uncomplicated trivial work as running a home which was well managed anyway.

'Perhaps she knows best,' he thought. 'But it's so boring, so stupid!'

> 'Before he had time to groan
> A bear came and knocked him prone,'*

Sergey said, snapping his fingers.

They finished their supper. Tatyana and Barbara made Podgorin sit down on a sofa in the drawing-room and, in hushed voices, talked about business again.

'We must save Sergey,' Barbara said, 'it's our moral duty. He has his weaknesses, he's not thrifty, he doesn't put anything away for a rainy day, but that's only because he's so kind and generous. He's just a child, really. Give him a million and within a month there'd be nothing left, he'd have given it all away.'

'Yes, that's so true,' Tatyana said and tears rolled down her cheeks. 'I've had a hard time with him, but I must admit he's a wonderful person.'

* From Krylov's fable *The Peasant and the Workman* (1815).

Both Tatyana and Barbara couldn't help indulging in a little cruelty, telling Podgorin reproachfully, 'Your generation, though, Misha, isn't up to much!'

'What's all this talk about generations?' Podgorin wondered. 'Surely Losev's no more than six years older than me?'

'Life's not easy,' Barbara sighed. 'You're always threatened with losses of some kind. First they want to take your estate away from you, or someone near and dear falls ill and you're afraid he might die. And so it goes on, day after day. But what can one do, my friends? We must submit to a Higher Power without complaining, we must remember that nothing in this world is accidental, everything has its final purpose. Now you, Misha, know little of life, you haven't suffered much and you'll laugh at me. Go ahead and laugh, but I'm going to tell you what I think. When I was passing through a stage of deepest anxiety I experienced second sight on several occasions and this completely transformed my outlook. Now I know that nothing is contingent, everything that happens in life is necessary.'

How different this Barbara was, grey-haired now, and corseted, with her fashionable long-sleeved dress – this Barbara twisting a cigarette between long, thin, trembling fingers – this Barbara so prone to mysticism – this Barbara with such a lifeless, monotonous voice. How different she was from Barbara the medical student, that cheerful, boisterous, adventurous girl with the red hair!

'Where has it all vanished to?' Podgorin wondered, bored with listening to her. 'Sing us a song, Ba,' he asked to put a stop to that conversation about second sight. 'You used to have a lovely voice.'

'That's all long ago, Misha.'

'Well, recite some more Nekrasov.'

'I've forgotten it all. Those lines I recited just now I happened to remember.'

Despite the corset and long sleeves she was obviously short of money and had difficulty making ends meet at that factory beyond Tula. It was obvious she'd been overworking. That heavy, monotonous work, that perpetual interfering with other people's business and worrying about them – all this had taken its toll and had aged her. As he looked at that sad face whose freshness had faded, Podgorin concluded that in reality it was *she* who needed help, not Kuzminki or that Sergey Losev she was fussing about so much.

Higher education, being a doctor, didn't seem to have had any effect on the woman in her. Just like Tatyana, she loved weddings, births, christenings, interminable conversations about children. She loved spine-chilling stories with happy endings. In newspapers she only read articles about fires, floods and important ceremonies. She longed for Podgorin to propose to Nadezhda – she would have shed tears of emotion if that were to happen.

He didn't know whether it was by chance or Barbara's doing, but Podgorin found himself alone with Nadezhda. However, the mere suspicion that he was being watched, that they wanted something from him, disturbed and inhibited him. In Nadezhda's company he felt as if they had both been put in a cage together.

'Let's go into the garden,' she said.

They went out – he feeling discontented and annoyed that he didn't know what to say, she overjoyed, proud to be near him, and obviously delighted that he was going to spend another three days with them. And perhaps she was filled with sweet fancies and hopes. He didn't know if she loved him, but he did know that she had grown used to him, that she had long been attached to him, that she considered him her teacher, that she was now experiencing the same kind of feelings as her sister Tatyana once had: all she could think of was love, of marrying as soon as possible and having a husband, children, her own place. She had still preserved that readiness for friendship which is usually so strong in children and it was highly probable that she felt for Podgorin and respected him as a friend and that she wasn't in love with *him*, but with her dreams of a husband and children.

'It's getting dark,' he said.

'Yes, the moon rises late now.'

They kept to the same path, near the house. Podgorin didn't want to go deep into the garden – it was dark there and he would have to take Nadezhda by the arm and stay very close to her. Shadows were moving on the terrace and he felt that Tatyana and Barbara were watching him.

'I must ask your advice,' Nadezhda said, stopping. 'If Kuzminki is sold, Sergey will leave and get a job and there's no doubt that our lives will be completely changed. I shan't go with my sister, we'll part, because I don't want to be a burden on her family. I'll take a job somewhere in Moscow, I'll earn some money and help Tatyana and her husband. You *will* give me some advice, won't you?'

Quite unaccustomed to any kind of hard work, now she was inspired at the thought of an independent, working life and making plans for the future – this was written all over her face. A life where she would be working and helping others struck her as so beautifully poetic. When he saw that pale face and dark eyebrows so close he remembered what an intelligent, keen pupil she had been, with such fine qualities, a joy to teach. Now she probably wasn't simply a young lady in search of a husband, but an intelligent, decent girl, gentle and soft-hearted, who could be moulded like wax into anything one wished. In the right surroundings she might become a truly wonderful woman!

'Well, why *don't* I marry her then?' Podgorin thought. But he immediately took fright at this idea and went off towards the house. Tatyana was sitting at the grand piano in the drawing-room and her playing conjured up bright pictures of the past, when people had played, sung and danced in that room until late at night, with the windows open and birds singing too in the garden and beyond the river. Podgorin cheered up, became playful, danced with Nadezhda and Barbara, and then sang. He was hampered by a corn on one foot and asked if he could wear Sergey's slippers. Strangely, he felt at home, like one of the family, and the thought 'a typical brother-in-law' flashed through his mind. His spirits rose even higher. Looking at him the others livened up and grew cheerful, as if they had recaptured their youth. Everyone's face was radiant with hope: Kuzminki was saved! It was all so very simple in fact. They only had to think of a plan, rummage around in law books, or see that Podgorin married Nadezhda. And that little romance was going well, by all appearances. Pink, happy, her eyes brimming with tears in anticipation of something quite out of the ordinary, Nadezhda whirled round in the dance and her white dress billowed, revealing her small pretty legs in flesh-coloured stockings. Absolutely delighted, Barbara took Podgorin's arm and told him quietly and meaningly, 'Misha, don't run away from happiness. Grasp it while you can. If you wait too long you'll be running when it's too late to catch it.'

Podgorin wanted to make promises, to reassure her and even he began to believe that Kuzminki was saved – it was really so easy.

' "And thou shalt be que–een of the world",'* he sang, striking a pose. But suddenly he was conscious that there was nothing he could do for these people, absolutely nothing, and he stopped singing and looked guilty.

Then he sat silently in one corner, legs tucked under him, wearing slippers belonging to someone else.

As they watched him the others understood that nothing could be done and they too fell silent. The piano was closed. Everyone noticed that it was late – it was time for bed – and Tatyana put out the large lamp in the drawing-room.

A bed was made up for Podgorin in the same little outhouse where he had stayed in the past. Sergey went with him to wish him goodnight, holding a candle high above his head, although the moon had risen and it was bright. They walked down a path with lilac bushes on either side and the gravel crunched underfoot.

> 'Before he had time to groan
> A bear came and knocked him prone,'

Sergey said.

Podgorin felt that he'd heard those lines a thousand times, he was sick and tired of them! When they reached the outhouse, Sergey drew a bottle and two glasses from his loose jacket and put them on the table.

'Brandy,' he said. 'It's a Double-O. It's impossible to have a drink in the house with Barbara around. She'd be on to me about alcoholism. But we can feel free here. It's a fine brandy.'

They sat down. The brandy was very good.

'Let's have a really good drink tonight,' Sergey continued,

* From Lermontov's narrative poem *The Demon*.

nibbling a lemon. 'I've always been a gay dog myself and I like having a fling now and again. That's a *must*!'

But the look in his eyes still showed that he needed something from Podgorin and was about to ask for it.

'Drink up, old man,' he went on, sighing. 'Things are really grim at the moment. Old eccentrics like me have had their day, we're finished. Idealism's not fashionable these days. It's money that rules and if you don't want to get shoved aside you must go down on your knees and worship filthy lucre. But I can't do that, it's absolutely sickening!'

'When's the auction?' asked Podgorin, to change the subject.

'August 7th. But there's no hope at all, old man, of saving Kuzminki. There's enormous arrears and the estate doesn't bring in any income, only losses every year. It's not worth the battle. Tatyana's very cut up about it, as it's her patrimony of course. But I must admit I'm rather glad. I'm no country man. My sphere is the large, noisy city, my element's the fray!'

He kept on and on, still beating about the bush and he watched Podgorin with an eagle eye, as if waiting for the right moment.

Suddenly Podgorin saw those eyes close to him and felt his breath on his face.

'My dear fellow, please save me,' Sergey gasped. '*Please* lend me two hundred roubles!'

Podgorin wanted to say that he was hard up too and he felt that he might do better giving two hundred roubles to some poor devil or simply losing them at cards. But he was terribly embarrassed – he felt trapped in that small room with one candle and wanted to escape as soon as possible from that breathing, from those soft arms that grasped him around the waist and which already seemed to have stuck to him like glue. Hurriedly he started feeling in his pockets for his note-case where he kept money.

'Here you are,' he muttered, taking out a hundred roubles. 'I'll give you the rest later. That's all I have on me. You see, I can't refuse.' Feeling very annoyed and beginning to lose his temper he went on, 'I'm really far too soft. Only please let me have the money back later. I'm hard up too.'

'Thank you. I'm so grateful, dear chap.'

'And please stop imagining that you're an idealist. You're as much an idealist as I'm a turkey-cock. You're simply a frivolous, indolent man, that's all.'

Sergey sighed deeply and sat on the couch.

'My dear chap, you *are* angry,' he said. 'But if you only knew how hard things are for me! I'm going through a terrible time now. I swear it's not myself I feel sorry for, oh no! It's the wife and children. If it wasn't for my wife and children I'd have done myself in ages ago.' Suddenly his head and shoulders started shaking and he burst out sobbing.

'This really is the limit!' Podgorin said, pacing the room excitedly and feeling really furious. 'Now, what can I do with someone who has caused a great deal of harm and then starts sobbing? These tears disarm me, I'm speechless. You're sobbing, so that means you must be right.'

'Caused a great deal of harm?' Sergey asked, rising to his feet and looking at Podgorin in amazement. 'My dear chap, what are you saying? Caused a great deal of harm? Oh, how little you know me. How little you understand me!'

'All right then, so I don't understand you, but please stop whining. It's revolting!'

'Oh, how little you know me!' Losev repeated, quite sincerely. 'How little!'

'Just take a look at yourself in the mirror,' Podgorin went on. 'You're no longer a young man. Soon you'll be old. It's time you stopped to think a bit and took stock of who and what you are. Spending your whole life doing nothing at all, forever indulging in empty, childish chatter, this play-acting and affectation. Doesn't it make your head go round – aren't you sick and tired of it all? Oh, it's hard going with you! You're a stupefying old bore, you are!'

With these words Podgorin left the outhouse and slammed the door. It was about the first time in his life that he had been sincere and really spoken his mind.

Shortly afterwards he was regretting having been so harsh. What was the point of talking seriously or arguing with a man who was perpetually lying, who ate and drank too much, who spent large amounts of other people's money while being quite convinced that he was an idealist and a martyr? This was a case of stupidity, or of deep-rooted bad habits that had eaten away at his organism like an illness past all cure. In any event, indignation and stern rebukes were useless in this case. Laughing at him would be more effective. One good sneer would have achieved much more than a dozen sermons!

'It's best just ignoring him,' Podgorin thought. 'Above all, not to lend him money.'

Soon afterwards he wasn't thinking about Sergey, or about his hundred roubles. It was a calm, brooding night, very bright. Whenever Podgorin looked up at the sky on moonlit nights he had the feeling that only he and the moon were awake — everything else was either sleeping or drowsing. He gave no more thought to people or money and his mood gradually became calm and peaceful. He felt alone in this world and the sound of his own footsteps in the silence of the night seemed so mournful.

The garden was enclosed by a white stone wall. In the right-hand corner, facing the fields, stood a tower that had been built long ago, in the days of serfdom. Its lower section was of stone; the top was wooden, with a platform, a conical roof and a tall spire with a black weathercock. Down below were two gates leading straight from the garden into the fields and a staircase that creaked underfoot led up to the platform. Under the staircase some old broken armchairs had been dumped and they were bathed in the moonlight as it filtered through the gate. With their crooked upturned legs these armchairs seemed to have come to life at night and were lying in wait for someone here in the silence.

Podgorin climbed the stairs to the platform and sat down. Just beyond the fence were a boundary ditch and bank and further off were the broad fields flooded in moonlight. Podgorin knew that there was a wood exactly opposite, about two miles from the estate, and he thought that he could distinguish a dark strip in the distance. Quails and corncrakes were calling. Now and then, from the direction of the wood, came the cry of a cuckoo which couldn't sleep either.

He heard footsteps. Someone was coming across the garden towards the tower.

A dog barked.

'Beetle!' a woman's voice softly called. 'Come back, Beetle!'

He could hear someone entering the tower down below and a moment later a black dog – an old friend of Podgorin's – appeared on the bank. It stopped, looked up towards where Podgorin was sitting and wagged its tail amicably. Soon afterwards a white figure rose from the black ditch like a ghost and stopped on the bank as well. It was Nadezhda.

'Can you see something there?' she asked the dog, glancing upwards.

She didn't see Podgorin but probably sensed that he was near, since she was smiling and her pale, moonlit face was happy. The tower's black shadow stretching over the earth, far into the fields, that motionless white figure with the blissfully smiling, pale face, the black dog and both their shadows – all this was just like a dream.

'Someone *is* there,' Nadezhda said softly.

She stood waiting for him to come down or to call her up to him, so that he could at last declare his love – then both would be happy on that calm, beautiful night. White, pale, slender, very lovely in the moonlight, she awaited his caresses. She was weary of perpetually dreaming of love and happiness and was unable to conceal her feelings any longer. Her whole figure, her radiant eyes, her fixed happy smile, betrayed her innermost thoughts. But he felt awkward, shrank back and didn't make a sound, not knowing whether to speak, whether to make the habitual joke out of the situation or whether to remain silent. He felt annoyed and his only thought was that here, in a country garden on a moonlit night, close to a beautiful, loving, thoughtful girl, he felt the same apathy as on Little Bronny Street: evidently this type of romantic situation had lost its fascination, like *that* prosaic depravity. Of no consequence to him now were those meetings on moonlit nights, those white shapes with slim waists, those mysterious shadows, towers, country estates and characters such as Sergey Losev, and people like himself, Podgorin, with his icy indifference, his constant irritability, his inability to adapt to reality and take what it had to offer, his wearisome, obsessive craving for what did not and never could exist on earth. And now, as he sat in that tower, he would have preferred a good fireworks display, or some moonlight procession, or Barbara reciting Nekrasov's *The Railway* again. He would rather another woman was standing there on the bank where Nadezhda was: this other woman would have told him something absolutely fascinating and new that had nothing to do with love or happiness. And if she did happen to speak of love, this would have been a summons to those new, lofty, rational aspects of existence on whose threshold we are perhaps already living and of which we sometimes seem to have premonitions.

'There's no one there,' Nadezhda said.

She stood there for another minute or so, then she walked quietly towards the wood, her head bowed. The dog ran on ahead. Podgorin could see her white figure for quite a long time. 'To think how it's all turned out, though . . .' he repeated to himself as he went back to the outhouse.

He had no idea what he could say to Sergey or Tatyana the next day or the day after that, or how he would treat Nadezhda. And he felt embarrassed, frightened and bored in advance. How was he going to fill those three long days which he had promised to spend here? He remembered the conversation about second sight and Sergey quoting the lines:

> 'Before he had time to groan
> A bear came and knocked him prone.'

He remembered that tomorrow, to please Tatyana, he would have to smile at those well-fed, chubby little girls – and he decided to leave.

At half past five in the morning Sergey appeared on the terrace of the main house in his Bokhara dressing-gown and tasselled fez. Not losing a moment, Podgorin went over to him to say goodbye.

'I have to be in Moscow by ten,' he said, looking away. 'I'd completely forgotten I'm expected at the Notary Public's office. Please excuse me. When the others are up please tell them that I apologize. I'm dreadfully sorry.'

In his hurry he didn't hear Sergey's answer and he kept looking round at the windows of the big house, afraid that the ladies might wake up and stop him going. He was ashamed he felt so nervous. He sensed that this was his last visit to Kuzminki, that he would never come back. As he drove away he glanced back several times at the outhouse where once he had spent so many happy days. But deep down he felt coldly indifferent, not at all sad.

At home the first thing he saw on the table was the note he'd received the day before: 'Dear Misha,' he read. 'You've completely forgotten us, please come and visit us soon.' And for some reason he remembered Nadezhda whirling round in the dance, her dress billowing, revealing her legs in their flesh-coloured stockings . . .

Ten minutes later he was at his desk working – and he didn't give Kuzminki another thought.

The Bet

ৡৢ

It was a dark autumn night and an elderly banker was pacing his study, reminiscing about a party he had given one autumn fifteen years ago. Many clever people had come and there had been a most interesting conversation, capital punishment being one of the topics they had discussed, among others. The great majority of the guests, who included many scholars and journalists, had been against it: in their view this form of punishment was outmoded, immoral and unfit for Christian states. Some thought that the death penalty should be replaced everywhere by life imprisonment.

'I don't agree,' the banker had told his guests. 'I've never tasted capital punishment or life imprisonment myself. But if I may offer an *a priori* judgement, I think that capital punishment is more moral and humane than imprisonment. Executions kill you right away, whereas life imprisonment does it slowly. Which kind of executioner is more humane? One who takes just a few minutes to kill you, or one who drags the life out of you during the course of many years?'

'Both are equally immoral,' remarked one of the guests. 'Both have the same purpose – to take life. The State isn't God. It has no right to take away what it can't give back, if it so chooses.'

Among the guests was a young lawyer of about twenty-five. When his opinion was asked he said, 'The death penalty and life imprisonment are equally immoral. But if I had to choose between execution or being locked away for life, I'd opt for the second, without any doubt. Any sort of life's better than none at all.'

A lively argument had broken out then. The banker, who was younger and more excitable in those days, suddenly lost his temper, banged his fist on the table and shouted at the young lawyer, 'That's not true! I bet you two million that you wouldn't even last five years in a cell on your own.'

'If you mean that seriously,' the lawyer replied, 'then I bet you I could stay locked up for fifteen years, not five.'

'Fifteen? Done!' shouted the banker. 'Gentlemen, I stake two million on it!'

'I accept! You're staking millions, I'm staking my freedom!' the lawyer said.

And so that preposterous, senseless bet was made. The banker, a spoilt, frivolous man at the time, who had more millions than he could count, was overjoyed at the bet. Over supper he made fun of the lawyer. 'Come to your senses, young man, before it's too late,' he said. 'Two million is chicken-feed to me, but you risk losing three or four of the best years of your life. I say three or four, because you won't last longer. And don't you forget, poor man, that voluntary confinement is much harder than compulsory incarceration. The thought that you could regain your freedom any minute will poison your whole existence in prison. I feel sorry for you!'

As the banker paced the room he now remembered all this.

'What was the point of that bet?' he wondered. 'What was the use of that lawyer losing fifteen years of his life or my throwing away two million? How could that prove that the death penalty is any better or worse than life imprisonment? Definitely not! Stuff and nonsense! On my part it was the whim of someone with too much money, on the lawyer's it was sheer greed.'

A little later he remembered the events following that evening. They had decided that the lawyer must serve his time under the strictest surveillance in one of the lodges in the banker's garden. The conditions were: for fifteen years he was not to be allowed to cross the threshold, to see a living soul or hear a human voice, to receive newspapers or letters. He was allowed a musical instrument and books to read, and to write letters, drink wine and smoke. His only communication with the outside world, they stipulated, was to be through a small, specially built window and he wasn't allowed to speak one word. Books, music, wine and so on – he could have anything he needed and as much as he liked, but only via the window and by writing little notes. To ensure his confinement was strictly solitary, the agreement covered every minute point of detail and compelled the lawyer to serve a term of *exactly* fifteen years, from twelve o'clock on 14 November 1870 until twelve o'clock on 14 November 1885. The least attempt to violate these conditions, even two minutes before the time was up, freed the banker from any obligation to pay the two million.

During the first year of his confinement the lawyer suffered dreadfully from loneliness and boredom – as far as one could judge from his brief notes. Day and night the sound of the piano came from the lodge. He refused wine and tobacco: wine, he wrote, stimulates desire and desire was a prisoner's worst enemy. Moreover, nothing was more depressing than drinking good wine on one's own. And tobacco polluted the air in his room. For the first year the lawyer mainly had light books sent in – novels with complicated love plots, crime fiction, fantastic tales, comedies and so on.

In the second year music no longer came from the lodge and the lawyer wrote and asked for the classics only. In the fifth year music was heard again and the prisoner asked for wine. People watching him through the window said that throughout that year he did nothing but eat, drink and lie on his bed, often yawning and talking angrily to himself. He didn't read any books. Some nights he would sit up writing and would keep at it for ages. But towards the morning he'd tear everything he'd written to shreds. More than once they heard him weeping.

In the second half of the sixth year the prisoner devoted himself with great zeal to the study of languages, philosophy and history. He applied himself so eagerly to these subjects that the banker was hard put keeping him supplied with books: in the course of four years nearly six hundred volumes had been obtained at his request. During this craze the banker happened to receive the following letter from his captive:

My dear Gaoler!

I'm writing these lines in six languages. Show them to the experts. Let them read them. If they don't find any mistakes I beg you to have a shot fired in the garden – that will prove to me that my efforts haven't been in

vain. Geniuses of all centuries and countries speak different languages,
but the same flame burns in all of them. If only you knew the heavenly
bliss I feel in my heart now that I can understand them!

The prisoner's wish was carried out – the banker ordered two
shots to be fired in the garden.

After the tenth year the lawyer sat motionless at his table,
reading nothing except the Gospels. The banker thought it
strange that someone who had mastered six hundred abstruse
tomes in four years should spend nearly a year reading one slim,
easily comprehensible volume. Then the Gospels were followed
by the history of religion and theology.

During the last two years of his incarceration the prisoner read
a vast amount, quite indiscriminately. First he read natural
science, then he asked for Byron or for Shakespeare. In some of
his notes he asked for books on chemistry, medical textbooks, a
novel and a philosophical or theological treatise – wanting them
all at the same time. His reading put one in mind of someone
swimming in the sea amidst the wreckage of his ship, eagerly
clutching at one piece of wood after the other to save his life.

II

As he recalled all this the old banker reflected, 'Tomorrow at
twelve he goes free. And I have to pay him two million, according
to the agreement. But if I pay up, I'm finished, I'll be absolutely
ruined.'

Fifteen years ago he had more millions than he could count,
but now he was afraid to ask which was the greater, his assets
or his debts. Gambling on the stock-exchange and very risky
speculation, combined with an impulsiveness that he had never
managed to control despite his advanced years, had gradually
brought a decline in his fortunes and that fearless, self-confident,
proud man of wealth was now just a small-time financier, trembling at every rise or fall in his assets.

'That damned bet!' the old man muttered, clutching his head.
'Why couldn't the man die? He's only just forty. He'll take my
last copeck, he'll marry, he'll enjoy life, he'll play the stock

market, while I jealously watch him like a beggar. Every day I'll hear him say the same thing. "I owe all my happiness to you, please let me help you." No, it's too much! My only salvation from bankruptcy and disgrace is that man's death!'

Three o'clock struck. The banker cocked an ear. The whole household was sleeping – the only sound was the rustling of the frozen trees outside. Trying not to make any noise, he took from a fireproof safe the key to the door that had been unopened for fifteen years, put on his coat and went out.

It was dark and cold outside and it was raining. A sharp, damp wind swept howling around the whole garden and gave the trees no peace. The banker strained his eyes but couldn't see the ground, the white statues, the lodge or the trees. As he approached the spot where the lodge stood he called out twice to his watchman. There was no reply – he was obviously sheltering from the weather and sleeping somewhere in the kitchen, or in the greenhouse.

'If I have the courage to carry out my intention,' thought the old man, 'then the first to be suspected will be the watchman.'

By groping about in the dark he found the dark steps and door, and entered the hall. Then he felt his way into a small passage and lit a match. No one was there – only some sort of bed without any bedding and the dark shape of a cast-iron stove in the corner. The seals on the door leading to the prisoner's room were intact.

When the match went out the old man, trembling with excitement, peered through the small window.

In the prisoner's room a candle burned dimly. The prisoner was sitting at the table. Only his back, the hair on his head and hands were visible. On the table, on two armchairs and on the rug near the table, lay open books.

Five minutes passed without the captive moving once. Fifteen years of confinement had taught him to sit still. The banker tapped on the window with one finger, but the prisoner made no movement in response. Then the banker carefully broke the seals on the doors and put the key in the key-hole. The rusty lock grated and the door creaked. The banker was expecting an immediate shout of surprise and footsteps, but three minutes went by and it was still absolutely quiet on the other side. He decided to go in.

A man quite unlike any normal human being was sitting motionless at the table. He was all skin and bones, with the long curly hair of a woman and a shaggy beard. His complexion was yellow, with an earthy tinge, his cheeks were hollow, his back long and narrow, and the hand with which he propped his bushy head was so thin and wasted it was painful to look at. His hair was already touched with grey and no one looking at that gaunt, senile face would have believed that he was only forty. He was sleeping . . . A sheet of paper with something written on it in small letters lay on the table in front of his bowed head.

'Poor man!' thought the banker. 'He's asleep and probably dreaming of those millions! All I have to do is take hold of this semi-corpse, throw it on the bed, just smother it gently with a pillow and the most meticulous examination won't find a trace of death by violence. However, let's first read what he's written . . .'

The banker picked up the sheet of paper and read the following:

Tomorrow at twelve o'clock I regain my freedom and the right to mix with people again. But before I leave this room and see the sun again there's some things I feel I should tell you. With a clear conscience, and with God as my witness, I declare that I despise freedom, life, health and everything that those books of yours call the blessings of this world.

I have spent fifteen years making a careful study of life on earth. True, I haven't *seen* anything of the earth, of people, but in your books I have drunk fragrant wine, sung songs, hunted deer and wild boar in forests, loved women . . . Beautiful creatures as ethereal as clouds created by the magic of your great poets have visited me at night and whispered marvellous tales in my ear, making my head reel. In your books I have scaled the summits of Elbruz and Mont Blanc and from them I have seen the sun rising in the morning, flooding the sky, ocean and mountain peaks with crimson gold in the evening. From there I have seen the lightning flash above me and cleave the clouds. I have seen green forests, fields, rivers, lakes, towns. I have heard the sirens sing and the music of shepherds' pipes. I have touched the wings of beautiful demons who flew down to talk to me about God. In your books I have hurled myself into bottomless abysses, wrought miracles, murdered, burnt cities, preached new religions, conquered entire kingdoms.

Your books have given me wisdom. Everything that man's indefatigable mind has created over the centuries is compressed into a tiny lump inside my skull. I know that I'm cleverer than the lot of you.

And I despise your books. I despise all the blessings of this world, all its wisdom. Everything is worthless, transient, illusory and as deceptive as a mirage. You may be proud, wise and handsome, but death will wipe you from the face of the earth, together with the mice under the floorboards. And your posterity, your history, your immortal geniuses will freeze or be reduced to ashes, along with the terrestrial globe. You've lost all reason and are on the wrong path. You mistake lies for the truth and ugliness for beauty. You'd be surprised if apple and orange trees suddenly started producing frogs and lizards instead of fruit, or if roses smelt of sweaty horses. I'm amazed at you people who have exchanged heaven for earth. I just don't *want* to understand you.

To show in actual practice how much I despise what you live by, I renounce the two million I once dreamed of, as though of paradise, but for which I feel only contempt now. To forfeit my right to them I shall leave this place five hours before the stipulated time and thus break the agreement . . .

After reading this the banker laid the piece of paper on the table, kissed the strange man's head and left the lodge weeping. At no other time, not even after heavy losses on the stock-exchange, had he ever felt such contempt for himself as now. Back in his house he went to bed, but he was kept awake for a long time by excitement and tears.

Next morning some white-faced watchmen came running to inform him that they had seen the man from the lodge climb through his window into the garden, make for the gate and disappear. The banker went to the lodge with his servants to make certain that the prisoner had in fact fled. To put paid to any unnecessary disputes later on he picked up the sheet with the renunciation from the table, returned to the house and locked it in his fireproof safe.

New Villa

ᘏᘏ

I

About two miles from the village of Obruchanovo a huge bridge was being constructed. Its steel skeleton could be seen from the village, which stood high on a steep bank. In misty weather and on calm winter days, when its thin iron trusses and surrounding scaffolding were covered in hoar frost, it made a picturesque, even fantastic sight. Kucherov, the engineer who was building the bridge (he was a stout, broad-shouldered, bearded man with a soft crumpled cap), would sometimes drive through the village in a racing drozhky or carriage. Now and then, when they had the day off, the navvies working on the bridge would turn up, beg for money, laugh at the village women and sometimes make off with something. But that happened rarely. Usually the days passed quietly and peacefully, as if no construction was taking place at all. Only in the evenings, when bonfires brightly burned near the bridge, were the sounds of the navvies' songs borne faintly on the wind. During the day a mournful, metallic, ringing sound could sometimes be heard.

One day Mrs Kucherov, the engineer's wife, drove out to see him. She took a fancy to the river banks and the splendid view over the green valley with its hamlets, churches and cattle, and she asked her husband to buy a small plot of land and build a villa on it. The husband did as he was asked. They bought fifty acres and, in a field high up on the bank where cows from the village had once wandered, they built a fine two-storey house with terrace, balconies, and a tower with a spire from which they flew a flag on Sundays. After taking about three months to complete it, they kept planting large trees throughout the winter. When spring came and all around was green, paths had already been laid in the new garden. A gardener with two assistants in white aprons dug near the house, a fountain flowed and a plate-glass globe gleamed so brightly that it hurt the eyes. And the estate already had a name: New Villa.

One bright, warm morning at the end of May, two horses were brought to Obruchanovo to be shod by Rodion Petrov, the local blacksmith. They were from New Villa, white as snow, grace-ful, well-fed and strikingly alike.

'Just like swans,' Rodion said, surveying them in awe.

His wife Stepanida, his children and grandchildren came out into the street to have a look. Gradually a crowd gathered. The Lychkovs, father and son, both naturally beardless, with bloated faces and without any caps, turned up. So did Kozov, a tall, skinny old man with a long, narrow beard and a walking-stick. He kept winking his cunning eyes and smiling supercilious, knowing smiles.

'So, they're white, that's all you can say about them,' he said. 'If mine had oats to eat they'd be just as sleek. They should be put to the plough . . . and whipped too.'

The coachman merely looked at him contemptuously and said nothing. While the smithy fire was being made up the coachman told them some news and smoked cigarettes. The peasants learned many details from him: his master and mistress were rich; the mistress, Yelena Kucherov, had lived poorly as a governess in Moscow before marrying and she was kind, warm-hearted and loved helping the poor. There wouldn't be any ploughing or sowing on the new estate, he said: they just wanted to enjoy life and breathe fresh air. When he had finished and was taking the horses back home, a crowd of urchins followed him. Dogs barked and Kozov winked sarcastically as he watched him go.

'Proper lords of the manor!' he said. 'They've gone and built a house, they own horses, but they probably can't make ends meet. Think they're God almighty, do they?'

Right from the start Kozov had somehow conceived a hatred for the new estate, the white horses and that well-fed, handsome coachman. He was a lonely man, a widower. He led a dull life – some ailment he called 'rumpture' or 'the worms' prevented him from working. He lived on the money sent by his son who worked for a Kharkhov confectioner and from dawn to dusk would idly wander along the river bank or through the village. If he saw some peasant carting a hefty log for instance, or fishing, he would remark, 'That wood's dead, rotten,' or 'The fish won't bite in weather like this.' During droughts he'd say that it wouldn't rain until the frosts came. And when it did rain he'd say that all the crops would rot, everything was ruined. And he would accompany these observations with that knowing wink of his.

In the evenings Bengal lights and rockets were set off on the estate and a boat with red lanterns would sail past Obruchanovo. One morning Yelena Kucherov, the engineer's wife, drove into the village with her little daughter in a yellow-wheeled trap drawn by a pair of dark bay ponies. Both mother and daughter wore broad-brimmed straw hats turned down over the ears.

It happened to be manuring time, and Rodion the blacksmith – a tall, skinny, capless, barefoot old man with a pitchfork over his shoulder – was standing near his dirty, ugly cart, gazing dumbfounded at the ponies. His face showed that he had never seen such small horses before.

'It's that Mrs Kucherov with 'er pony and trap,' came the whisper from all around. 'Just look at the fine lady!'

Yelena Kucherov looked at the huts inquiringly, then brought the ponies outside the poorest one, where a host of children's heads – fair, dark or red – appeared at the windows. Rodion's wife Stepanida – a plump old woman – came running out of the hut and her kerchief fell from her grey hair. She looked at the trap against the sun, frowning as if she were blind.

'That's for the children,' Yelena said, handing her three roubles.

Stepanida suddenly burst into tears and bowed down to the ground. Rodion also sank down, displaying his broad brown skull and almost catching his wife in the side with his pitchfork in the process. Yelena Kucherov felt awkward and drove back home.

II

The Lychkovs, father and son, found two cart-horses, one pony and a broad-muzzled Aalhaus steer straying in their meadow and drove them off to the village, assisted by red-haired Volodka, Rodion the blacksmith's son. They summoned the village elder, rounded up witnesses and went to inspect the damage.

'Let 'em try!' Kozov said, winking. 'Just let 'em try! Let's see them engineers get out of this! Do they think the law don't concern 'em? All right, we'll send for the constable and make out a charge.'

'Make out a charge,' repeated Volodka.

'I won't forget this,' Lychkov senior shouted, louder and louder, so that his puffy face swelled even more. 'Whatever will they think of next? Give 'em half the chance and they'll let their cattle trample all over our meadows. They've no right to harm us ordernary folk. People don't own no serfs no more!'

'People don't own no serfs no more!' echoed Volodka.

'We made do without a bridge before,' Lychkov senior said morosely. 'They didn't come and ask if we needed one and we don't want one!'

'Yes lads! We're not going to take this lying down!'

'Let 'em try,' Kozov winked. 'Let 'em try and get out of this! Think they're God almighty!'

They turned back towards the village and on the way Lychkov's son kept beating his chest with his fist and shouting, while Volodka shouted too, repeating everything he said. Meanwhile a large crowd had gathered in the village round the pedigree steer and horses. The steer was confused and looked sullen, but then it suddenly dropped its head to the ground and tore off, kicking up its hind legs. Kozov was frightened and waved his stick at it, making everyone laugh. After that they locked the animals up and waited.

That evening the engineer sent five roubles to pay for the damage and both horses, the pony and the steer returned home unfed and unwatered, their heads bowed guiltily, like prisoners being led to execution.

After receiving the five roubles, the Lychkovs, father and son, the village elder and Volodka crossed the river by boat and when they were on the other side made for the village of Kryakovo, where there was a pub. They spent a long time making merry there. Their singing and young Lychkov's shouting could be heard and the women in the village were so worried they didn't sleep the whole night. Rodion couldn't sleep either.

'It's a nasty business,' he said, tossing from side to side and sighing. 'If the squire gets mad about it he'll have 'em up in court, he will. They've gone and done him an injury, they have. Oh, it's a nasty business.'

One day the peasants, Rodion among their number, went into their wood to settle who should reap which portion of land and on their way back they met the engineer. He was wearing a red calico shirt and high boots. A setter with its long tongue sticking out followed him.

'Hallo, lads!' he said.

The men stopped and doffed their caps.

'I've been wanting to have a talk with you lads for some time,' he continued. 'The thing is this. Every day since early spring your cattle have been coming into my garden and woods. Everything's trampled on, your pigs have dug up the meadow, they're wrecking the kitchen garden and all the saplings in my woods are ruined. I can't hit it off with your shepherds – ask them something and they jump down your throat. Every day your cattle trespass on my land, but I take no notice and don't make you pay fines. I don't complain. And on top of all this, you went and confiscated my horses and steer and then took five roubles off me. Is that nice, is that being good neighbours?' he continued. His voice was soft and earnest and he didn't look very stern. 'Is that how honest men carry on? A week ago one of you chopped down two young oak trees in my wood. You've dug up the road to Yeresnevo and now I have to make a two-mile detour. Why are you always trying to do rotten things to me? Have I ever been nasty to you, for God's sake? The wife and I are doing our utmost to live in peace and harmony with you and we help the people in the village as much as we can. My wife is a kind, warm-hearted woman, she doesn't refuse you any help, all she wants is to be useful to you and your children. But you repay good with evil. You're unfair, my friends. Think about it, I beg you. Please think it over. We're treating you like human beings, so please repay us in the same coin.'

He turned and walked away. The peasants stood there a little longer, put their caps on and moved off. Rodion, who always got the wrong end of the stick and interpreted things his own way said, 'We've got to pay up, lads. 'E says we have to pay *in coin* . . .'

Silently they walked to the village. Back home Rodion said his prayers, took off his boots and sat next to his wife on the bench. He and Stepanida always sat side by side at home and they always walked down the street side by side. They always ate and drank and slept together, and the older they became the stronger grew their love. It was cramped and hot in their hut and everywhere there were children – on the floor, window-ledges and stove.

Despite her advanced years Stepanida was still having children and it was hard to tell which of that bunch were Rodion's and which Volodka's. Volodka's wife Lukerya, an unattractive young woman with bulging eyes and a bird-like nose, was kneading dough in a tub. Volodka was sitting on the stove, his legs dangling.

'On the road, not far from Nikita's buckwheat . . . hm . . . that engineer and that dog of his . . .' Rodion began after a little rest, scratching his sides and elbows, ''e said we got to pay . . . In coin he said. I'm not sure about coins, but we should collect ten copecks from each hut. We're being very nasty to the squire, that we are. I feel right sorry . . .'

'We've made do without a bridge till now,' Volodka said, not looking at anyone. 'And we don't want one now.'

'What are you on about? It's a government bridge.'

'We don't want it.'

'And who's asking *you*? What's it got to do with you?'

'"Who's asking *you*?"' mimicked Volodka. 'We don't have nowhere to go, so what do we want a bridge for? If need be we can cross by boat.'

Someone banged on the window from outside so hard that the whole hut seemed to shake.

'Is Volodka home?' came Lychkov junior's voice. 'Volodka, come out, we're leaving now.'

Volodka leapt down from the stove and started looking for his cap.

'Don't go, Volodka,' Rodion said timidly. 'Don't go with them, son. You're so stupid, a real baby. They won't teach you anything good. So don't go!'

'Don't go, son!' begged Stepanida, blinking and on the verge of tears. 'Most likely they'll take you to the pub.'

'"To the pub",' mimicked Volodka.

'You'll come back drunk again, you filthy dog,' Lukerya said, looking at him furiously. 'Go then, go! I hope the vodka burns you up inside, you tailless devil!'

'And you shut yer face!' Volodka yelled.

'It's an idiot I'm married to. I'm ruined. I'm just a wretched orphan! Oh, you red-haired boozer!' Lukerya wailed, wiping her face with a dough-covered hand. 'I wish I'd never set eyes on you!'

Volodka hit her on the ear and went out.

III

Yelena Kucherov and her little daughter walked into the village – they were out for a stroll. It happened to be a Sunday and the women and girls were walking about in their bright dresses. Rodion and Stepanida, sitting side by side in their porch, bowed and smiled to Yelena and her little girl as if they were old friends. More than a dozen children were peering out of the windows at them, their faces displaying bewilderment and curiosity. Whispering could be heard.

'It's that Mrs Kucherov! Mrs Kucherov!'

'Good morning,' Yelena said, stopping. After a brief silence she asked, 'Well then, how are you?'

'Not too bad, thank God,' Rodion answered rapidly. 'We get by, of course.'

'It's a dreadful life we lead!' laughed Stepanida. 'You can see how poor we are, dear. There's fourteen in the family, but only two bring home money. We're just blacksmiths. People bring horses for shoeing, but we've no coal – got no money for it. It's a wretched life, lady,' she continued, laughing. 'It's a real dog's life!'

Yelena Kucherov sat in the porch, put her arms around her little girl and became thoughtful. Judging from her expression, the little girl's head was filled with gloomy thoughts too.

Pensively she played with the elegant lace parasol she had taken from her mother's hands.

'We're terribly poor!' Rodion said. 'We've so many worries and we have to keep slaving away. God doesn't send any rain now . . . It's a dog's life, no mistake.'

'It's hard for you in this life,' Yelena said, 'but in the next you'll be happy.'

Rodion didn't understand and just coughed into his fist. But Stepanida said, 'It's all right for the rich in the next world too, lady. The rich man has candles burning in church and his own services said and he gives money to the poor. But what about the peasant? He's got no time to make the sign of the cross over his forehead, he's a pauper, so how can he save his soul? And being poor brings about so much sinning, we're like dogs howling in our misery. We don't have a good word for no one. As for the goings-on here, dear lady – God save us! We're not happy in this world and we won't be in the next. The rich have all the happiness.'

She spoke cheerfully. Evidently she had long been used to talking about her wretched life. Rodion smiled too. He liked his old woman being so clever, so good with words.

'But the rich only *seem* to have an easy time of it,' Yelena said. 'Everyone has his own cross to bear. Now we – my husband and I – don't live badly, we have means, but are we happy? I'm still young, but I've already had four children. They're always ill and I'm ill too. I'm always going to the doctor's.'

'What's wrong with you?' Rodion asked.

'It's a woman's complaint. I can't sleep. My headaches don't give me a moment's peace. I'm sitting here talking to you, but my head feels dreadful. I feel weak all over, and I'd prefer the hardest physical work to being in this state. And I'm really terribly worried. I always fear for the children and my husband. Every family has its own burden to bear and we're no exception. I don't come from a family of gentlefolk myself. My grandfather was a simple peasant, and my father was a tradesman in Moscow, just an ordinary working man too. But my husband's parents are rich, out of the top drawer. They didn't want him to marry me, but he wouldn't listen, fell out with them and they still haven't forgiven us. This worries my husband and he gets upset. He's always on tenterhooks. He loves his mother, loves her very much. Well, I get worried too. It comes hard for *me*.'

Some men and women were standing listening near Rodion's hut now. Kozov came up, stopped and shook his long narrow beard. Then the Lychkovs, father and son, came up.

'And there's something else. You can't be happy and contented if you feel out of place,' Yelena continued. 'Every one of you has his own little plot of land, every one of you slaves away and knows what he's working for. My husband builds bridges. In a word, everyone has his own trade. But I fritter away my time, I don't have any plot, I don't do any work, and I feel like a fish out of water. The reason I'm telling you all this is so that you won't judge from appearances any more. If someone is expensively dressed and has money it still doesn't mean he's satisfied with his life.'

She got up to leave and took her daughter's hand. 'I like it very much here with you,' she said smiling, and one could tell from that weak, timid smile how ill she really was, and how young and pretty. She had a pale, thin face, dark eyebrows and fair hair. The little girl was just like her mother, thin, fair-haired and slim. They both smelt of scent.

'I like the river, the woods, the village,' Yelena continued. 'I could live my whole life here – I think I might get better and find the right place for myself. I dearly want to help you, to be useful and close to you. I know all about your hardship and what I don't know I can guess at and feel intuitively. I'm ill and weak, and perhaps it's too late for me to change my way of life to what I'd like it to be. But I have children and I'm trying to bring them up to grow used to you and to like you. I'll always see they don't forget that their lives don't belong to themselves – they belong to *you*. But I urge you, beg you, to trust us, live with us in friendship. My husband's a kind, fine man. Don't upset him, don't irritate him. He's very sensitive to the least little thing. Yesterday, for example, your cattle strayed into our kitchen garden and one of you broke the fence near the beehives. That kind of behaviour reduces my husband to despair.

'I beg you,' she implored, crossing her hands on her breast, 'I beg you to be good neighbours. Let's live in peace! As they say, a rotten peace is better than a good war and it's your neighbours you buy, not houses. I repeat, my husband is a good, kind man. If all goes well I promise you we'll do everything we can. We'll mend roads, we'll build a school for your children, I promise you.'

'We thanks you from the bottom of our hearts, lady, of course we do,' Lychkov senior said, looking down at the ground. 'You're educated, you knows best. But it's only that a rich villager called "Raven" Voronov once promised to build a school in Yeresnevo. He was always saying I'll give you this and that as well and all he did was put up the framework and then cleared off. The peasants had to do the roof and finish the work, they had to stump up a thousand roubles. Raven couldn't have cared less, all he did was stroke his beard, which got up the lads' noses all right.'

'It was a raven what did that, now we've a rook!' Kozov said, winking.

There was laughter.

'We don't need no school,' Volodka said gloomily. 'Our children go to Petrovskoye and let 'em. We don't want no school.'

Yelena suddenly quailed. She turned pale, her face grew pinched and she shrank back, as if touched by some rough object. Without another word she went on her way. She walked faster and faster, without looking round.

'Lady!' Rodion called, going in pursuit. 'Lady, please wait, there's something I want to tell you.'

Hatless, he kept following her, talking in a low voice, as if begging for charity, 'Lady, please wait. I've something to tell you.'

They walked out of the village and Yelena stopped in the shadow of an old mountain-ash, near someone's cart.

'Please don't take offence, lady,' Rodion said. 'Don't let all this get you down. Be patient, try and stick it for a couple of years and everything'll turn out all right. We're honest, law-abiding folk here. The villagers are good people, I swear it. Don't take no notice of Kozov or the Lychkovs or that Volodka – he's an idiot and does the first thing anyone tells him. The others are peaceful folk. They don't say very much. Some of them would be glad to stand up for you but they can't. They've a soul and conscience, but no tongues. Don't take offence, please be patient. Don't let it get you down.'

Yelena looked thoughtfully at the broad, peaceful river and the tears flowed down her cheeks. Rodion was embarrassed at her tears and he almost wept himself.

'Now, don't you worry,' he muttered. 'Try and stick it for a couple of years or so. And we'll have that school, and roads, but not right away. Let's suppose, for example, you'd be wanting to sow wheat on this little hillock. First you'd have to get all the roots out, clear all the stones away. Then you'd have to plough it and you'd be forever going backward and forward. It's the same with village folk, there's a lot of to-ing and fro-ing before you come out on top.'

The crowd moved away from Rodion's hut and went up the street towards the mountain-ash. They started singing, an accordion played and they came nearer and nearer.

'Mummy, let's go away from this place!' the little girl said, pale-faced, pressing close to her mother and trembling all over.

'Where to?'

'To Moscow. Let's go away, Mummy.'

The little girl burst into tears. Rodion, his face bathed in sweat, was completely nonplussed. He took a small, twisted, crescent-shaped cucumber covered in rye crumbs from his pocket and put it in the girl's hands.

'Now there,' he muttered, frowning sternly. 'Take this cucumber and eat it. You shouldn't cry. Your mummy will smack you and she'll tell Daddy when you're home. There, there.'

They walked on and he followed them the whole time, wanting to tell them something nice and reassuring. When he saw that they were both preoccupied with their own thoughts and troubles and were ignoring him, he stopped. Shielding his eyes from the sun, he watched them for a long time, until they disappeared into their wood.

IV

Evidently the engineer had become irritable and crotchety, for in every trifle he could now see only robbery or some kind of criminal act. He kept the gates locked even during the day and at night two watchmen kept a look-out in the garden, beating boards. No more day-labourers from Obruchanovo were taken on. As luck would have it someone – no one knew if it was a villager or one of the navvies – took the new wheels off his cart and replaced them with old ones. Not long after that, two bridles and a pair of pincers were stolen, which made tongues wag even in the village. They said that the Lychkovs' and Volodka's huts should be searched, but then the pincers and bridles were found under the engineer's garden hedge, someone having thrown them there.

One day a crowd of peasants met the engineer as they were coming out of the wood. He stopped and, without greeting them, stared angrily first at one, then another.

'I asked you not to pick mushrooms in my park or near the house, to leave them for my wife and children. But your girls come at the crack of dawn and there's not one left after that. Whether we ask or not it's always the same. Requests, kind words, persuasion – all that's a waste of time. That's how I see it.'

Fixing his outraged look on Rodion he continued, 'My wife and I have treated you like human beings, as equals. But what about *you*? Oh, what's the use of talking! In the end we'll probably do nothing but *despise you*. We won't have any choice!'

Making a great effort to control his temper in case he said too much, he wheeled round and strode off.

When he arrived home, Rodion prayed, took off his boots and sat on the bench next to his wife.

'Yes,' he began after he had rested. 'We were out walking just now when along comes Mr Kucherov. Oh yes . . . He saw them girls at dawn . . . He asks why they didn't pick no mushrooms for his wife and kids. Then he gives me a look and says, "The wife and I'll do nothing *to spite you*." I felt like falling at his feet, that I did, but I was too shy. May God grant him good health . . . God bless him.'

Stepanida crossed herself and sighed.

'Him and his lady wife are good people, no side about *them*, there ain't. "We won't do nothing *to spite you*" – he promised that in front of everyone. In our old age . . . hm . . . that wouldn't be too bad. I'd always say a prayer for them. May the Holy Mother send Her blessing . . .'

On 14 September – the Feast of the Exaltation of the Cross – there was a festival in the parish church. In the morning the Lychkovs, father and son, had crossed the river and in the afternoon they came back drunk. For a long time they roamed around the village, singing and exchanging obscenities, after which they had a fight and then went to the villa to complain. Lychkov senior was first to enter the gardens and he was carrying a long aspen stick. He hesitated, then doffed his cap. Just then the engineer was having tea with his family on the terrace.

'What do you want?' he shouted.

'Squire, please . . .' Lychkov began and burst into tears. 'Please be kind to me, help me . . . My son's making my life hell. He's ruined me. He's always starting a fight with me, that he is, sir . . .'

Then Lychkov junior appeared, also with a stick. He stopped and fixed his drunken, asinine gaze on the terrace.

'It's not for me to sort your problems out,' the engineer said. 'Go to the council, or the district police officer.'

'I've been trying everywhere, making complaints,' Lychkov senior sobbed. 'Where can I go now? I suppose he can murder me, eh? Can do anything he likes, eh? And to his father? His *father?*'

He raised his stick and struck his son on the head. His son raised his stick and hit the old man so hard on his bare skull that the stick bounced off. Lychkov senior didn't move an inch and hit his son on the head again. And there they stood, whacking each other on the head and it seemed more of a game than a fight. Peasant men and women crowded at the gates and peered silently into the yard – all looking very serious. They had come to wish the family happy holiday, but the moment they saw the Lychkovs they felt ashamed and stayed outside.

Next morning Yelena left for Moscow with the children and it was rumoured that the engineer was selling the villa.

V

The villagers are used to the bridge now and it is hard even to visualize this stretch of river without one. The heaps of rubble left by the builders have long been overgrown with grass, the navvies are forgotten and instead of their songs the sounds of passing trains are heard almost every hour.

New Villa was sold long ago. Now it belongs to some civil servant who comes here with his family when he has the day off, drinks tea on the terrace and then travels back to Moscow. He has a cockade on his hat and he speaks and coughs like someone of importance, although he's only a low-ranking official. When the peasants bow to him he just ignores them.

Everyone in Obruchanovo has grown old. Kozov is dead and there are more children than ever in Rodion's hut. Volodka has grown a long red beard. They're just as badly off as before.

Early one spring the inhabitants of Obruchanovo are sawing wood near the station. There they are now, going home slowly from work, in single file. The broad saws bend over their shoulders, reflecting the bright sun. Nightingales sing in the bushes along the river bank, skylarks pour out their song in the sky. It's quiet at New Villa, not a soul to be seen, only golden pigeons – golden as they fly in the sunlight, high above the house. Everyone – Rodion, both Lychkovs and Volodka – re-member those white horses, little ponies, fireworks, the boat with its lanterns. They remember the engineer's beautiful, elegant wife coming into the village and talking so warmly to them. But it seems as if none of this ever happened, everything is like a dream or fairy-tale.

They wearily drag themselves along and take to brooding. They think that the people in their village are good, peaceful, reasonable and God-fearing. Yelena was quiet, kind and gentle too, and they had felt sorry to see her in such a predicament. But why hadn't they all got on with one another and had parted enemies? What kind of mist was shrouding the most important things, so that all they could see now were straying animals, bridles, pincers and things of so little importance that they seemed nonsensical when one thought about them now? Why do they get on so well with the new owner, but never managed to hit it off with the engineer?

Not knowing the answer to these questions, everyone is silent. Only Volodka mutters something or other.

'What did you say?' asks Rodion.

'We've got by in the past without no bridge,' Volodka says gloomily. 'We never asked for it and we don't need it now.'

No one answers and silently they go their way, heads bowed.

At a Country House

ༀༀ

Paul Rashevich paced the room, softly treading on the floor covered with Ukrainian rugs, casting his long, narrow shadow on wall and ceiling. Meyer, his guest, an acting coroner, was sitting on the sofa, one leg tucked beneath him, smoking and listening. The clock showed eleven and they could hear the servants laying the table in the room next to the study.

'All right then,' Rashevich was saying, 'from the point of view of brotherhood, equality and so on, Mitka the swineherd is perhaps just as good as a Goethe or Frederick the Great. But if you look at things scientifically and have the courage to face the facts, you'll soon see that fine breeding is no prejudice or old wives' tale. Fine breeding, dear man, is justified by Nature and to deny it is as strange – in my opinion – as denying a stag its antlers. You must face the facts! You're a lawyer and since you've never studied anything besides the arts you can flatter yourself with illusions about equality, fraternity and the rest of it. I'm an incorrigible Darwinist, however, and such words as breeding, aristocracy and pedigree are not just empty sounds!'

Rashevich was excited and spoke enthusiastically. His eyes shone, his pince-nez kept falling from his nose, he nervously twitched his shoulders and winked – and when he said 'Darwinist' he had jauntily glanced at the mirror and smoothed his grey beard with both hands. He was wearing a very short, shabby jacket and narrow trousers. The speed of his movements, his jauntiness and that over-short jacket were out of character, and this large handsome head with long hair that put one in mind of some bishop or venerable poet seemed to have been stuck on to the body of a tall, skinny, affected young man. As he stood there with feet apart his long shadow had the shape of a pair of scissors.

He really loved holding forth and always thought that whatever he said was novel and original. In Meyer's presence he felt exceptionally stimulated, just brimming with ideas. He was fond of the coroner and felt inspired by his youthfulness, health, refined manners, reliability – and above all by the warmth of his feelings for himself and his family. On the whole Rashevich wasn't liked by his acquaintances and they steered clear of him: as he very well knew, they maintained that he had driven his wife to her grave by all his talking and called him a misanthrope and an 'Old Toad' behind his back. Only Meyer, that unbigoted man of enterprise, was an eager and frequent visitor, and he had even said somewhere that Rashevich and his daughters were the only people in the province with whom he really felt at home. Rashevich also liked him because he was a young man who might be a good match for Zhenya, his elder daughter.

As he savoured his own thoughts and the sound of his own voice, now looking with pleasure at the rather stout, respectable Meyer with his beautifully trimmed hair, Rashevich dreamt of settling his Zhenya with a good man like him, so that the son-in-law would then have to shoulder all the worries with the estate – and quite nasty ones they were too. He owed the bank two interest payments and his various arrears and penalties amounted to more than two thousand roubles.

'There's no doubt about it,' Rashevich continued, growing even more carried away. 'If some Richard the Lion-Heart or Frederick Barbarossa happens to be brave and magnanimous, these qualities are transmitted by heredity to the son, together with cranial convolutions and bumps. If – by dint of education and exercise – this bravery and magnanimity are preserved in the son and if he marries a princess who is just as high-minded and brave, then these qualities will be transmitted to the grandson and so on, until they become a generic feature so to speak and are organically transmuted into flesh and blood. Thanks to rigid sexual selection, thanks to noble families instinctively avoiding misalliances, thanks to upper-class youngsters not marrying God knows whom, lofty mental attributes have been transmitted, undefiled, from generation to generation. They have been preserved and with the passage of time have become perfected and

205

more refined through being put into practice. For all the blessings of mankind we are indebted to Nature, to that well-ordered, efficient evolutionary process which, over the centuries, has so diligently kept the upper classes apart from the rabble. Yes, my dear chap! It wasn't your proles, your labourers' sons who gave us literature, science, the arts, law, concepts of honour and duty . . . For all this, humanity is indebted to blue-blooded men. From a biological standpoint, your nasty brutish landowner, precisely because he has blue blood in his veins, is more useful and refined than your most successful businessman who might have built fifteen museums. Say what you like, my dear sir, but if I refuse to shake hands with some little upstart or common oaf, if I don't have him at my table, what I'm doing is preserving all that is finest in this world and helping to fulfil one of Mother Nature's noblest designs for the perfection of mankind.'

Rashevich stopped for a moment and stroked his beard with both hands; his scissors-shaped shadow stopped still on the wall.

'Just consider our Mother Russia,' he continued, putting his hands in his pockets and standing first on his heels, then on his toes. 'Who are the *cream*? Take our first-class artists, writers, composers. Who are they? All of them, my dear chap, were from the aristocracy. Pushkin, Gogol, Lermontov, Turgenev, Goncharov, Tolstoy – they weren't sextons' sons.'

'The Goncharovs were business people,' Meyer said.

'All right! Exceptions only prove the rule, though. And in any case Goncharov's talent is highly debatable. But let's forget individuals and look at the facts again. What would you say to this most eloquent fact, my dear sir? As soon as your common lout has managed to insinuate himself into spheres where he was never allowed before – high society, science, literature, local government, the courts – then Nature herself has always been the first to intercede on behalf of humanity's noblest vested rights, she has been first to declare war on this riff-raff. In fact, the moment this prole of yours ventures beyond his proper place in life he begins to waste away, go insane, degenerate. Nowhere will you find so many neurotics, mental cripples, consumptives and assorted weaklings as among these birds. They die like flies in autumn. Were it not for this salutary degeneracy, our civilization would have gone to pot ages ago, your dirty little upstarts would have gobbled it up. Please tell me, what has this invasion so far given us? What have the proles contributed?'

Rashevich assumed a mysterious, frightened expression and went on, 'Science and literature have never been at such a low ebb as now. These days people have no ideas or ideals, my dear sir, their sole thought is grabbing all they can while ruining everyone else in the process. These days anyone claiming to be progressive, decent, can be bought for just one rouble. That's exactly what singles out your present-day intellectual – when you talk to him you have to keep your hand on your pocket or he'll pinch your wallet.'

Rashevich winked and laughed. 'By God, he'll have your wallet off you,' he said joyfully, in a shrill little voice. 'And what about morality? How does that stand?' Rashevich looked round at the door. 'No one's surprised nowadays when a wife robs and deserts her husband – that's a mere trifle! These days twelve-year-old girls are already looking for lovers and all these amateur theatricals and literary evenings have been invented solely to make it easier to hook some rich peasant farmer and then be kept by him. Mothers sell their daughters, and husbands are asked point-blank how much they're asking for their wives. You can even haggle with them about the price, my dear chap . . .'

Meyer, who had remained silent and still all this time, suddenly rose from the couch and glanced at his watch.

'I'm sorry, Pavel, I must be off.'

Rashevich wasn't done yet, however. He put his arm round Meyer, forced him to sit on the couch again and vowed not to let him go without supper. So Meyer sat down again and listened. But this time he looked at Rashevich in bewilderment and alarm, as though only now was he beginning to understand him. Red blotches broke out on his face. Finally, when the maid entered and announced that the young ladies wanted them to come in for supper, he sighed faintly and was first to leave the study.

At the table in the next room sat Rashevich's daughters, Zhenya and Iraida, twenty-four and twenty-two years old; they were black-eyed, very pale and of identical height. Zhenya wore her hair down, Iraida's was done up high. Before eating they both drank a glass of some bitter, home-made liqueur and gave the impression they did this accidentally, for the first time in their lives. Both were embarrassed and they burst out laughing.

'Now girls, don't be naughty,' Rashevich said.

Zhenya and Iraida spoke French to each other, but Russian to their father and his guest. Interrupting each other and mixing French and Russian, they gave a rapid account of how, in the old days, at precisely this time of year (August), they had always gone away to boarding-school – and how they had enjoyed themselves there! But now there was nowhere to go and they had to live in that country house the whole summer and winter without ever leaving the place. What a bore that was!

'Now girls, don't be naughty!' Rashevich repeated.

He wanted to hold the stage. If others spoke in his presence he'd feel twinges of jealousy.

'So that's how it is, dear chap,' he started afresh, looking affectionately at the coroner. 'From the kindness of our hearts and out of naïvety, and because we're afraid of being considered backward-looking, we hob-nob with all kinds of trash, if you'll pardon the expression. We preach fraternity and equality with upstart country bumpkins and publicans. But if we stop to think a moment, we'd see how criminal this kindness is. We've put civilization in dire jeopardy. My dear fellow! What took our ancestors centuries to achieve will not be desecrated and ruined now by this latest type of vandal.'

After supper everyone went into the drawing-room. Zhenya and Iraida lit candles on the piano and prepared the music. But their father went on and on and there was no telling when he would stop. Now they looked wearily and irritably at their egotistical father, to whom the pleasure of talking and displaying his intellect was evidently dearer, more important, than his daughters' happiness. Meyer – the only young man who ever called at the house – visited them only for their charming female company. But that irrepressible old boy had him under his thumb and didn't let him out of his sight for one minute.

'In the same way that western knights repelled the Mongol invasion, so we must join forces before it's too late – and united we must strike the enemy!' Rashevich continued in a preacher's voice, raising his right arm. 'If only I could confront that rabble, not as Pavel Rashevich, but as the mighty and formidable Richard the Lion-Heart. Let's not pull any punches with them, we've had enough! Let's all agree that the moment one of these oafs comes anywhere near us we'll hurl words of scorn right in his mug: "Clear off! The cobbler should stick to his last." Right in the mug!' Rashevich continued rapturously, prodding the air with bent finger. 'Right in the mug!'

'I couldn't do that,' Meyer said, turning away.

'Why not?' Rashevich asked in a lively voice, anticipating an interesting and lengthy argument.

'Because I'm from the working classes myself.'

Having said this, Meyer blushed, even his neck swelled and tears glistened in his eyes.

'My father was a simple workman,' Meyer added in a rough, brusque voice, 'but I don't see anything bad in that.'

Rashevich felt dreadfully embarrassed. He was stunned, like a criminal caught in the act, and he looked at Meyer in dismay, lost for words. Zhenya and Iraida blushed and bent over their music – they were ashamed of their tactless father. A minute went by in complete silence and it was all unbearably embarrassing. Then, quite suddenly, an anguished, tense, grating voice rang out, 'Oh yes, I'm working-class and proud of it.' With this, Meyer made his farewell, stumbled awkwardly against the furniture and rushed into the hall, even though his carriage hadn't yet been brought round.

'It'll be rather dark travelling tonight,' Rashevich muttered, following him. 'The moon rises late now.'

Both stood there in the dark porch waiting for the carriage. It was chilly.

'There's a falling star,' Meyer said, wrapping himself tightly in his coat.

'There's a lot of those in August.'

When the carriage came round, Rashevich peered intently at the sky and sighed. 'A phenomenon worthy of Flammarion's pen.'

After seeing his guest off, he strolled round the garden, gesticulating in the dark and not wanting to believe that such a strange, stupid misunderstanding had just taken place. He was ashamed, and annoyed with himself. In the first place it had been extremely indiscreet and tactless on his part to have started that damned conversation about blue blood without having ascertained beforehand what kind of person he was dealing with. Something similar had happened to him before. Once, in a railway compartment, he had started belittling Germans and all his travelling companions turned out to be German. Secondly, he had the feeling that Meyer would never come again. Those working-class intellectuals were such a morbidly conceited, obstinate, rancorous lot.

'That's bad, very bad,' Rashevich muttered, spitting. He felt awkward and sick, as if he had just eaten some soap. 'Oh, that's very bad!'

From the garden he could see Zhenya through the drawing-room window, standing by the piano, her hair hanging loose. She looked very pale and frightened and she was talking very quickly. Iraida was pacing the room, deep in thought. But then she too started talking very fast and she looked indignant. Both were speaking at once. He couldn't hear a word, but he guessed what they were saying. Zhenya was probably complaining that her father had driven away all respectable people from the house with his interminable talking and that today he had deprived them of their only friend – of a husband, perhaps – and now there was nowhere in the whole province for that young man to go and relax. From the way she was raising her hands in despair Iraida was probably talking about their boring life, about her wasted youth.

When he was in his room, Rashevich sat on his bed and slowly undressed. He felt very low, still plagued by that sensation of eating soap. He was ashamed of himself. After undressing he looked at his long, sinewy, old man's legs and recalled that he had been nicknamed Old Toad in the district and that he always had feelings of shame after every long conversation. As if it were ordained by fate, he would always start gently, kindly, with every good intention, calling himself an old university student, an idealist, a Don Quixote. But then, without even realizing it, he would suddenly resort to abuse and slander. Most amazing of all.

he would criticize the arts, science and morality, in all sincerity, although it was twenty years since he had last read a book or travelled further than the main town in the district, and he really didn't have any idea of what was going on out in the wide world. If he sat down to write something, even a letter of congratulation, that too would turn out abusive. All this was most peculiar, as he was in fact a sensitive man, easily moved to tears. Did he have some demon inside him which was spreading hatred and slander, against his will?

'It's all very bad, very bad,' he sighed underneath his quilt. 'Very bad!'

His daughters couldn't sleep either. There was the sound of loud laughter and shouting, as if they were chasing someone – Zhenya was having hysterics. Soon afterwards Iraida started sobbing too. A barefoot maid ran up and down the corridor several times.

'God, what a mess!' Rashevich muttered, sighing and tossing from side to side. 'It's *bad*.'

He had a nightmare in which he was standing in the middle of a room, naked and tall as a giraffe, poking his finger out and saying, 'Right in their fat mugs. Let them have it right in their fat ugly mugs!'

He awoke terrified and the first thing he remembered was that misunderstanding of yesterday. Of course, Meyer would never call again. He remembered too that he had to pay some bank interest, marry off his daughters, eat and drink. And there were illnesses, old age and other things to worry about – soon it would be winter and there was no firewood.

It was past nine in the morning. Rashevich slowly dressed, drank his tea and ate two large slices of bread and butter. His daughters didn't appear at breakfast – they wanted to avoid him and this offended him. He lay on the couch in his study, then sat at his desk and began to write his daughters a letter. His hand shook and his eyes itched. He wrote that he was old now, unwanted and unloved, and he asked his daughters to forget him and, when he died, to bury him in a simple pine coffin, without any fuss, or to send his body to the dissecting theatre at Kharkov. He felt that every line breathed malice and play-acting, but he couldn't stop and kept writing, writing . . .

Beauties

༕

I

When I was in the fifth or sixth form at high school I remember travelling with my grandfather from the village of Bolshaya Krepkaya, in the Don region, to Rostov-on-Don. It was a hot day in August, wearying and depressing. Our eyelids seemed glued together, our mouths were parched from the heat and dry scorching wind that drove clouds of dust towards us. We had no inclination to look, speak or think, and when Karpo, our dozing Ukrainian driver, caught me on the cap as he struck out at his horses, I did not protest or make a sound. All I could do when I woke from my half-sleep was look dejectedly, feebly, into the distance to see if I could make out a village through the dust. We stopped to feed the horses at the large Armenian village of Bakhchi-Salakh, at the house of a rich Armenian friend of Grandfather's. Never in my life have I seen anything more grotesque than that Armenian. Imagine a small, close-cropped head with thick, beetling eyebrows, a bird-like nose, long grey whiskers and a wide mouth with a long, cherrywood chibouk sticking out of it. This small head was clumsily stuck on to a scraggy, hunchbacked torso garbed in fantastic costume: a short red jacket with sky-blue, baggy trousers. This person walked around with legs wide apart, shuffling his slippers, speaking with the pipe still in his mouth – but at the same time bearing himself with typical Armenian dignity, never smiling, goggling his eyes and trying his hardest to ignore his visitors.

The Armenian's place wasn't windy or dusty, but it was just as unpleasant, stuffy and dreary as the steppe and the highway. I remember sitting on a green trunk in one corner, dusty and exhausted by the heat. The unpainted wooden walls, the furniture and the ochre-stained floorboards smelled like dry wood scorched by the sun. Wherever I looked there were flies, flies, flies. Grandfather and the Armenian were talking in hushed voices about pasturage, grazing and sheep. I knew that they would take a whole hour to get the samovar boiling, that Grandfather would spend no less than an hour over his tea, after which he would lie down to sleep for two or three hours. A quarter of my day would be taken up waiting, and then there would be the heat, dust and bumpy cart once more. As I listened to those two voices muttering away I felt that I had seen the Armenian, the crockery cupboard, the flies, those windows with the hot sun beating on them a long, long time ago and that I would only stop seeing them in the far distant future. And I was filled with loathing for the steppe, the sun, the flies . . .

A Ukrainian woman with a shawl brought in a tray of tea things, then the samovar. Without hurrying, the Armenian went out into the hall and shouted, 'Masha! Come and pour the tea! Masha, where are you?'

There were hurried footsteps and then a sixteen-year-old girl in a simple cotton print dress and white shawl came in. She stood with her back to me as she rinsed the crockery and poured the tea and all I noticed was that she had a slim waist, was barefoot and that her small bare heels were covered by her low trousers.

The master invited me to drink some tea. As I sat at the table I peered into the face of the girl who was handing me a glass and suddenly I felt as if a breeze had swept over my heart and blown away all the impressions of that day, all that boredom and dust. I saw the enchanting features of the most beautiful face I have ever seen, whether awake or dreaming. A true beauty was standing before me – this flashed on me like lightning, at the very first glance.

I am ready to swear that Masha, or 'Massya' as her father called her, was a true beauty, though I cannot prove it. Sometimes clouds mass haphazardly on the horizon and the sun, hidden behind them, paints them and the sky every conceivable colour – crimson, orange, gold, lilac, muddy pink. One cloud looks like a monk, another a fish, a third resembles a Turk with turban. The sunset glow has embraced one third of the sky, it glitters on a church cross, on manor-house windows, is reflected in the river, in small ponds, it quivers on trees. Far, far away, against the setting sun, a flock of wild ducks flies off somewhere for the night. The boy with his herd of cows, the surveyor driving in his trap over the mill-dam, ladies and gentlemen out walking – all of them look at the sunset, finding it stunningly beautiful. But no one knows, no one can say in what that beauty actually resides.

I was not the only one who found the Armenian girl beautiful. My eighty-year-old grandfather, a harsh old man, indifferent to women or the beauties of nature, looked at Masha affectionately for a whole minute and then asked, 'Is that your daughter, Avet Nazarovich?'

'Yes, she's my daughter,' the Armenian replied.

'A fine young lady,' said Grandfather.

An artist would have termed the Armenian girl's beauty classical and severe. The contemplation of just this type of beauty, God knows why, thoroughly convinces you that the features before you are regular, that hair, eyes, nose, mouth, neck, bosom and all the movements of this young body have been fused by nature into perfect harmony and she had not erred, not even in the most minute detail. Somehow you imagine that the ideally beautiful woman should have a nose just like Masha's, straight but slightly aquiline, the same large, dark eyes, the same long lashes and that same languid glance. Her curly black hair and eyebrows are the perfect match for the delicate white colour of her forehead and cheeks, just as green reeds suit a quiet stream. Masha's white neck and young bosom are not fully developed, but you feel that only a great artist could sculpt them. Looking at her you are gradually filled with the desire to tell the girl something particularly pleasant, sincere and beautiful, something as beautiful as herself.

At first I was offended and rather put out by Masha completely ignoring me and looking down the whole time. There seemed to be some special air about her, happy and proud, that isolated her from me, jealously shielding her from my glances.

'That's because I'm covered in dust, sunburnt and just a young boy,' I thought.

But after that I gradually forgot about myself and gave myself up completely to the sensation of beauty. I no longer thought of the dreary steppe, the dust, I no longer heard flies buzzing or tasted my tea: I was conscious only of that beautiful girl standing on the other side of the table.

The effect her beauty had on me was rather strange. It was not desire, rapture or any feeling of delight that Masha aroused in me, but a deep sadness that was none the less pleasant, and vague and hazy as a dream. I rather felt sorry for myself, for Grandfather, for the Armenian and for the girl even. I felt as if all four of us had lost something of the greatest importance in our lives which we would never recover. Grandfather became sad too. He no longer discussed grazing or sheep, but remained silent, glancing pensively at Masha.

After tea Grandfather had his sleep, while I went outside and sat in the porch. Like all the other houses in Bakhchi-Salakh, this one stood in the full glare of the sun. There were no trees, no awnings, no shadows. The Armenian's large yard, overgrown with goosefoot and mallow, was full of life and cheerful, despite the intense heat. Behind one of the low wattle fences criss-crossing the spacious yard, threshing was in progress. Twelve horses, harnessed abreast and forming one long radius, were moving round a pole set in the dead centre of the threshing-floor. In his long waistcoat and baggy trousers, a Ukrainian walked beside them, cracking his whip and shouting as if he meant to tease the horses and display his power over them.

'Get a move on, damned horses! Oh, rot your guts! Are you all *scared*?'

Not understanding why they were being compelled to keep turning on the same spot and tread wheat straw, the bay, grey and skewbald horses trotted reluctantly, as if it were too hard for them, and they flicked their tails indignantly. The wind raised large clouds of golden chaff from under their hooves, carrying it far away across the wattle fences. Near the tall, newly made ricks, women swarmed with rakes, and bullock carts went to and fro. In another yard, beyond the ricks, another dozen similar horses were trotting around a pole, while a similar Ukrainian cracked his whip and laughed at them.

The steps on which I was sitting were hot. The heat was

making glue ooze from the wood here and there on the banisters and window-frames. Tiny red insects crowded together in the strips of shade under the steps and shutters. The sun baked my head, chest and back, but I was oblivious of it, aware only of bare feet scuttling over the floorboards of the hall and other rooms in the house. After clearing away the tea things, Masha ran down the steps, making a little draught as she passed me, and flew like a bird towards a small, soot-blackened outbuilding – the kitchen, no doubt – from which came the smell of roast mutton and the sound of angry Armenian voices. She vanished through a dark doorway and in her place appeared an old, hunchbacked, red-faced Armenian woman in green baggy trousers. She was angrily telling someone off. Masha soon reappeared in the doorway, flushed from the heat of the kitchen and carrying a large black loaf on her shoulder. Bending gracefully under the weight of the bread she ran across the yard to the threshing-floor, darted over one of the fences, plunged into a cloud of golden chaff and disappeared behind the carts. The Ukrainian who had been urging on the horses lowered his whip, stopped speaking and looked silently in the direction of the carts for a minute. Then, after the girl had again flashed past the horses and leapt over a fence, he followed her with his eyes and shouted at his horses, as if highly annoyed, 'To hell with you devils!'

Afterwards I kept hearing her bare feet and saw her rushing round the yard with a serious, worried look. First she would tear down the steps, sending currents of air towards me, then into the kitchen, then to the threshing-floor, after which she went through the gates and I could hardly turn my head quickly enough to follow her.

The more I glimpsed this beautiful creature, the sadder I became. I felt sorry for myself, for her and for the Ukrainian mournfully watching her every time she dashed through a cloud of chaff to the bullock carts. Did I envy her beauty? Or was it that I regretted that the girl wasn't mine, would never be mine and that I was a stranger to her? Did I have the vague feeling that her rare beauty was something quite accidental, unnecessary and ephemeral, like everything in this world? Or was my sadness that particular sensation the contemplation of real beauty arouses in people? Heaven alone knows!

The three hours' wait passed unnoticed. I felt that I'd hardly had time to look at Masha when Karpo rode down to the river, bathed the horse and started harnessing it. The wet horse snorted with pleasure and banged its hooves on the shafts. Karpo shouted 'Get back!' at it. Grandfather woke up, the gates creaked as Masha opened them, we climbed into the carriage and drove out of the yard. We didn't speak, as if we were angry with one another.

When Rostov and Nakhichevan appeared in the distance, after about two or three hours, Karpo, who hadn't said a word the whole time, quickly looked round and said, 'A wonderful girl, that old Armenian's daughter!'

And he whipped the horse.

II

On another occasion, when I was a student, I was travelling south by train. It was May. At one station – possibly between Belgorod and Kharkov – I got out for a walk along the platform.

Evening shadows already lay over the station garden, platform and fields. The station buildings blotted out the sunset, but the highest, delicate pink puffs of smoke from the engine told me that the sun hadn't yet completely disappeared.

As I wandered down the platform I noticed that most of the passengers who had left the train for some fresh air were walking or standing near one second-class carriage in particular. Their expressions suggested some celebrity must be sitting in it. Among the inquisitive onlookers by this carriage was my travelling companion, an artillery officer – a bright young man, likeable and charming, like anybody you chance to meet briefly on journeys.

'What are you looking at?' I asked.

He didn't reply, merely indicating a female figure with his eyes. It was a young girl of about seventeen or eighteen, in Russian national costume, without any hat and with a lace scarf nonchalantly draped over one shoulder. She wasn't a passenger and was probably the stationmaster's daughter or sister. She was standing near a carriage window talking to some elderly lady passenger. Before I realized it, I was overwhelmed by that same sensation I had once experienced in the Armenian village.

The girl was strikingly beautiful and neither myself nor the other onlookers could have any doubts about it.

If one were to describe her appearance in the usual way, detail by detail, only her fair, wavy, thick hair could really be called beautiful – it hung loose and was tied back on her head by a ribbon. Everything else was either irregular or very ordinary. It may have been her way of flirting or shortsightedness, but she kept screwing her eyes up. Her nose was retroussé, her mouth small, her profile flat and featureless, her shoulders narrow for one of her age. For all that, the girl gave the impression of true beauty. As I gazed at her I was convinced that a Russian face needs no regularity of features to appear beautiful. Moreover, even if this girl's upturned nose were to be replaced by another, regular and impeccably moulded like the Armenian girl's, I imagine her face would have lost all its charm.

As she stood talking at the window, shrinking from the evening chill, the girl kept looking round at us. First she would place hands on hips, then raise them to her head to smooth her hair. She talked and laughed, displaying surprise and horror in turn, and I can't recall a single moment when her body and face were still. The whole mystery and magic of her beauty lay in these tiny, infinitely refined movements, in her smile, in the play of her expression, in her swift glances at us; and also in the combination of these delicate, graceful movements both with the youthfulness and freshness and purity of heart that rang out in her speech and laughter, and with that defencelessness so lovely to see in children, birds, fawns and young trees.

She had a butterfly-like beauty which goes hand in hand with waltzing, with fluttering about the garden, with laughter and gaiety, and which is far removed from seriousness, sadness or calm. I felt that if a strong gust of wind had rushed down that platform, or if it had suddenly started raining, then that fragile body would have faded at once and that capricious beauty scattered like pollen.

'Ah well,' the officer muttered with a sigh as we returned to our carriage after the second bell. I do not presume to know the meaning of that 'Ah well.' Perhaps he was sad and reluctant to leave that beautiful creature and the spring evening for the stuffy compartment. Or perhaps, like myself, he felt inexplicably sorry for the beautiful girl, for himself, for me, and for all the passengers who were lifelessly, unwillingly creeping back to their compartments. As we passed one of the station windows, behind which a pale, pasty-faced telegraphist with red curls sticking up and prominent cheekbones sat at his apparatus, the officer sighed and said, 'I bet this telegraphist is in love with that pretty little thing. Living out here in the wilds, under the same roof as that ethereal creature and not to fall in love is beyond human power. How sad, my friend, what a mockery, to be round-shouldered, scruff dull, respectable, intelligent, and in love with that pretty, silly little thing who completely ignores you! Even worse: imagine that this telegraphist who's in love with her is married to a woman just as round-shouldered, scruffy and respectable as himself! That must be sheer hell!'

A guard was standing on the little open platform at the end of our carriage, his elbows propped on the railings. He was looking towards the girl and his flabby, unpleasantly puffy face, exhausted by sleepless nights and the jolting of the train, expressed intense joy and the deepest sorrow, as if he were seeing his own youth, his happiness, sobriety, purity, his wife and children in that girl. He was regretting his sins, it seemed, and he apparently felt with his whole being that the girl was not his and that for him, with his premature ageing, his clumsiness and flabby face, the happiness enjoyed by ordinary people, by train passengers, was as far away as the heavens.

The third bell rang, whistles blew and the train lazily moved out. First a guard, then the stationmaster and garden flashed past our windows, then the beautiful girl with her magical, childishly cunning smile.

As I leaned out to look back, I could see her watch the train leave, then walk down the platform past the window where the telegraphist was at work. She smoothed her hair and ran into the garden. The station no longer blotted out the sun – we were in open country. But the sun had set now and black puffs of smoke drifted over the new velvety-green corn. There was a sadness in the spring air, in the dark sky, in the compartment.

That familiar guard entered the compartment and started lighting the candles.

His Wife

ನಾ

'I asked you not to take anything from my desk,' Nikolay said. 'After you've been tidying up it's impossible to find a thing. Where's that telegram? Where did you put it? Please have a look. It's from Kazan, dated yesterday.'

The maid, who was very slim and pale, with an apathetic expression, found several telegrams in the basket under the desk and silently handed them to the doctor. But they were all local, from patients. Then they searched the drawing-room, and Olga's room.

It was past midnight. Nikolay knew that his wife wouldn't be back for ages, not until five in the morning at the earliest. He didn't trust her and felt miserable and couldn't sleep if she was out late. At the same time he despised his wife, her bed, her mirror, her boxes of sweets and those lilies-of-the-valley and hyacinths that someone sent to her every day and which filled the house with the cloying smell of a flower-shop. On nights like these he would become touchy and moody, and find fault with everything. Now he felt that he really must get hold of that telegram his brother had sent yesterday, although all it contained was the compliments of the season.

On the table in his wife's room he did discover a telegram under a box of writing-paper and he looked at it. It was from Monte Carlo and was addressed to his wife, care of his mother-in-law, and signed *Michel*.

The doctor couldn't understand one word, since it was in some foreign language, apparently English.

'Who is this *Michel*? Why from Monte Carlo? Why care of my mother-in-law?' he wondered.

After seven years of marriage he had become used to suspecting everything, hazarding guesses and sifting evidence, and he often thought that with all this practice he might have made an excellent detective. He went back to his study to take stock. He recalled being with his wife in St Petersburg eighteen months ago and lunching at Cubat's with an old school-friend, a transport officer who had introduced a young man of twenty-two or twenty-three, by the name of Michael, with the brief, rather odd surname – Rees. Two months later the doctor saw a photograph of this young man in his wife's album, with an inscription in French: 'In memory of the present and with hopes for the future.' Afterwards he twice met this same young man at his mother-in-law's. That was almost exactly the same time as his wife had started going out a great deal, returning in the early hours. She had kept asking him to get her a passport, so that she could go abroad, and he had refused her. As a result such a battle royal was waged for days on end in their house that he was too ashamed to face the servants.

Six months ago his medical colleagues had decided that he was developing T.B. and advised him to drop everything and leave for the Crimea. On hearing this, Olga pretended to be very alarmed, and started being nice to her husband, assuring him that the Crimea was cold and boring and that Nice would be better. She would travel with him, nurse him there and see that he got a good rest.

Now he understood why his wife was so keen on Nice: this *Michel* lived in Monte Carlo.

He picked up an English–Russian dictionary and, by translating words here and there, or guessing at their meaning, he eventually put the following together:

I DRINK TO MY DEARLY BELOVED I KISS SWEET LITTLE FOOT THOUSAND TIMES IMPATIENTLY AWAIT ARRIVAL.

He realized what a ludicrous, pathetic role he would have played had he agreed to take his wife to Nice. His feelings were so hurt that he was close to tears and he started walking from room to room in great agitation. His pride had been wounded, his touchiness about his humble origins had been aroused. Clenching his fists and frowning with disgust he asked himself: how could he have allowed himself – a village priest's son, educated in a church school, a blunt, uncouth person and a surgeon by profession – to become a slave, shamefully subjugating himself to this weak, worthless, mercenary, vile creature?

'Sweet little foot!' he muttered, crumpling up the telegram. 'Sweet little foot!'

Only the memory of long, fragrant hair, masses of soft lace and that tiny foot – which actually was very small and pretty – remained from the time when he had fallen in love, proposed and then had seven years of marriage. Now all that seemed to be left of those embraces was the sensation of silk and lace on his hands and face, nothing more. Nothing more, unless you counted hysterics, screams, reproaches, threats and lies – barefaced, treacherous lies . . . He remembered how birds sometimes happened to fly into his father's house in the village and start furiously beating against the windows and knocking things over. In exactly the same way this woman had flown in from a completely different environment and had wrought utter havoc.

The best years of his life had gone and they had been a living hell. His hopes of happiness had been dashed and ridiculed, his health had gone, his house was filled with a vulgar coquette's bric-à-brac. Out of the ten thousand roubles he earned every year he couldn't even muster ten to send to his elderly mother – and he was already fifteen thousand in debt. If a gang of bandits had taken up residence in his house they wouldn't have wrecked his life so completely as that woman had, it seemed.

He started coughing and gasping for breath. He should have gone to bed to keep warm, but he couldn't, and he kept walking round the house or sitting down at his desk, nervously running pencil over paper and writing automatically: 'Writing practice . . . Little foot.'

By five o'clock he felt weak and thought that he was to blame for everything. Had Olga married someone else who would have exerted a good influence on her, so it seemed, then she might have developed into a decent, honest woman in the end. But he was a rotten psychologist, ignorant of the female heart, and so dull and thick-skinned into the bargain.

'I haven't much longer,' he thought. 'I'm a corpse and I shouldn't get in the way of the living. It would be terribly odd and stupid of me to try and claim my rights now. I'll have it out with her. Let her go to her lover . . . I'll give her a divorce. I'll be the guilty party.'

At last Olga arrived. Without taking off her white cloak, hat and galoshes, she came straight into the study and collapsed into an armchair. 'That revolting, fat boy!' she said, sobbing and breathing heavily. 'It's downright dishonest, it's so low!' She stamped her foot. 'I can't, I won't stand for it!'

'What's wrong?' Nikolay asked, going over to her.

'That student Azaberkov was seeing me home and he's lost my purse with the fifteen roubles Mother lent me.'

She was crying in real earnest, just like a little girl, and not only her handkerchief but even her gloves were wet with tears.

'What can one do?' sighed the doctor. 'If it's lost, then it's lost and to hell with it. Now calm yourself, I must have a word with you.'

'I'm not a millionairess and I can't afford to be so careless with money. He said he'd give it back to me, but I don't believe him, he's so poor.'

Her husband asked her to calm down and listen to him, but she went on and on about that student and those lost fifteen roubles.

'All right, I'll give you twenty-five tomorrow, only please shut up!' he said, irritably.

'I have to change now,' she said, crying. 'How can I talk seriously in a fur coat? That *would* be odd!'

As he helped her remove her fur coat he could smell white wine, the kind she liked with oysters. Despite her delicate appearance she over-ate and drank far too much. She went to her room and soon returned changed and powdered. Her eyes were red from crying. She seemed to vanish into her flimsy lace négligé and in that ocean of pink waves all her husband could make out was her loose hair and that tiny slippered foot.

'What did you want to say?' she asked, rocking in the armchair.

'I just happened to see this,' the doctor said, handing her the telegram.

'What of it?' she asked, rocking harder. 'It's just an ordinary

New Year's greeting, nothing else. It's no secret.'

'You're counting on my not knowing English. No, I don't know it, but I do have a dictionary. That telegram's from Rees, he drinks the health of his beloved and sends you one thousand kisses. But let's forget that,' the doctor continued hastily. 'I haven't the least intention of telling you off or making a scene. We've had enough scenes and reproaches, it's time to call it a day. Now, this is what I want to say: you are free and you can go and live as you like.'

A short silence followed. She wept softly.

'I'm freeing you from any need to pretend and lie,' Nikolay went on. 'If you love that young man, then go and love him. If you want to go abroad and live with him, then go. You're young and healthy, but I'm a cripple. I'm not long for this world. In brief – you know what I want to say.'

He was so excited he couldn't continue. Olga cried and admitted in a self-pitying voice that she loved Rees, had driven out of town with him, had been to his flat and very much wanted to join him abroad now.

'So, you see, I'm keeping nothing from you,' she sighed. 'I've opened my heart. And I beg you once again, please be kind to me, *please* give me a passport.'

'I repeat: you're free.'

She moved to another chair that was closer so that she could watch the expression on his face. She didn't trust him and wanted to read his innermost thoughts. She never really trusted anyone, always suspecting that people were acting from petty, base motives and that they were only interested in themselves, however noble their intentions. And when she gazed quizzically into his face her eyes seemed to have a green glint, like a cat's.

'When will I get the passport?' she asked softly.

He suddenly felt like saying 'never' but restrained himself and replied, 'Whenever you like.'

'I'm only going for a month.'

'You're going to stay with Rees for good. I'll give you a divorce, I'll take the blame, then Rees will be able to marry you.'

'But it's not a divorce I want!' Olga replied spiritedly, looking amazed. 'I'm not asking for a *divorce*! All I want is a passport.'

'But why don't you want a divorce?' the doctor asked, losing his temper. 'You *are* a strange woman! If you're so crazy about him and if he feels the same way, then the best thing for people in your position is marriage. Surely you're not still undecided whether to opt for marriage or adultery?'

'I understand you,' she said, moving away, and her face assumed an evil, vindictive look. 'I understand you perfectly. You're tired of me and you just want to get rid of me and saddle me with a divorce. Thanks very much, I'm not the idiot you take me for. I won't accept a divorce and I won't leave you. I won't, I won't! In the first place, I don't want to lose my social position,' she continued, hurrying as if scared he might interrupt. 'Secondly, I'm twenty-seven and Rees is twenty-three. In a year's time he'll be fed up and he'll drop me. Thirdly, if you really want to know, I wouldn't like to swear that this infatuation is going to last very long. So there! I won't leave you.'

'Then I'll throw you out of the house!' Nikolay shouted, stamping his feet. 'I'll throw you out, you vile, disgusting woman!'

'We'll see about that!' she said and left.

It had been light outside for some time, but the doctor still stayed at his desk, doodling and writing mechanically, 'My dear sir ... tiny foot ...'

Or he would walk around, stopping in front of a photograph in the drawing-room that was taken seven years before, shortly after his wedding. He looked at it for quite a while. It was a family group: his father-in-law, mother-in-law, his wife – then twenty years old – and himself in the role of a young, happy husband. His father-in-law was a close-shaven, plump, dropsical, high-ranking government official, both cunning and money-grubbing. His mother-in-law was a fat woman with the fine predatory features of a polecat – she loved her daughter madly and helped her in everything she did. If her daughter had strangled someone the mother wouldn't have breathed a word to her, but would merely have hidden her in her skirts. Olga's features were fine and predatory as well, but more expressive and bold than her mother's. She was no polecat but a far more formidable proposition! Nikolay himself looked such a simple, pleasant, straightforward person in this photograph. That good-natured, schoolboy smile was written all over his face and *he* had been naïve enough to believe that this bunch of vultures, with which fate happened to have landed him, would bring him romance and happiness and all he had ever dreamed of when he used to sing 'Without love, young life lies in ruins . . .' as a student!

Once again he asked himself in bewilderment: how could a parish priest's son like himself, brought up in a church school, such a simple, coarse and blunt person, so feebly capitulate to that petty-minded, lying, vulgar, worthless creature who was so diametrically opposed in temperament?

When he put on his coat at eleven to leave for the hospital the maid entered the study.

'What do you want?' he asked.

'Madam is up and is asking for the twenty-five roubles you promised her yesterday.'

The Student

∾

At first the weather was fine and calm. Thrushes sang and in the marshes close by some living creature hummed plaintively, as if blowing into an empty bottle. A woodcock flew over and a shot rang out, echoing cheerfully in the spring air. But when darkness fell on the forest, an unwelcome, bitingly cold wind blew up from the east and everything became quiet. Ice needles formed on puddles and the forest became uninviting, bleak and empty. It smelt of winter.

Ivan Velikopolsky, a theology student and parish priest's son, was returning home along the path across the water meadows after a shooting expedition. His fingers were numb and his face burned in the wind. It seemed that this sudden onset of cold had destroyed order and harmony in all things, putting Nature herself in fear and making the evening shadows thicken faster than was necessary. All was deserted and somehow particularly gloomy. Only in the widows' vegetable plots by the river did a light gleam. Far around, though, where the village stood about three miles away, everything was completely submerged in the chill evening mists. The student remembered that when he left home his mother had been sitting barefoot on the floor of the hall, cleaning the samovar, while his father lay coughing on the stove. As it was Good Friday no cooking was done at home and he felt starving. Shrinking from the cold, the student thought of similar winds blowing in the time of Ryurik, Ivan the Terrible and Peter the Great – during their reigns there had been the same grinding poverty and hunger. There had been the same thatched roofs with holes in them, the same ignorance and suffering, the same wilderness all around, the same gloom and feeling of oppression. All these horrors had been, existed now and would continue to do so. The passing of another thousand years would bring no improvement. He didn't feel like going home.

The vegetable plots were called 'widows' because they were kept by two widows, mother and daughter. A bonfire was burning fiercely, crackling and lighting up the ploughed land far around. Widow Vasilisa, a tall, plump old woman in a man's sheepskin coat, was standing gazing pensively at the fire. Her short, pock-marked, stupid-faced daughter Lukerya was sitting on the ground washing a copper pot and some spoons. Clearly they had just finished supper. Men's voices could be heard – some local farm-workers were watering their horses at the river.

'So, winter's here again,' the student said as he approached the bonfire. 'Good evening.'

Vasilisa shuddered, but then she recognized the student and gave him a welcoming smile.

'Heavens, I didn't know it was you,' she said. 'That means you'll be a rich man one day.'

They started talking. Vasilisa, a woman of the world, once a wet-nurse to some gentry and then a nanny, had a delicate way of speaking and she always smiled gently, demurely. But her daughter Lukerya, a peasant woman who had been beaten by her husband, only screwed up her eyes at the student and said nothing. She had a strange expression, as if she were a deaf-mute.

'It was on a cold night like this that the Apostle Peter warmed himself by a fire,' the student said, stretching his hands towards the flames. 'That is to say, it was cold then as well. Oh, what a terrible night that was, Grandma! A dreadfully sad, never-ending night!'

He peered into the surrounding darkness, violently jerked his head and asked, 'I suppose you were at the Twelve Readings from the Gospels yesterday?'

'Yes,' Vasilisa replied.

'You'll remember, during the Last Supper, Peter said to Jesus, "I am ready to go with Thee, both into prison and to death." And the Lord replied, "I say unto thee, Peter, before the cock crow twice thou shalt deny me thrice." After the Supper, Jesus prayed in the garden, in mortal agony, while poor Peter was downhearted and his eyes grew heavy. He couldn't fight off sleep, and he slept. Then, as you know, Judas kissed Jesus on that night and betrayed Him to the torturers. They led Him bound to the High Priest and they beat Him, while Peter, exhausted and sorely troubled by anguish and fear – he didn't have enough sleep, you understand – and in expectation of something dreadful taking place on earth at any moment, followed them. He loved Jesus passionately, to distraction, and now, from afar, he could see them beating Him.'

Lukerya put the spoons down and stared intently at the student.

'They went to the High Priest,' he continued, 'they started questioning Jesus and meanwhile the workmen, as it was so cold, had made a fire in the middle of the hall and were warming themselves. Peter stood with them by the fire, warming himself as well, as I am now. One woman who saw him said, "This man was also with Jesus." So she really meant that this man too had to be led away for questioning. And all the workmen around the fire must have looked at him suspiciously and sternly, as he was taken aback and said, "I know him not." Soon afterwards someone recognized him as one of Jesus's disciples and said, "Thou also wast with Him." But again he denied it and for the third time someone turned to him and asked, "Did I not see you in the garden with Him this day?" He denied Him for the third time. And straight after that a cock crowed and as he looked on Jesus from afar Peter remembered the words He had spoken to him at supper. He remembered, his eyes were opened, he left the hall and wept bitterly. As it is said in the Gospels, "And he went out and wept bitterly." I can imagine that quiet, terribly dark garden, those dull sobs, barely audible in the silence . . .'

The student sighed and became deeply pensive. Still smiling, Vasilisa suddenly broke into sobs and large, copious tears streamed down her cheeks. She shielded her face from the fire with her sleeve as if ashamed of her tears, while Lukerya stared at the student and blushed. Her face became anguished and tense, like someone stifling a dreadful pain.

The workmen were returning from the river and one of them, on horseback, was quite near and the light from the bonfire flickered on him. The student wished the widows goodnight and moved on. Again darkness descended and his hands began to freeze. A cruel wind was blowing – winter had really returned with a vengeance and it did not seem as if Easter Sunday was only the day after tomorrow.

Now the student thought of Vasilisa: she had wept, so everything that had happened to Peter on that terrible night must have had some special significance for her.

He glanced back. The solitary fire calmly flickered in the darkness and no one was visible near it. Once again the student reflected that, since Vasilisa had wept and her daughter had been deeply touched, then obviously what he had just been telling them about events centuries ago had some significance for the present, for both women, for this village, for himself and for all people. That old woman had wept, but not at his moving narrative: it was because Peter was close to her and because she was concerned, from the bottom of her heart, with his most intimate feelings.

His heart suddenly thrilled with joy and he even stopped for a moment to catch his breath. 'The past,' he thought, 'is linked to the present by an unbroken chain of events, each flowing from the other.' He felt that he had just witnessed both ends of this chain. When he touched one end, the other started shaking.

After crossing the river by ferry and climbing the hill, he looked at his native village and towards the west, where a narrow strip of cold crimson sunset was glimmering. And he reflected how truth and beauty, which had guided human life there in the garden and the High Priest's palace and had continued unbroken to the present, were the most important parts of the life of man, and of the whole of terrestrial life. A feeling of youthfulness, health, strength – he was only twenty-two – and an inexpressibly sweet anticipation of happiness, of a mysterious unfamiliar happiness, gradually took possession of him. And life seemed entrancing, wonderful and endowed with sublime meaning.

FOR THE BEST IN PAPERBACKS, LOOK FOR THE 🐧

In every corner of the world, on every subject under the sun, Penguin represents quality and variety – the very best in publishing today.

For complete information about books available from Penguin – including Pelicans, Puffins, Peregrines and Penguin Classics – and how to order them, write to us at the appropriate address below. Please note that for copyright reasons the selection of books varies from country to country.

In the United Kingdom: Please write to *Dept E.P., Penguin Books Ltd, Harmondsworth, Middlesex, UB7 0DA*

If you have any difficulty in obtaining a title, please send your order with the correct money, plus ten per cent for postage and packaging, to *PO Box No 11, West Drayton, Middlesex*

In the United States: Please write to *Dept BA, Penguin, 299 Murray Hill Parkway, East Rutherford, New Jersey 07073*

In Canada: Please write to *Penguin Books Canada Ltd, 2801 John Street, Markham, Ontario L3R 1B4*

In Australia: Please write to the *Marketing Department, Penguin Books Australia Ltd, P.O. Box 257, Ringwood, Victoria 3134*

In New Zealand: Please write to the *Marketing Department, Penguin Books (NZ) Ltd, Private Bag, Takapuna, Auckland 9*

In India: Please write to *Penguin Overseas Ltd, 706 Eros Apartments, 56 Nehru Place, New Delhi, 110019*

In Holland: Please write to *Penguin Books Nederland B.V., Postbus 195, NL–1380AD Weesp, Netherlands*

In Germany: Please write to *Penguin Books Ltd, Friedrichstrasse 10–12, D–6000 Frankfurt Main 1, Federal Republic of Germany*

In Spain: Please write to *Longman Penguin España, Calle San Nicolas 15, E–28013 Madrid, Spain*

In France: Please write to *Penguin Books Ltd, 39 Rue de Montmorency, F-75003, Paris, France*

In Japan: Please write to *Longman Penguin Japan Co Ltd, Yamaguchi Building, 2–12–9 Kanda Jimbocho, Chiyoda-Ku, Tokyo 101, Japan*

Netochka Nezvanova Fyodor Dostoyevsky

Dostoyevsky's first book tells the story of 'Nameless Nobody' and introduces many of the themes and issues which will dominate his great masterpieces.

Selections from the Carmina Burana A verse translation by David Parlett

The famous songs from the *Carmina Burana* (made into an oratorio by Carl Orff) tell of lecherous monks and corrupt clerics, drinkers and gamblers, and the fleeting pleasures of youth.

Fear and Trembling Søren Kierkegaard

A profound meditation on the nature of faith and submission to God's will which examines with startling originality the story of Abraham and Isaac.

Selected Prose Charles Lamb

Lamb's famous essays (under the strange pseudonym of Elia) on anything and everything have long been celebrated for their apparently innocent charm; this major new edition allows readers to discover the darker and more interesting aspects of Lamb.

The Picture of Dorian Gray Oscar Wilde

Wilde's superb and macabre novella, one of his supreme works, is reprinted here with a masterly Introduction and valuable Notes by Peter Ackroyd.

A Treatise of Human Nature David Hume

A universally acknowledged masterpiece by 'the greatest of all British Philosophers' – A. J. Ayer

FOR THE BEST IN PAPERBACKS, LOOK FOR THE 🐧

PENGUIN CLASSICS

A Passage to India   E. M. Forster

Centred on the unresolved mystery in the Marabar Caves, Forster's great work provides the definitive evocation of the British Raj.

The Republic   Plato

The best-known of Plato's dialogues, *The Republic* is also one of the supreme masterpieces of Western philosophy whose influence cannot be overestimated.

The Life of Johnson   James Boswell

Perhaps the finest 'life' ever written, Boswell's *Johnson* captures for all time one of the most colourful and talented figures in English literary history.

Remembrance of Things Past (3 volumes)   Marcel Proust

This revised version by Terence Kilmartin of C. K. Scott Moncrieff's original translation has been universally acclaimed – available for the first time in paperback.

Metamorphoses   Ovid

A golden treasury of myths and legends which has proved a major influence on Western literature.

A Nietzsche Reader   Friedrich Nietzsche

A superb selection from all the major works of one of the greatest thinkers and writers in world literature, translated into clear, modern English.

PENGUIN CLASSICS

Benjamin Disraeli	**Sybil**
George Eliot	**Adam Bede**
	Daniel Deronda
	Felix Holt
	Middlemarch
	The Mill on the Floss
	Romola
	Scenes of Clerical Life
	Silas Marner
Elizabeth Gaskell	**Cranford** and **Cousin Phillis**
	The Life of Charlotte Brontë
	Mary Barton
	North and South
	Wives and Daughters
Edward Gibbon	**The Decline and Fall of the Roman Empire**
George Gissing	**New Grub Street**
Edmund Gosse	**Father and Son**
Richard Jefferies	**Landscape with Figures**
Thomas Macaulay	**The History of England**
Henry Mayhew	**Selections from London Labour** and **The London Poor**
John Stuart Mill	**On Liberty**
William Morris	**News from Nowhere** and **Selected Writings and Designs**
Walter Pater	**Marius the Epicurean**
John Ruskin	**'Unto This Last'** and **Other Writings**
Sir Walter Scott	**Ivanhoe**
Robert Louis Stevenson	**Dr Jekyll and Mr Hyde**
William Makepeace Thackeray	**The History of Henry Esmond**
	Vanity Fair
Anthony Trollope	**Barchester Towers**
	Framley Parsonage
	Phineas Finn
	The Warden

FOR THE BEST IN PAPERBACKS, LOOK FOR THE 🐧

PENGUIN CLASSICS

BY THE SAME AUTHOR

The Duel and Other Stories

The six stories in this collection were written between 1891 and 1895 when Chekhov was at the zenith of his powers as a short-story writer. Chekhov once said that a writer should not provide solutions but describe a situation so truthfully that the reader can no longer evade it. In these stories he deals with a variety of themes – religious fanaticism and sectarianism, megalomania, scientific controversies of the time – as well as provincial life in all its tedium. And through his portraits of men and women afflicted with inertia, selfishness and spiritual emptiness, he illustrates the questions of his day. But Chekhov never abandons his belief in the capacity for human progress through education and knowledge.

Also published

THE KISS AND OTHER STORIES
LADY WITH LAPDOG AND OTHER STORIES
THE PARTY AND OTHER STORIES
PLAYS: IVANOV/THE CHERRY ORCHARD/THE SEAGULL/
UNCLE VANYA/THREE SISTERS/THE BEAR/THE PROPOSAL/
A JUBILEE